DARKEST DESIRE

"Night Walker?"

He turned to look at Brittany and felt his breath catch. In the dusky twilight she was like a dream...misty and golden. He fought for control of his senses, refusing to let them interfere with logic.

"My sister and I come in friendship, Night Walker...Your village has greeted us as friends. Your family is generous and very kind."

"Have you told them why you are here?"

"Why do you think I'm...we're here?"

"You are here in our village for the same reason the whites are on our land. To take what belongs to us. Only you are worse, for you would change us. We are not white and you want us not to be ourselves. What would you have us be then? We would end up as nothing."

"You're unfair. You have decided before you understand. Why can't you give us a chance, give me a chance?"

Her voice was like velvet and she reached out to lay her hand on his arm. He fought a surge of desire he was not prepared for. He was prepared to fight her...he wasn't prepared to want her.

Other *Leisure* books by Sylvie Sommerfield:
NOAH'S WOMAN
WINTER SEASONS

NIGHT WALKER

Sylvie SOMMERFIELD

LEISURE BOOKS NEW YORK CITY

Dedicated to my great-grandaughter Chelsea

A LEISURE BOOK®

March 1998

Published by

Dorchester Publishing Co., Inc.
276 Fifth Avenue
New York, NY 10001

ISBN 0-8439-4359-9

Prologue

It was certain that neither Tempest nor Brittany Nelson had ever been more excited in their young lives. They'd barely slept the night before, lying together in the huge four-poster bed they shared. They had whispered and giggled long into the night.

Now they rode toward the railway station with their parents and their older brother, James, who had recently passed his eighteenth birthday. Today they would take their first train ride!

Their father traveled a great deal as a railroad executive, and had promised his children time and time again a trip by train. Now, at last, the promised trip had finally come about.

As they boarded the train, the girls caught the eyes of several young men. Just fourteen and eleven, Brittany and Tempest already held the promise of great beauty. From their mother Brittany had acquired red-gold hair and green eyes. In Tempest the brilliant color was muted; her hair was a paler gold and her eyes a soft blue. From their father they'd acquired a streak of stubbornness accompanied by a wicked sense of humor.

But as much as they resembled each other in looks, the two differed in personality. Whereas Brittany was adventuresome and inquisitive, Tempest was shy and gentle.

Some time later they were seated in their compartment, laughing together, when Brittany saw the first station flash by. She wondered if the train was supposed to be going so fast.

It was moving downhill and the scenery outside was whizzing by quicker and quicker. She could hear the screech of brakes being uselessly applied.

Suddenly the compartment began to bounce and buck like a horse out of control. The passengers all seemed to be lifted out of their seats and caught up in a mad, senseless jumble of arms and legs, and cascading luggage.

Tempest was catapulted from her seat and the sound of their mother's long, terrified scream obliterated all else. Then a rush of suction seemed to scoop them up and swirl them about like leaves in a gale.

It seemed to go on and on, the noise getting more deafening, and the gyrations of the compartment more violent. It rumbled and creaked ... then cracked and splintered as the train car went over the crest of a bank. Then a strange silence followed.

Brittany blinked and became aware of a numbness in her head. She raised her hand to touch it and was surprised when it came away bloody. She felt no pain.

Gradually her mind began to function, and to clear, and when she could view what was around her, she moaned with both fright and agony.

Her parents lay covered with blood, and even as inexperienced as she was, she knew they were dead.

She searched about for her brother and Tempest and found them huddled in a corner. James, stunned, bruised and bleeding from small wounds, cradled Tempest's head in his lap. There was a frightful bruise on her temple, and a slow stream of blood ran from her nose, mouth and ears. James and Brittany exchanged looks of disbelief ... and fear.

Chapter One

Boston, Massachusetts, 1873

Daniel Nixon pushed his chair back and rose to his feet. He walked to the window of his law office two floors above the bustling city. From here he had a spectacular view of the place he both loved and hated.

Loved because it was the cradle of culture, wealth and what aristocracy America could claim. Hated because everything he wanted was slipping out of his reach and everyone of consequence in the city must be laughing at him.

Daniel was highly efficient and he knew his capabilities. Knew them and did not hesitate to take advantage of unsavory methods to achieve what he wanted.

He was a tall man, well over six feet, and an extremely handsome one, whose easy smile and lazy blue eyes seduced most people. He had a charm that could win people to his way of thinking with little effort.

His hair was thick and the color of rich mahogany. He was trained in the law and a descendant of a well-to-do family; he meant to use both to get what he wanted. He considered what he wanted: position, power and control. All of these took one thing, wealth . . . and his wealth was something that might be ripped away from him at any moment.

His father! His damnable father! Lawrence Nixon had remarried when Daniel was twenty. Now, dissatisfied with his thirty-six year old son, Lawrence had hinted that he might will everything he had to his wife. Daniel's stepmother hated him as much as he hated her.

She walked around these days with a knowing smile, a look of satisfaction. She always spoke softly and tauntingly in a way his father never understood. She knew . . . she must know.

Daniel considered the meeting that was planned for later tonight. He had made a number of very influential friends, but with his funds growing shorter he had no way to keep bribing and buying his way into favor with the politicians he wanted to join. It had surprised him when Senator John Gifford had said he wanted to see him . . . privately. Daniel had invited him to his house late that night and he had had all day to consider what Gifford might want.

When the day's work was over, Daniel had joined his father and stepmother for dinner, then gone to his own home to await Gifford's arrival.

He had gone to dinner at his father's home only because he didn't mean to retreat before his step-mother and her knowing smiles.

At home he had drunk three brandies before he could control the anger this woman could stir in him.

When he heard the carriage stop outside, he had reached some semblance of control. He had dismissed the two servants he kept, a destitute married couple he had hired for a pittance, and now answered the door himself.

Although he was surprised that the senator was accompanied by others, he said nothing. He ushered them into his small sitting room and offered them brandies, which they accepted.

"Daniel," John said, "this is Major Lee Cline, and Robert Preston, who publishes the *Sentinel*.

"Yes, I know. Good evening, gentlemen. How can I be of service to you?"

"I like your attitude, Daniel," John said, "but I think we can all be of service to each other."

"I don't understand," Daniel replied.

"Please . . . allow me to ask you a question first," Robert Preston said. "Had you thought to run for political office next year?"

Daniel was surprised, but he retained his control. "Yes, with my father's help."

"Well, I've been put on notice. Your father intends to give his money and his support to James MacBride."

Daniel was stunned; his face went white. Without his father's money and support, he might as well acknowledge that his political aspirations were gone.

"But there are ways around your father, and Major Cline may have found one."

"What? What way?"

Major Cline said nothing. He simply reached into his pocket, withdrew what to Daniel looked like a small rock and laid it on the table. For a minute Daniel could only gaze at it; then the import of what it was came to him.

"Gold," he whispered. "That's gold."

"From out west," Robert replied. "And it assays so high, it's unbelievable. It's rich. Rich enough for all of us. You won't need your father anymore."

Daniel was shaken . . . then suspicious. Why did they need him? He asked the question and saw respect for his pragmatism in their eyes.

"Because there is a small problem that stands between that gold and us, and we need you to help take care of it," Major Cline said. "The military cannot be involved."

"Tell me . . . what do I have to do?"

The men smiled, and Major Cline answered. "There are two problems: one is Indians, and the other is a mission and school in the area built by one Aaron Abbott."

"What are you suggesting?"

"That we find a way to get rid of the mission, put the blame on the Indians and have them moved . . . to a reservation far from where we want to be."

"Get rid of the mission?"

"Any way you can . . . preferably permanently. The military commander out there is trying to keep trouble from brewing. If the Indians destroy the mission, he will have little recourse but to retaliate. We will have a clear field before others know there's gold there."

"And my share?"

"You'll get a fair share of course. But better yet, you'll get all of our support politically," Robert said. "And the support of my paper."

"Agreed."

The men looked at each other, then slowly nodded.

"Just one more question," Daniel said. "Where is the gold?"

"In the **Black Hills of Dakota.**"

Chapter Two

Lieutenant Cole Young stepped out onto the hotel porch in Sioux Falls and squinted at the sun. He had enjoyed his few days' leave and, in fact, would have welcomed a few days more. But he had an assignment. He was to escort Aaron Abbott and his supplies back to Fort Pierre, deep in Indian territory.

He adjusted his hat, squared his blue-clad shoulders and started across the street. At thirty-three, Cole was a tall, broad-shouldered man whose purposeful stride would have proclaimed him a military man even if he had not been in uniform. His eyes were the same blue as the cloudless sky above, and his hair was deep gold, as was the mustache he wore with aplomb.

Cole was a man who found easy amusement in

things and had a flexible nature that made leadership natural.

The headache he fought was a result of the past night's revelry and he wasn't looking forward to the rough and dusty trip. But Aaron's company would compensate for any discomfort. He had always found the missionary a stimulating companion. He was intelligent and amusing and, in Cole's eyes, he'd done a pretty remarkable thing by establishing his mission in the wilderness of the Dakotas and befriending the Sioux who lived nearby.

Cole had a desire to learn more about the Indians himself, but he wasn't in command at the fort, and neither could he seem to make contact with the Sioux. He'd tried, lord knew he'd tried, but they were as elusive as fireflies.

He'd been intrigued by Aaron's stories of the inquisitive children and daring warriors, especially the legendary Night Walker. But the missionary's tales were as close as he was likely to get to the Sioux. He had never come face to face with any of them.

When he reached Aaron's hotel he took the steps two at a time, crossed the porch and went inside.

"What room is Aaron Abbott's?" he questioned the clerk.

"Number twenty-six, up the stairs and four doors down."

"Thanks."

At the door he knocked and waited only a few seconds before Aaron opened the door.

"Aaron, you old reprobate. It's about time you

got back from Philadelphia," Cole said, grinning.

"And you, you young whippersnapper. I take it you're my escort again."

"Yep. I asked for the duty. You owe me a game of checkers or two, and besides, I'm going to convince you to introduce me to your friend Night Walker, if it's the last thing I do."

"Now you know that's not up to me."

"So, convince the Sioux of what an amiable chap I am."

"And harmless?"

"Hell, yes, harmless. What does that mean?"

"I think you have a pretty good idea what I mean. Separation might be the best thing between the native people and the military."

"But that doesn't apply to you."

"No."

"Aaron . . ."

"Cole, they need more time. They don't exactly trust the military. They really have no reason to."

"I know. But why can't I prove to them that some white people are trustworthy? Why is it they trust only you and your missionaries?"

"Oh," Aaron chuckled, "I'm hoping they'll learn to trust a few outsiders."

"Oh, really?"

"Yes, really."

"Who?"

"I'd rather show you than tell you. Your men ready to go soon?"

"Whenever you and your wagons are."

"Then let's go down the hall. I want you to meet some of my troops."

"Troops?"

"Come on." Aaron shrugged into his jacket. "Skinner will have the wagons ready."

Cole followed Aaron with a puzzled look on his face. They walked down the hall, where Aaron knocked on a door, and then smiled a bit wickedly at Cole, who had to laugh in return.

When the door opened, Cole's smile froze on his face and his eyes widened in surprise. He had expected another missionary, hardly the beauty who stood in the open doorway and returned his smile. Her hair glistened like a gold coin caught in the morning sun, and her eyes were the color of fresh spring leaves. He'd never seen skin so soft and dewy fresh looking, and it stirred his senses as did her slender yet womanly body.

"Good morning, Aaron," the beauty sang out.

"Good morning, Brittany. My, you do look pretty today."

"Thank you. Tempest and I are almost ready."

"Ready?" Cole repeated, stunned.

"Oh—" Aaron's voice was filled with humor— "Cole, my friend, I'd like to introduce you to my new teacher, Miss Brittany Nelson."

"Teacher," Cole repeated and watched with a touch of embarrassment as Brittany tried to contain the laughter he saw dancing in her eyes.

"Brittany, this young man is our military escort to the fort, Lieutenant Cole Young."

"Hello, Lieutenant. Aaron has told me a great

20

deal about you. My sister and I are looking forward to the balance of the journey."

Cole finally regained his equilibrium, and smiled at Brittany. "Sorry. You were a bit of a shock to say the least. You're going to teach at the mission?"

"Yes, I am. Come in, please. Tempest and I will be ready to leave in a few minutes."

"Ah . . . if you don't mind, Aaron and I will wait here. I have a few things to discuss with him before we leave," Cole said.

"No, of course not. We won't be long." Her smile still intact, Brittany closed the door between them.

Cole turned to face Aaron with a dark scowl on his face.

"Are you crazy, Aaron?"

"Crazy? It's a debatable point," Aaron said, amusement in his voice. "Depends on who you ask."

"You know perfectly well what I mean. You can't do this!"

"This what?"

"You can't bring an . . . unmarried woman like her out here to live in that wilderness you call home. I take it she and her sister are both single?"

"Yes, and I might add, very properly chaperoned. You wait, you have a treat in store for you. You have yet to meet Aunt Claudia and Uncle Myron, who accompanied us all the way from Philadelphia. Besides that, you're jumping to conclusions. You have no idea what they're like.

21

Brittany is a dedicated teacher and a very courageous woman. She's looking forward to teaching at the mission."

"Why don't you bring your school into the fort? There are a lot of children there that need schooling, too."

"Cole, you know why," Aaron said gently. "The Sioux would never send their children to a school inside the fort. No, the school must remain at the mission. I've been living out there for years, and no harm has come to me yet."

"Aaron, you can't keep on doing this."

"Oh, but I can, Cole. You'll just have to face the truth. There is no danger, and the Nelson girls are going to prove that fact."

"I suppose her sister is as pretty as she is," Cole said half in disgust and half in amusement.

"She is that."

"Wonderful," Cole said dryly. "This really ought to make my job easier."

"I told you. You have no reason to worry. Let me assure you, improving the lives of the Sioux is my only goal. When I met Brittany at the home of a friend in Philadelphia, she became interested in the same goal."

Before Cole could answer, the door was opened again and Brittany appeared, with her sister behind her. Cole at once saw that there was something unique about this fragile looking girl.

"Good morning." He spoke directly to her, but she only smiled and inclined her head slightly.

"We're as ready as we'll ever be, Aaron," Brittany said.

"Cole," Aaron said in a voice that held a note of warning Cole did not yet understand. "This young lady is Brittany's sister, Tempest. I'm afraid she neither speaks nor hears."

Cole's shocked look made Brittany square her shoulders and defiantly lift her chin.

"I'm sorry," he said, uncertain what else to say.

"My sister needs no sympathy, Lieutenant. She lost her hearing as the result of a train wreck seven years ago. She is quite capable of taking care of herself, however, and she will handle whatever Aaron needs to have done in his infirmary. You might be surprised at what a fine nurse she is."

"I'm sorry again. I didn't mean to imply pity. It was a bit of a surprise. I'm sure she'll be an asset to Aaron."

"Shall we go and gather your aunt and uncle?" Aaron said, and Cole wasn't too sure he didn't hear laughter in his voice. He gritted his teeth in a smile and promised a bit of revenge on Aaron as soon as possible.

Aaron's assistant, Skinner Mackenzie, was waiting for them, as were the men under Cole's command. As they approached the wagons, a ripple of movement went through the entire group as men straightened their shoulders, adjusted equipment and shot surreptitious and pleased glances at the two women who accompanied Cole. He, in turn, began to think it was going to be a long, long trip back to the fort. But the stiff back and forbidding

23

presence of their chaperone, Aunt Claudia, kept the men at a safe distance.

There were many hands to help as the last of the travelers' baggage was put into the wagons. For a while Tempest rode with Aaron on one wagon, and Brittany went in the other with Skinner, who was too shy to talk to her at first. Aunt Claudia and Uncle Myron rode in the third wagon with one of Skinner's men, while Cole and his men rode surrounding the wagons, with one man going on ahead to scout. Aaron seemed amused at this. He made it clear that as far as he was concerned, they were perfectly safe from attack. Secretly, Cole agreed with him, but that wouldn't make this trip into the wilderness with two beautiful women one bit easier.

Brittany and Tempest were fascinated by the countryside around them. The land was majestic in its vast undulating plains and endless blue sky.

Brittany gazed about in awe. It seemed she could see forever, and she felt like a diminutive speck on the landscape.

For the first time she was a little scared . . . not for herself, but for how Tempest would function in the vast wild place they were going to. When Brittany had made the decision to come west, Tempest had insisted on accompanying her. Ever since the accident, Tempest had withdrawn from the world, relying on Brittany to interpret life for her. She knew Tempest would follow her anywhere. But this time, had she led her sister down the wrong road just to satisfy her own hunger for . . . ?

Brittany didn't know the word to describe what she sought in Sioux territory, or what she expected to find. She knew she was more adventuresome than most. But it was one thing to seek adventure for herself, and another to lead her sister into the unknown. She closed her eyes and prayed she wasn't doing Tempest more harm than good.

They traveled slowly, and both Brittany and Tempest were grateful. Besides the fact that the wagons were not exactly comfortable, neither woman wanted to miss anything.

Cole kept his distance, which amused Brittany. She knew he could see the laughter in her eyes every time he got within speaking distance of Aunt Claudia. Her aunt seemed to expect him to do something to alleviate her many discomforts, everything from the bumping wagon to the heat of the sun.

Myron, on the other hand, seemed resigned to suffer the journey in stoic silence, but now and then Brittany got the feeling he might have been enjoying himself a bit . . . and enjoying Claudia's discomfort a bit more.

Aaron was a constant source of information, and what he couldn't supply, Cole or Skinner did.

Skinner was the tallest, skinniest man Brittany had ever seen. Beside being over six and a half feet tall, Skinner Mackenzie was painfully shy. His skin was leathered, and it was hard to guess his age, but his eyes were young. His head had a scruff of dark hair surrounding a bald pate, and his ears protruded like miniature wings. His smile was a jack-o'-lantern grin that threatened to slice his face from ear to ear.

Skinner lost some of his shyness when he discovered how much Brittany enjoyed the tales he could weave. When she had occasion to ride with him over the next few days, he seemed to take pleasure in her company and her enthusiasm. He made it clear that he felt Aaron had made an excellent choice in his new teacher. Skinner seemed to have an endless supply of anecdotes that made her hours pass contentedly.

When they crested the hill that led to the fort, they paused to let Brittany and Tempest get a good view of the place where they would spend the next three or four days before they began the last leg of their journey to the mission.

Fort Pierre lay before them. Its high walls were the guardians of nearly four hundred people, soldiers, their wives and children. From this vantage point the fort bustled with activity and looked like a small city.

In the distance the vague blue shadows of the Black Hills could be seen.

The fort contained a number of buildings besides the individual accommodations for military wives. It had a good doctor and some hospital facilities. Stables and storage places were more than adequate, as was the commander's office.

"It's larger than I thought it would be," Brittany said.

"It houses quite a number of men and families, not to mention the supplies necessary to provide sustenance for them," Cole replied.

"Sustenance." Aaron chuckled, and Cole laughed.

"I know. The Indians live off the land and live well . . . so you say. I've never been welcome in the village, so I wouldn't know."

"You mean you've never been there?" Brittany questioned. "I thought you . . . and the fort were here to keep peace between Indians and whites."

Cole and Aaron exchanged a glance and smiled. "Keep peace?" Cole said. "The government doesn't need us out here to keep the peace. But the army ought to closely monitor the people who pull duty out here."

"I don't understand."

"Some people," Aaron said quietly, "just don't like Indians on general principle."

"What general principle?" Brittany said indignantly.

"The principle that the Indians are on the land and somebody else wants it. All in the name of progress, of course," Cole responded.

"Why, Cole," Aaron chuckled, "you talk like that and the lady will believe you are a visionary who sees injustice."

"No. I'm no visionary. I'm just a soldier. Besides, I'm no authority on Indian affairs." He urged his horse into a trot and rode on ahead of the wagons.

27

"He wasn't angry with me, was he, Aaron?" Brittany asked.

"No. He's not angry at all. It's just that the Sioux nearby are very good friends of mine . . . but they are a bit elusive when it comes to the military."

"Elusive?"

Aaron chuckled. "It seems they have no inclination to visit the fort, nor to fraternize with the other whites. In fact, they never are where anyone expects to find them."

"And you've decided to create a school for their children."

"Rather presumptuous of me, isn't it?" He laughed. "I just can't rid myself of the idea that it's children and education that can bring two such different cultures together."

"I do like your presumptuous attitude. I hope you're right."

"So do I, my dear, so do I."

Aaron slapped the reins against the horses' rumps and they moved slowly down toward the fort. As they approached the fort, the huge gates swung open. The new arrivals were met with enthusiasm. After all, mail and news arrived with Aaron.

Aaron aided Brittany down from the wagon, and Cole went to Tempest to do the same while Skinner went to the aid of Claudia and Myron. Aaron's name was called out, and he turned to see a tall man walking toward him. Brittany watched Aaron hesitate for a second, then extend his hand and move to meet the other man.

"Steven, it's good to see you again, sir."

"Aaron, you've been gone quite some time. Welcome back. I see you've brought us some visitors. Do the ladies have relatives here at the fort? A pretty face is most welcome."

"Let me introduce you. Colonel Brady, this is Brittany Nelson, her sister, Tempest, and their Aunt Claudia and Uncle Myron Davis. I'm afraid, though, they are not just visitors here."

"Good afternoon," he said. "You are not visitors . . . then you intend to stay."

"Well . . . ah . . ." Brittany began.

"We are still uncertain of our plans," Claudia said with a jut of her firm chin. "It depends upon how safe my nieces will be."

Colonel Brady regarded Claudia and tried not to smile. She looked like a ship under full sail, her eyes gleaming beacons searching out any danger in the distance. Beside her, Myron looked exactly like what he was, an uprooted bookkeeper. One would never guess the two loved each other completely.

"Actually, Colonel," Aaron cut in, "Brittany, her sister and her . . . family will go on with me. You see, Brittany will be my new teacher, and Tempest will be invaluable in the infirmary."

"Aaron, I cannot believe this. You intend to keep these two young ladies at your mission! That is unthinkable! It's also dangerous."

"Dangerous!" Claudia fairly shrieked in alarm. "I knew it. I warned your brother this would hap-

29

pen. I don't know why he agreed to let you girls come to this wilderness at all."

"Now, Claudia," Myron said mildly, "there are other women out here, and I know Brittany and Tempest are very courageous." Claudia cast him a withering look.

"Dangerous?" Aaron replied mildly. "I have made that mission my home for years and have yet to have any kind of a problem."

Steven's jaw stiffened, and Aaron could see the light of battle in his eyes. Steven had come to the fort out of ambition to gain a promotion and the desire to add luster to his name. He had come when he was forty. He was now forty-six, and it seemed to him his stay at Fort Pierre might last until his retirement. Aaron often suspected that he was downright annoyed that the Indians didn't rebel or cause any problems.

Still, Aaron knew that basically Steven was a good man, and his wife, Esther, was a strong and level-headed woman who would take Brittany and Tempest under her wing for the short time they would be here.

As if she had known his feelings, Esther came bustling across the compound. She was a small woman with bright, intelligent green eyes and a mass of black hair of which she was extremely proud. Her smile was open and given freely and, as everyone in the fort knew, her temper was just as open and just as freely given.

Compared to Steven, who was nearly six feet tall, she was like a miniature. But Esther ran her home, and most often her husband with an unbelievable will, an iron hand, and more love than one could believe she contained.

"Aaron, my friend, it's good to see you back out here. I haven't heard a good devil-smiting sermon since you left," Esther laughed.

"Well, I'll be here for Sunday service if you like. But for now I want to introduce you to my newest and most welcome acquisitions. My teacher, Brittany Nelson, and her sister, Tempest."

"Welcome," Esther said. "My, what lovely creatures. Miss Nelson." She smiled at Brittany as she shook her hand. "And you—" she fairly beamed at Tempest—"you're still a child."

"I'm afraid my sister can't hear you, Mrs. Brady. She's been deaf since she was eleven. An accident."

"Oh, what a shame," Esther said, but her smile never wavered. She did not need to be told Tempest had a bright and inquiring mind; she could see it in her eyes. "Come to my home and let me make you some tea and get acquainted. You ladies are just in time for my husband's birthday party Sunday night. I think I'd better get you safely ensconced in the guest quarters before there's a stampede of young men. Come, Miss Nelson."

"Please, call me Brittany." Brittany turned to her aunt and uncle and introduced them.

"Yes, I think we'll get along fine. Aaron, I hope to have a nice long chat with you before you leave."

"Why did I have no doubts about that, dear Esther? I shall be here whenever you want."

Esther bundled the three women away. Claudia's protesting voice seemed to echo behind after all of them had disappeared. Aaron and Steven could do little but exchange smiles of amusement. There were few things Esther Brady couldn't handle.

When Aaron, Cole and the women rode through the gates of the fort, word was already winging its way to the Sioux camp. Word that their friend Aaron was on his way home.

Night Walker heard the news that Aaron traveled with a military escort, and that with him came several women. The presence of the women he ignored: they were most likely brides or wives of men already at the fort or working farms nearby. It was the wagons that interested him. Surely they brought more supplies for Aaron's dwelling place and for the place he called a hospital. Night Walker did not understand the word, but he did know that Aaron had helped his people, had even saved the lives of several.

The next three days were both informative and fun for Brittany and Tempest. Esther was an endless supplier of lore about the area in which they were to live, and even Aunt Claudia became interested and lost some of her cold reserve. Esther fascinated Brittany with her down-to-earth acceptance of Tempest's infirmity and a unique ability to reach Tempest, who smiled more when Esther was present. Brittany realized just how dreadfully Tempest had missed the loving touch of a mother.

Steven's birthday supper was enjoyable, but the following dance was awkward for Tempest until she realized that the soldiers were so hungry for feminine company that they would not shun her as the young men in Philadelphia had done. Then she began to relax. Both women were besieged by young men hungry for the sight, scent and smile of a pretty girl.

Although Claudia tried to hover over both girls like a hen with only two chicks, she was thwarted over and over again by an equally determined Esther, who always seemed to be between her and the girls.

Myron was pleased at his own small taste of freedom and took advantage of it by stationing himself beside a bowl full of spiked punch near a group of men whose stories interested him.

They went back to their quarters very late. Aaron warned them that morning was going to come faster than they thought . . . and it did.

Esther and many others were unhappy to see Aaron and the girls leave. Both Brittany and Tempest were torn. They wanted to stay, yet they wanted to see what promise the future held.

It was mid-morning by the time the fort vanished in the distance behind them. Now it was only Aaron, Skinner, Brittany and Tempest, and the "bodyguards" as Brittany referred to her aunt and uncle, and Skinner's men.

Aaron's mission was only a few hours' ride from the fort, yet the vastness of the plains made them feel as if they were nearly alone in the world.

"It's as if civilization doesn't exist," Brittany said.

"The civilization you know doesn't, not out here. But a whole new one is there to enjoy."

"How will you let the Indians know you're back?"

"Brittany, they knew the day we arrived. They knew when the fort doors opened this morning that we were on our way and who was with us. I wouldn't be a bit surprised if they didn't have a pretty good idea what's in the wagons by now."

"Good heavens"—Brittany looked about her—"I don't see any sign of anybody."

"And you won't. They're seen when they want to be seen. That's what seems to frustrate Cole so much. A Sioux brave can blend with nature so well that if you were walking in the woods you wouldn't know he was there, until he tapped you on the shoulder. If you're an enemy, it's too late by then."

"How frightening," Brittany murmured.

"No, Brittany, not frightening. I brought you out here to understand. The Sioux are not war seekers. They are a warm and friendly people, and very interesting. You will probably receive from them as much or more than you give."

Brittany craned her neck to look behind her. "I hope Tempest is all right. I wouldn't want her to be frightened."

"Stop worrying. Skinner will make sure she's fine. I wouldn't be surprised to learn he's found a way to communicate with her."

Brittany may have been doubtful, but Aaron's words were very true. Tempest was awed by the things Skinner's astute eyes had been able to point out to her.

Hawks soaring in the blue sky. A deer leaping away in startled bounds. When Tempest laughed, Skinner laughed, too, though she couldn't hear it. Tempest felt a comfortable comradeship with Skinner.

When they arrived at Aaron's mission there was a bustle of activity, laughter and shouts. People seemed to converge from several different locations.

Introductions were made, and Brittany and Tempest were surrounded by a sea of welcoming faces. Brittany was first introduced to the doctor, Thomas Hammond. Then they met the cook, Jake White, a grizzled man, who grinned when Aaron assured Brittany he was the best cook in the territory. The blacksmith, Joseph Miles, his wife, Meg, and their daughter, Samantha, came next, followed by Thomas Hammond and his small staff of three. Next to them were the four men who had been originally hired by Aaron to help build the mission; they had decided to stay on and work there.

"Aaron," Thomas said, "we hadn't thought you'd be back until next week. But I'm grateful you are and that you've renewed our supply of medicines.

There's been a rash of the influenza and I've been afraid it would get out of hand."

"I hope we are in time to stop it."

Thomas nodded acknowledgment to the women, but his worried look remained.

"Don't worry so, Tom. I've brought plenty of everything. I have even brought your assistant, Tempest. I bought all I could afford, but we'll have to thank the girls here for a lot of what we have. They have donated a great deal toward our supplies. How many cases have you come across?"

"The little Carter girl is still here in the infirmary. I've treated both her brothers and they seem to be hearty and well. There were about six other cases as well. I don't believe there's a homestead around that's not been touched."

"And . . . any Indian children?" Aaron asked worriedly.

"Well, you know they've got a lot of damn good cures of their own. But they might come if it gets out of hand."

"Influenza could be deadly to them," Aaron said thoughtfully. "Perhaps they're all well."

"I hope so."

"Come, girls, let me show you around my little world."

The compound was made up of a number of buildings. One, a building about fifteen by twenty-five feet, was where they would take their communal meals. Aaron's small house sat nearby, along with other dwellings shared by those who worked with Aaron. Near the edge of the forest was the schoolhouse Aaron had so carefully built.

"It gets cold here, but we'll keep you well supplied with wood, and the stove will keep the room quite comfortable."

"How many children will I have?" Brittany asked.

"Probably about nine or ten. I'm still having some trouble convincing Laughing Thunder and Running Cougar that they should attend school. They are young men who still believe hunting comes before learning."

"I'll do everything I can to help convince them."

"Come." Aaron smiled at Tempest as he took hold of her arm. "I'll show you my little hospital. It's not much, but I hope to see it flourish one day, too."

The hospital was a long, narrow room with cots lining both sides. Aaron went directly to one on which a girl of about ten lay. The man who sat beside her kept squeezing out a cloth in cool water and wiping the child's face.

"How is she, Joseph?" Aaron whispered.

"She seems to be getting better."

"Brittany, this is Joseph Carter, Amy's brother. He is a helper here also."

Tempest had sat down on the other side of the bed and taken Amy's small hands in hers. Amy's eyes fluttered open and she gazed up at Tempest. Amy believed she was seeing an angel. She smiled, sighed and drifted back to sleep. Joseph smiled at Tempest, who returned it.

Once they had seen the hospital, they went on

37

to the rest of the cluster of buildings. They were welcomed by Aaron's friends as they made their rounds of the other buildings.

"Where will all of us stay?" Brittany questioned.

"Come with me and I'll show you. Now, I want no arguments from you. I have had all my possessions moved to other quarters. I'm turning my small house over to you and your sister. Your aunt and uncle will have the little cottage just across the compound. It's small but comfortable. Brittany, my house will give you privacy and still have you within walking distance of the school."

"Your house . . . but, Aaron—"

"No, no arguments. You have given up a great deal to come here and help me. If I can give you a small bit of comfort in return, then I take great pleasure in it. Before you see the house, I would like you all to come with me to the church. I've many thanks to give and I'd like to ask a blessing on you both for your unselfish and giving natures."

The church was small, with several rows of wooden benches for the worshipers and a hand-hewn wooden pulpit that Brittany guessed had been carved from one huge tree. The ceiling was of the same rough-hued timbers as the walls and very high.

There was an aura of warmth, peace and tranquility here, and Brittany felt that it emanated as much from Aaron as from the church itself. This was the first time in several days that some of her trepidations were washed away. She began to think of what Aaron was trying to build here, and it excited her to think she was going to be part of it.

That night Aaron, his guests and several of the missionaries ate a communal meal, but only after Aaron assured all three women that all of their personal belongings had been safely delivered.

Aaron's house was, as he had said, small. Especially if one were to compare it to the luxury the women were used to. It consisted of four rooms: two bedrooms, a third that would serve as a small library since Aaron had filled it with books and a large desk where Brittany could make lessons, and a small sitting room. A cozy fireplace and rough but comfortable furniture gave the room a warm feeling. There had never been need of a kitchen since Aaron and the entire staff ate communal meals.

Brittany began to imagine how livable she and Tempest could make this place. They would be more than comfortable. The challenge of it thrilled her.

Tempest, too, had been walking through the house and when she and Brittany exchanged a look, Brittany was pleased to see Tempest smile. She, too, felt how truly useful they could be here.

Brittany drew out the small notepad she always carried.

What do you think? she wrote.

It is certainly isolated, was Tempest's answer.

Are you afraid?

No, actually I'm not. This place . . . it's so big, and so beautiful.

It is vast. But Aaron has assured me there's little danger.

What of the Indians? I have not seen any.

Aaron says they come when they choose.

I wonder what they look like.

I don't know, Brittany wrote. *But I have a terrible curiosity. I really want to know what they are like.*

I know we have no idea if it's safe here or not, Tempest wrote, *but I'd like to take a short walk . . . to be alone for a while. Can you understand?*

Of course. I don't suppose there is really any great danger. Please don't go too far.

I won't.

Tempest brushed Brittany's cheek with a swift kiss and left the small house. Brittany stood in the open doorway and watched her walk slowly to the edge of the surrounding woods.

There was no doubt in her mind about Tempest's courage. Still, she did battle with her conscience and prayed she had not made a costly mistake. Not for herself, she was very pleased with where she was. But she wondered if she was ever going to be able to justify dragging Tempest out here to the back of beyond.

Tempest enjoyed her walk that day, but she forgot her promise to keep close to the mission. Enchanted by this new vision of a beautiful world, she drifted some distance away from the mission and found herself in a small verdant glen. The small stream that flowed through it was an invitation for her to pause. She sat to consider her innermost feelings.

She couldn't put into words what she felt. There was a spirit of freedom here that lightened her heart. It was hard when you could not tell anyone the depths of your feelings. She loved Brittany completely, but there were times when she could not convey even to her how she felt.

She hated the silence in which she lived, yet in some way she took pleasure in it, because it was a wall she could hide behind.

She remembered well the teasing of some of her schoolmates and how hurt she had been. She had not been able to trust strangers from that point on.

She knew she had become reclusive and had enjoyed being solitary. Yet she had also seen the excitement and hope in Brittany's eyes at the prospect of going west, and could not bear the thought of Brittany going away . . . possibly forever. At home she had felt she was a useless burden to her family. But here, in this vastness, she could find a way to contribute and to use some of the energy that made her nights so sleepless, or worse, stimulated nightmares about the terrible accident. She couldn't bear these visions of her parents and the sound of the scream torn from her mother before silence—the awful yet protective silence—descended.

Tempest inhaled the mingled scents, felt the breeze brush her skin and flutter through her hair, and enjoyed the warmth of the sun. She meant to find peace here, to find a way to make her life worthwhile, perhaps to stay forever.

Laughing Thunder had never seen a woman with hair the color of this one's. It was like strands of corn silk. He'd been watching the mission for some time, hoping to catch a glimpse of the newcomers. Their arrival had been whispered about by the scouts. Now he had seen one of them and she was different from any woman he had ever seen before. He could hardly wait to get back to the village to let his older brothers know.

When Tempest finally disappeared from his sight, Laughing Thunder raced to where he had hidden his horse. Night Walker and Soaring Eagle would be interested in his news. He would be the center of attention, and to get Night Walker and Soaring Eagle's undivided attention was rare. He urged his horse into a run toward the village.

Chapter Three

A vivid red sunset silhouetted two riders against the horizon as they crested a hill above the Indian village and drew their horses to a halt. The vista before them was breathtakingly beautiful.

At least twenty painted tepees sat among a sparse stand of trees, and nearby a stream rippled over its rocky bed. Even in the dying light, curling tendrils of pale grey smoke could be seen coming from each dwelling. Beyond the village, the forest was thick and dark with the shadows cast by the setting sun.

The laughter of children at play carried on a light breeze, and the sharp bark of a dog joined it.

The younger of the two men smiled at his brother Night Walker. Though they taunted and challenged each other constantly, there was a great love between the brothers. As far as Soaring Eagle was concerned, there was no more accomplished brave in the tribe than Night Walker.

"I can smell meat roasting from here," Soaring Eagle said.

"You can smell any kind of food cooking from any distance. I believe your stomach has no bottom."

"I need all my strength if I am going to beat you."

"Beat me?"

"In a race—" Soaring Eagle grinned—"to see who gets the first piece of meat."

Night Walker looked at his brother with amusement. He saw a younger reflection of himself. Ebony hair hung as sleek as mink past his shoulders. Eyes so brown they were nearly black were set below a broad forehead. His wide, sensual mouth was quick to smile and reveal strong, white, even teeth. Night Walker was taller than his brother's six feet by two inches. Both were strong-muscled men. Their long legs and narrow waists were accentuated by a breadth of shoulder that spoke of latent strength.

Both were dressed in soft, well-cured deerskin pants, and moccasins that laced nearly to their knees. They were bare-chested except for the longbows they carried strung across their chests with a matching strip of leather that held a quiver of arrows.

"The sun has not risen on the day that you can beat me," Night Walker laughed.

"Do not brag tonight," Soaring Eagle chuckled in response, his dark eyes sparkling. "I am very hungry."

"Then let's race." Night Walker's laugh was easy. "Since you are younger, I will let you call the start."

Soaring Eagle laughed and bent forward to affectionately pat the arched neck of his horse. "I thought you were going to ask for that."

"Say the word," Night Walker answered.

The two bent slightly forward, prepared to kick their horses into action. Then, with a shout from Soaring Eagle, they were suddenly in motion.

They raced down from the hill neck and neck, and as the sound of their horses reached the village, people turned to watch in admiration. None of them were surprised: they were used to the competition between the brothers.

Night Walker pulled to a dirt-scattering stop near their father's tepee, with Soaring Eagle only a hand's breadth behind him.

As the two men dismounted, there was an explosion of young people from the tepee. Two girls, one nearing twelve and another fifteen, and two boys, one close to fourteen and one trying to appear a bit more reserved than the others, since he neared his sixteenth birthday.

"So," Night Walker boasted, "now I get the first piece of meat."

"Your luck is remarkable."

"Luck!" Night Walker was going to say something a bit more forceful until the young girl tugged at his arm and he remembered her presence. He looked down at her and his eyes softened and grew warm. His smile was gentle. "What is it?" he questioned.

"Night Walker, will you let me ride with you the next time you race?"

"And have our father take the skin from my back? No. Besides, Never Quiet, you can find your way into enough trouble all by yourself."

Never Quiet's eyes revealed her disappointment, but only for a minute. She was not one to be stopped for long by any problem, even the tormenting of her older brothers.

"Never Quiet," her older sister, Star Dancer, teased. "You are not a boy child. Why do you not do as our mother says, and carry the water bags and learn to be a good wife?"

"Yes," Running Cougar said, grinning. "You've been punished enough to make you remember. Besides, the next race will be with me."

"You must say that to Soaring Eagle," Night Walker laughed. "I do not want to shame two of my brothers on the same day." Never Quiet laughed, too.

"I will outride you when I get my new pony broken," Running Cougar claimed.

"And I will beat you both," Laughing Thunder said.

Before any of them could speak again, a man stepped from the tepee, and all attention was centered on him. There was no doubt of the emotions that pervaded the group. The tall, powerful man who stood before them commanded respect and deference by his mere presence. He exuded an aura of strength, and more . . . a sense of leadership that told of his immense charisma.

Sleeping Wolf was the father of the brood that gathered before him, and reflections of him could be seen in many ways: in the gift of humor, and the smiles of contentment; in the brilliance of dark eyes, and the glow of health.

He smiled at his two older sons. "Racing again? May I ask who won?"

"Since Night Walker could stand his hunger no longer," Soaring Eagle said with surprising calm, "I decided to let him win. You know how difficult he is to live with when he does not win. Is the food ready?" he added quickly, before his brother could make any retort. He stepped inside the tepee with a smile on his face, content at having the last word.

Sleeping Wolf chuckled, and Night Walker surrendered to his slight defeat with a grin. He turned to Laughing Thunder as his father and the other children drifted away.

Night Walker could see the sparkle in his younger brother's eyes and the broad smile on his face. He almost laughed. Laughing Thunder was so full of life that he could become excited over the simple fact that the sun had risen. Obviously he had something to tell, and couldn't wait to tell it.

"Where have you been today, little brother?"

"I was hunting. But I have seen something I have never seen before."

"There is an animal in the forest you have never seen before?" Night Walker laughed.

"Do not make fun of me or I will not tell you what I have seen and you will be the one to regret it," Laughing Thunder said smugly.

"Well then," Night Walker replied casually, "I will go inside for my food, if you are not going to tell me anything."

He turned his back on his brother and, trying to keep from laughing aloud, bent to enter the tepee. He could only imagine the look on Laughing Thunder's face, and was not surprised when he felt his brother's detaining hand.

"Night Walker, you are not funny," he complained. "Stop and listen to me."

"All right." Night Walker stopped and faced him again. "Tell me of such an animal as you have never seen before and how it managed to escape you."

"It was not an animal," he said. "If it were, it would not escape me. What I saw was a woman."

"Now, that is something of great mystery," Night Walker said in pretended awe.

"Not one of our women." Laughing Thunder was becoming exasperated.

Night Walker looked at him with a grin, and Laughing Thunder had to laugh.

"Aaron is back and the woman with him is young and very pretty. She has hair the color of—" he paused to think of an appropriate color—

"the sun when it first comes up in the morning. I have never seen a woman with hair that color. I wonder if she belongs to Aaron. He is an old man for a woman as young and beautiful as she was."

"I would not say those words in front of Aaron," Night Walker said. "As for the woman, maybe she is the wife or the daughter of one of his people. Whatever she is, she is not for us to think of," he counseled, ignoring his own curiosity at his brother's news.

"But Aaron is our friend."

"Yes, and he will most likely come visit us to explain."

"Night Walker—"

"It is time to eat, Laughing Thunder. It would be better if you talked this over with our father. And it would be even better if you took his words very seriously and tried to obey for a change."

Chastened, Laughing Thunder followed him into the tepee and Night Walker greeted his mother. As Night Walker began to eat, he considered Aaron's position in their lives.

Aaron had been a friend to all the village. Night Walker remembered well the first time he had met Aaron Abbott. It was a matter of saving Aaron's life.

Afterward, Aaron had related in vivid detail his version of the incidents that had brought them together.

Unaware of the dangers of the territory he had chosen to work in, Aaron had arrived at Fort

Pierre brimming with enthusiasm and a desire to work among the Indians.

Against the wishes and the strenuous arguments of the fort commander, he had set out alone to find the tribe. Steven Brady had tried to convince Aaron that he was going into territory that would swallow him up before he saw one sign of any Indians.

"They're elusive as hell, and if they don't want to be found, they won't be. Aaron, you've got to change your plans. The military can't run around this country trying to guard you while you pursue an impossible dream."

"Why impossible?" Aaron had inquired.

"Because," Steven replied, as if talking to a child, "you won't find them. Trust me. Aaron, you're taking your life in your hands. Please, don't go."

"My life is in God's hands," Aaron answered calmly, "and I have to go. I absolve you of any blame for what may happen. But . . . I want you to be prepared to apologize if I succeed."

"My pleasure," Steven said, in an exasperated tone. "Don't say I didn't try to warn you."

What Aaron had thought would be an easy ride turned to near disaster when he promptly became lost. His situation rapidly deteriorated when his horse stumbled into a hole and broke its leg.

It was three days later when Night Walker found him, badly shaken, thirsty and frightened to death by the circling wolves. Aaron's canteen of water had long since run dry and he was unable to prepare any food. He was certain he was about to meet his Maker when Night Walker appeared.

When the young brave had bent over him, Aaron was sure it was an apparition. He had never even seen an Indian. All he knew of them had come from stories other white men had brought back from the frontier, and most of them had been so exaggerated that Aaron could hardly discern truth from fiction.

He looked up at Night Walker and prayed silently, first that he was not as savage as he appeared, and next that he spoke a word or two of English. When Night Walker smiled, Aaron was relieved to think his first prayer had been answered. But when he spoke to Night Walker, he got no response.

"I don't know how to talk to you," Aaron groaned, "but I'm going to give it my best effort."

Night Walker had been younger then, and had not had much occasion to come face to face with any white man. He was on his way home from a successful hunt, and was annoyed at having to hang the deer he had killed in a tree, so that he could help Aaron back to the village. It had never even occurred to him to leave Aaron where he found him. No man of his village would leave a man to fend for himself if he needed help. At sixteen, Night Walker was too aware of his pride to do anything so unmanly.

Aaron tried several times to talk to Night Walker on the journey to the village, but he received no answer. To say he was frightened would have been a drastic understatement. And to say Night Walker was not aware of it would have been another. He could feel Aaron shaking; he just couldn't figure out why.

When they arrived at the village, both Aaron and Night Walker were the center of attention, which pleased Night Walker immensely.

During the time that Aaron spent in the village, he became aware of many things. The most important was that the Sioux were not savages at all.

He heard the laughter, saw the pride and the closeness of the tribe . . . and he began to understand them. He also began to teach them the rudiments of his language, and was pleased when they reciprocated. He sent word back to the fort by way of an Indian scout, a man not of the village, but one who was just passing through. He told Steven Brady he was well, that he was safe, and not to worry about him.

Aaron began to understand many of the things the people said. He was also pleased at the quick way the children picked up the words he spoke. He was quickly accepted by the little children, whose curiosity was unlimited, but not by the tall, powerful warriors, who seemed to watch every move he made with suspicion.

Night Walker was grimly determined not to speak the white tongue. But, inherently intelligent, he could not help absorbing what he heard. Soon he could understand, even though he still chose not to speak the English language.

Despite his determination not to respond to the

friendship Aaron offered, there came a moment when Night Walker had no choice. It happened early one morning. Never Quiet was a small child then, and had drifted from her mother's sight while she was kneeling at the river to fill water sacks. Aaron always rose early and went to the river to wash, and to pray in quiet. He was the only one who spotted Never Quiet when she tumbled into the swift-moving water and was swept from her feet. She cried out in fear, and her mother screamed and ran toward the spot. But it was clear she could never reach her in time. Aaron was farther downstream, and he dove into the water without thinking twice.

When Aaron finally dragged the child up onto the shore several minutes later, half the tribe had gathered. Sleeping Wolf, hearing his wife scream, had raced to the river. Night Walker and the others were not far behind him. They arrived in time to see an exhausted Aaron lift Never Quiet from the shallows and carry her ashore.

Night Walker was the first one to reach Aaron, and when Aaron put the limp little girl into his arms, he embraced the white man.

It led to a period in their lives that both Aaron and Night Walker would always cherish. It was a learning time as the days turned into weeks, then to months before they realized it. When Aaron saved Never Quiet, it was late summer. Through the fall and winter Aaron remained with them, learning their ways.

When he made his wish known that he had to

return to his people and let them know he was still alive, his decision was accepted. He was free to do as he chose. His stature in the tribe had risen with the rescue of Never Quiet. He wondered if another request would be granted to him, so he asked Night Walker to accompany him to the fort.

"To see that I make it safely," he said. "I am not equipped to travel that distance alone."

To Night Walker's surprise, they became even closer friends on that journey. Aaron found Night Walker to be extremely intelligent. Night Walker found Aaron to be a source of novel and intriguing ideas.

But Night Walker adamantly refused to go into the fort. He stopped when the fort was in sight, and bade Aaron farewell. No matter how much Aaron pleaded, Night Walker would go no further.

But Aaron was determined that this would not be his last contact with the Indians. There was much he could learn from them and much he could do to improve their lives, as well. He hoped he had made a connection that could be developed.

For the next few years, Aaron spent his time traveling between the village and the fort. A day's ride from the fort he was always joined by Night Walker, Soaring Eagle and often several more braves from the village. Often, he'd told Night Walker that it was beyond him how they knew he was coming.

Eventually, he built his mission so as to be nearer the village. Then he planned a school, but he knew that eventually he would have to go east to find someone who would consider teaching in it. He had told the tribe of his plan several months before. On the day of his departure, Night Walker and a number of his people had ridden to the hill beyond the mission to watch him leave.

Night Walker considered all this as he finished the evening meal. And now, Aaron was back. He was both pleased and somehow concerned about this. He'd had a strange feeling for some time, a portentous feeling, as if something of great importance was about to happen. He wasn't sure it was going to be something he would like, but he sensed that it was something that was going to change his life.

Later that night a council was called, and they sat about the fire discussing the different viewpoints held by the assorted men. Some were for the cultivation of the white men and favored acceptance of the new school. Others were for staying as far away from the white men as possible. The arrival of the young white women was also discussed. The chief, Flying Horse, sat silent, listening carefully, but offering nothing until he had all the differing points of view to weigh.

Night Walker watched both his father's face and that of his chief, but he could not tell what thoughts were passing through the minds of either. Both faces were expressionless, yet he could see they did not miss a word. He sat considering how he felt about the matter. He had been told by his father many times not to make decisions hastily, nor to voice them until they had been thought through. Now he was grateful for that advice. He was confused, and he knew it.

There had been too many arguments on both sides of the question, and he needed answers. Answers he could only find one way. He would go to speak with his old friend Aaron.

After the council he walked with his father.

"You have some thoughts you wish to discuss with me?" Sleeping Wolf questioned.

"I am going to see Aaron. It has been too long since our friend has joined us at our fire."

"Then invite him to come back to us."

"I will. All in the village will be pleased to have him with us again."

"I hope the bluecoats do not disagree with Aaron about this school. It might draw them here," Sleeping Wolf said.

"Aaron would do nothing to bring any harm to us."

"I think he takes his mission very seriously. He speaks of his God . . . and his God is not ours."

"It does not matter. He is our friend and he has done much for us. I will go and speak with our old friend. Maybe I can tell if he has changed since he went away."

"It would be a very painful thing to find Aaron was different, that he was no longer the man who lived among us. He had become like a brother. He slept with us, ate at our fire, hunted with us," Sleeping Wolf said, shaking his head. "Night Walker, it is best that someone from our camp does go to find out what is truth. Maybe . . . Maybe it would be best if you went alone. But you will not go into the white man's fort. You will go to Aaron when he is in his own home, so no one knows of your visit. Ask Aaron questions; watch his face. Soon you will be able to tell if the words he speaks are true."

"I will be very careful."

"And say nothing to Soaring Eagle. He will be the first to reach out and try to find bridges even if there are none. You know his heart will make room for reasons. He would trust before we are all sure trust is warranted."

"Soaring Eagle will not be pleased."

"It is how it must be," Sleeping Wolf said. His words were declared firmly; Night Walker understood they were to be the last spoken on the subject. He nodded his understanding, and Sleeping Wolf turned away.

Night Walker watched his father's tall form as he walked away; then he ducked his head and went inside.

Rolled in his furs, he found sleep slow in coming. When it did come, it was filled with disassociated dreams he could not begin to understand. . . .

He was hunting, and in his hand he carried one of the coveted long guns of the white man. The forest floor was covered with snow, and fine flakes were falling softly as he made his way slowly between the trees.

Suddenly he found himself at the edge of a

clearing. From where he stood, through the falling snow, he could see something huge standing in the center of the clear space.

He felt no fear as he moved toward it. But when he grew close he felt his heart begin to pound. It was a white buffalo! The sacred sign . . . But he did not understand.

The buffalo turned its shaggy head toward him and snorted, pawing the ground. Night Walker was awed that this sacred sign had been revealed to him. He was just as mystified when the buffalo began to back away from him. Its huge form was soon veiled by the falling snow.

Then, out of the mist of white, another form appeared. It was a golden, ethereal figure, and he could not stop himself from wanting to move closer. A woman! He could not believe what he was seeing, nor could he understand it. She smiled, and the huge buffalo appeared at her side.

Then, as suddenly as they had appeared, both vanished and he was left with a feeling of emptiness and loneliness so profound that it drew him up from the depths of sleep.

Chapter Four

Night Walker had considered his thoughts and his dreams all day. Then he had gone off alone to meditate. Still he was uncertain of what he would say to Aaron, and worried about what Aaron might say to him. Despite everything, Aaron was still a white man. Why had he brought two white women to the mission? If he had changed during his time away, then Night Walker knew a lot of problems faced them all.

Whatever the situation, he had to go and find out for himself. That was the only way he'd be satisfied.

Night Walker rode slowly, pondering the golden woman of his dream . . . the woman with hair like a sunrise that Laughing Thunder had described. Could there be a connection between the two?

The sun had set before Night Walker reached the outskirts of Aaron's settlement. From there he would move cautiously. He wanted to talk to Aaron, but not necessarily to any of the others. It would be better if they didn't know he'd come at all.

Tempest had returned from her daily walk to find Aaron and Brittany conferring over future plans. When she came in, both smiled, a bit surprised that they had been so involved in their conversation they'd forgotten the time.

Brittany snatched up her pad and pencil at once.

I'm sorry, Tempest, I know you must be starved. Aaron and I got so caught up in our plans, I forgot he came over to take us to dinner. Aunt Claudia and Uncle Myron have already gone to eat.

I am hungry, Tempest wrote. *This place is so beautiful. I guess I walked longer than I thought.*

I want to wash and change my clothes, Brittany wrote rapidly. *Why don't you and Aaron go on over? I'll join you in a few minutes.*

"That sounds like a good idea," Aaron said. He'd read over Brittany's shoulder. He smiled at Tempest, who smiled in return. "Come on, little one," he said to Tempest as he extended his arm. "Let's see what we can do about keeping those roses in your cheeks."

Tempest didn't know what he'd said, but she liked the openness of his smile and the friendliness in his eyes. She took his arm.

Brittany watched them leave. She'd seen Tempest's smile, and a slow feeling of hopeful warmth uncoiled within her. *Be happy, Tempest*, she thought silently. *Let fate give you something in return for all it has taken from you.*

She sighed and closed the door; then she walked to the bedroom, where she poured water from the pitcher into a bowl and washed her face and hands. Her hair, coiled tightly at the nape of her neck, needed to be brushed, so she unpinned it and brushed it, then decided to let it hang loose. She had to light a lamp before she found a comfortable cotton dress to wear, and she changed quickly. Just as she buttoned the last button, she heard a light rap on the door. She smiled. She had been too long, and Aaron had either come back or sent someone after her. She would have to watch that she didn't worry him too much. She had a feeling he meant to be overprotective with both her and Tempest.

She walked to the door with a smile and an apology on her lips. She grasped the handle and opened the door quickly.

For a moment she couldn't speak; in fact she couldn't seem to get her next breath. A man filled the doorway and every sense she possessed.

At first she thought she might scream, but she was sure if she opened her mouth, she wouldn't be able to get a squeak out. She was shocked to feel herself shaking. She had never in her life even imagined a man who looked like the one framed in the doorway.

He was big, yet lean and sleek, with rippling muscle under glistening amber skin, giving him a look of overpowering strength. His eyes were as dark as the night and seemed to be piercing her.

But if he was a shock to her, she could have no idea of the shattering experience Night Walker was going through.

He had been smugly satisfied when he'd tied his horse in the shadows of the trees and made his way to Aaron's. He knew he hadn't been seen and hoped to surprise Aaron. But when the door was opened, he was stricken to absolute silence.

A woman, Laughing Thunder had said, a woman! This was a vision, something he could hardly believe. Her hair was like a golden cloud and flowed about her shoulders. Her eyes were the color of fresh spring leaves.

It took him some moments to realize that she was staring at him with wide, shocked eyes. She was afraid.

Yes, Brittany was terrified. He was close to naked, wearing only a breechclout and moccasins because the weather was so warm. Brittany stood eye level with the broadest expanse of naked chest she had ever seen. In fact, she was so aware of his nakedness she didn't know where to look, so she chose what she thought was the lesser of two evils: to look up into his eyes.

Night Walker caught himself before he spoke to her in his own language. She looked frightened enough without his making it worse.

"I seek Aaron Abbott."

"Who . . . ah . . . who are you?" Brittany was more than annoyed with the fact that her voice quavered like a little girl's. His half smile didn't make her feel any happier.

"I am called Night Walker. Is Aaron here?" His voice was deep and strong.

"No, he's not here right now. He's eating."

"Go, and bring him to me," Night Walker said firmly, stepping inside. Brittany backed up as he closed the door behind him. "I will wait."

It was the arrogant command and the uninvited entrance, combined with the flat statement that he would wait, that brought Brittany out of her almost mesmerized condition.

"Was he expecting you?" she asked coolly.

Night Walker turned a dark look her way, raising one eyebrow in a show of surprise. This was certainly not the way for a woman to act. He would overlook it. She was a visitor to his land and Aaron's guest. Since he was in Aaron's house, he would not remind this woman of her place.

But Brittany did not back away from his dark look; instead she was returning it with an icy one of her own. She expected an answer. He was shocked.

"Yes. If you ask him, he will tell you that when he is here, in this house . . . he expects me. It is important that I speak with him." Night Walker continued to watch her. "Do you belong to Aaron?"

"Me? Belong? No, I do not belong to Aaron."

"Then who do you belong to?" He was totally

puzzled now. Why was she here if she did not belong to someone?

"I do not belong to anyone," Brittany said stiffly. "I belong to myself." She smiled now. "I've come to help Aaron."

Pieces of this puzzle began to assemble themselves in his mind.

"Bring Aaron to me. There is much we have to talk about."

Brittany struggled to remember that she was as much a guest in Aaron's house as this savage was, and to remember some of the things Aaron had told her about the Sioux. Still, she could not quite equate this tall and—yes, she had to admit—extremely handsome man with the gentle and affectionate people Aaron had described. He was much more the savage she had read about back East.

She nodded her agreement, but then realized she had to pass him to get to the door. He looked as immobile as a mountain. She would be damned if she'd circle around him like a frightened little girl.

She missed entirely the sparkle of laughter in Night Walker's eyes. He was reading her well and found her dilemma humorous.

Of course he was teasing her, but Brittany had no way of knowing that. She took a step or two toward him and he remained still. She was close enough to touch him, to smell his unique scent, a clean mingling of pine, cedar and leather. A heady, masculine smell that did her equilibrium little good.

His teasing had gone further than he'd intended. He'd expected her to back away. Instead
she raised her eyes to meet his. They were brilliant
green like sunlight on a new spring leaf, and something deep within him responded in a way he'd
least expected. He caught himself fighting the distinct urge to reach out and touch the spun gold of
her hair to see if it was as soft as it looked. He
didn't quite like this unwelcome feeling. He was
more aware of her than he had ever been of any
other woman, from the soft peach glow of her skin
to the pink-tinged mouth that seemed to beg to be
kissed.

Angry at himself, he stepped aside to let her
pass, which she did as rapidly as she could. Brittany would never admit that her heart was pounding so loud she was surprised he couldn't hear it.
She was shocked at herself and the sudden intensity of her reaction. She knew her cheeks were
pink and that unreasonable thoughts had crossed
her mind when their eyes met. Like . . . what
would it feel like if he put those hard-muscled
arms around her, and would his mouth be so firm
and unyielding if . . . oh Lord, she thought, this is
not real. I can't think thoughts like that.

Once she closed the door behind her, she lifted
her skirts and almost ran across the compound.
Then she paused to catch her breath before she
lifted the latch and walked inside.

Aaron saw Brittany first and motioned her to
join the small group at the table. But Brittany hesitated. She had no idea if Aaron would want the

others to know that Night Walker was there. After all, it seemed Night Walker had taken some precautions to see that his visit remained secret. She motioned Aaron to come to her.

Tempest and her aunt and uncle looked up questioningly at Aaron as he rose from his seat, then followed his gaze to see Brittany. But Aaron put a restraining hand on Tempest's shoulder as she started to rise. He smiled at all three and motioned them to remain where they were.

Aaron crossed the room to Brittany's side, sensing at once that something unusual had occurred.

"Brittany, is there some problem?"

"You have a visitor, Aaron."

"A visitor?"

"It's your friend Night Walker, and he asked . . . no, he commanded that I go and get you at once. What is he, a chief or something?"

"No," Aaron laughed. "He is perhaps one of my best friends. I hope the young man didn't frighten you. Really he is a charming fellow."

"I'm afraid his charm was lost on me," Brittany said wryly.

By this time Tempest was certain something was wrong. She rose quickly, leaving her aunt and uncle gazing after her silently. Tempest crossed the room quickly. She looked at Brittany with a questioning frown, but after Brittany had spoken a few words to Aaron, she smiled and motioned Tempest to come along.

As they crossed the compound, Brittany could sense an aura of excitement in Aaron. He seemed to be looking forward to seeing the implacable man Brittany had just met.

When Brittany had left the house, Night Walker smiled to himself. She'd been highly annoyed with him, and he wondered just what she was telling Aaron.

He looked around him and soon realized the woman must be living here, too. After he'd walked from familiar room to familiar room, he grew more puzzled. The bedroom was full of petticoats and dresses, and Night Walker was even more curious about the relationship between Aaron and this woman.

He'd returned to the main room and was standing before the fireplace when he heard someone approaching. When the door opened he got his second shock of the day. There were two of them!

He must have shown his surprise, for Aaron, who was following behind Brittany and Tempest, laughed. He walked toward Night Walker, his hand outstretched.

Aaron was so delighted to see his young friend, he could have embraced him, except he knew that Night Walker's reserved pride would not accept such a gesture. Instead, he shook his hand enthusiastically.

"Night Walker, my friend, it is good to see you again."

"It is good to see you, too, Aaron." Night Walker smiled. "You have been gone a long time. The whole village has missed you."

Brittany was watching the exchange, and she was again aware of how strikingly handsome Night Walker was. When he smiled, she thought, he was downright beautiful. She laughed to herself at the thought, but it was the only word that applied.

Brittany caught a glimpse of Tempest from the corner of her eye and could see she was gazing at Night Walker in amazed fascination. But there was no fear in her eyes, and Brittany was glad of that.

"What brings you here tonight, Night Walker?" Aaron was asking. "There is nothing wrong in the village, is there?"

"No, all is well there."

"How do you always know when I get back?"

Night Walker laughed. "We had scouts close by."

"And you came rushing over to see me." Aaron's eyes sparkled, and Night Walker had the grace to look a bit sheepish. The last thing he would admit was that he was curious . . . or even interested in seeing a golden-haired woman. He resorted to speaking his own language.

"Laughing Thunder was filled with tales and I was curious to see if what he said was true. He said there was a woman with hair like the sun. You know how excitable he can be."

"Yes, I do," Aaron replied in the same tongue. "Now you see for yourself."

"Have you taken a wife, Aaron? Or perhaps two?"

"No," he laughed, "I have not."

"Then where are their husbands, and why would they allow their wives to live with you?"

"Neither of the young ladies are married. I do not want to be rude and speak a language they do not understand. They are my guests—no, more than guests. Let me introduce them to you." Aaron turned to Brittany and Tempest. "Brittany, Tempest, my dears, this young man is the one I have told you about. The one who saved my life when I first came here. I owe a great deal to Night Walker and his people." Aaron turned to Night Walker. "This is Brittany Nelson. She has come to be my assistant in some new endeavors I have planned."

Aaron was well aware of Night Walker's puzzlement that he had not introduced both women, and of Brittany's surprise that he had not mentioned she was here to teach in his school.

"Night Walker," Brittany said softly, "I have heard a great deal about you. I am very happy to meet you." She extended her hand to him. He took her hand and felt its soft delicacy as he engulfed it in his large one. The contact created a unique sensation he wasn't quite prepared for. It was as if the room faded away from them and they stood alone. Again he was displeased with himself. He was acting like a young boy.

"And this young lady is Brittany's sister, Tempest. She does not hear. Nor does she speak."

For a second Night Walker paused. Then he smiled warmly at Tempest, who blushed and smiled. Night Walker made the hand gesture for "Welcome, friend."

"I'm afraid she does not know the signs," Aaron said.

"Then how—" He wanted to ask a million questions, but he didn't want to upset Brittany, who was regarding him closely.

"She reads well," Brittany answered calmly, but Night Walker could sense . . . not hostility . . . but some form of resistance. He regarded her closely. She stood close to her sister, and finally he had his answer. She was protective . . . very protective. That was what he sensed.

Softening his words with a cautious smile, he spoke gently. "And what if you are too far away from her to use this . . . writing? Or . . . perhaps she never gets that far away from you?"

Tempest watched Brittany's cheeks pinken and her eyes glow with indignation. Whatever this tall man had said to Brittany, it had roused her anger. Tempest had a feeling they were discussing her, and she didn't want to be the cause of a problem for Brittany. It had happened too often in the past. She laid one hand gently on Brittany's arm and extended the other to Night Walker.

Night Walker took it with a warm smile. This woman had spirit, maybe more than her sister thought. Although Night Walker knew she could not understand, he made the rapid signs that expressed his pleasure at her presence in his land.

Tempest smiled, reading his eyes well. They

were friendly and had no hint of the pity she had read so often in the eyes of others.

"I believe she understands your meaning without understanding the sign." Aaron spoke with pleasure.

"She seems to be a very intelligent woman. My people will welcome her here," Night Walker replied to Aaron, but he was watching Brittany again and his words seemed to disturb her even more.

"My sister and I are not here to socialize," she said firmly. "I am here to teach in Aaron's school, and Tempest is here to help in the infirmary." Her words sounded much more defensive than she'd wanted, but it was too late to call them back.

Night Walker looked at Aaron, and Aaron knew exactly what he was thinking. For a moment he closed his eyes. Brittany's bald statement had only made the situation worse. He had known there was resistance to the idea of a formal school, but now he realized the Sioux might utterly reject a female teacher unless she was introduced in the right way.

"You plan to teach our children?" Night Walker's voice was like ice. "It is a father's duty to teach his sons, and a mother's to teach her daughters," he replied.

"And that is all?" Brittany asked casually.

"That is all that is needed."

"That's not true any longer. Things are changing."

"My people were on this land long before the

71

time of my great-grandfather's grandfather. And we will be here when you are gone."

Brittany was on the verge of battle, and Aaron and Tempest could read her as easily as they could Night Walker, who didn't try to hide his contempt for the intrusion of white men in a territory he considered already claimed.

"Night Walker, are you hungry? I'm being very remiss as a host," Aaron interrupted.

"No, I'm not hungry. I will go now. I came only to invite you back to the village."

Night Walker had realized he had been on the verge of doing more than insulting Aaron's guests. In fact, he'd been tempted to shake some sense into Brittany and might have if Aaron hadn't been there.

He smiled in satisfaction at the knowledge that Brittany had not misunderstood him. She wasn't welcome here, and he felt he'd made that clear enough. Despite her beauty, Brittany Nelson could be a disturbing force. And she had so great an effect on him, he had to bring up every defense he knew.

"Well, thank you," Aaron replied coolly, determined to beat Night Walker at his little game. He was going to get Brittany and Tempest accepted within the tribe if it took his last breath. "And I'm sure your people would welcome my guests, also. I want the girls to meet them."

"Of course, they would be welcome," Night Walker replied. Pride would not allow him to refuse them his people's hospitality, yet the gleam of mischievous laughter in Aaron's eyes made him respond with a clenched smile.

He walked to the door, opened it and turned to look back at the three who watched him with very different attitudes. Aaron was smiling, Tempest was regarding him with interest, and Brittany . . . Brittany was seething with contained emotions.

Once he'd closed the door between them and had blended into the night, alone with his thoughts, he again allowed Brittany and Tempest into his mind.

The silent one was interesting. He saw no cowardice in her. But he saw no challenge either. She seemed . . . enclosed in a shell.

But Brittany was different. What puzzled him was that he couldn't really figure out what the difference was. Maybe it was because he saw the light of battle in her eyes and knew instinctively she was a woman of strength who would fight for what she wanted.

He tried to ignore the unique effect she'd had on him, but his senses wouldn't allow it. As if she were close to him, he could still smell the delicate scent of her and feel the soft texture of her skin. She was dangerous to him in a way he refused to define.

It would be best, he decided, to keep as distant from her as possible. He wished it were in his power to keep them from his village. But Aaron was too much of a friend for him even to consider that.

Still, he meant to fight for one thing. He was not

going to allow any white woman to force white ways into the minds of his people's children. Here he drew the line of battle and he would not allow anyone to sway him . . . even the beautiful Brittany Nelson.

Brittany gazed at the closed door for a minute and then realized she was actually trembling with anger.

She had the feeling Night Walker's obstinacy wasn't caused by a lack of intelligence. No, she could see a quick mind behind those penetrating eyes. But he also had a streak of pure male superiority and meanness, and she had the urge to do something violent just to watch his attitude change.

She turned to look at Aaron in time to see him trying to control his amusement, and she had to smile.

Tempest finally relaxed. For a minute she had imagined Brittany was going to attack the tall and very formidable man who had just left. But Brittany was now laughing.

"Brittany, my dear, you didn't get a chance to eat anything and I'm sure Tempest didn't finish her meal. Shall we go back and continue our dinner?" Aaron suggested.

"Yes," Brittany said. "I have a lot of questions to ask you."

"I have no doubt of that, at all," Aaron laughed.

The three of them again crossed the compound. Most of the others had already finished their meals and had gone about their evening's work.

They ate together while Aaron answered Brittany's questions. He told her about Flying Horse's village and the people's daily habits. Occasionally Brittany would write rapid notes for Tempest's benefit.

When the sisters finally walked back to their small house, both were enjoying the warm evening air. The moon was a huge, orange-gold ball in a midnight sky sprinkled with millions of diamond-bright stars. Out here the stars seemed much closer than they had in Philadelphia. Brittany felt that if she reached up, she could touch one.

She inhaled scents for which she had no name, and would never be able to describe. She was almost reluctant to go inside when they reached the house. But she knew her days would be overflowing from now on, and they had not yet finished unpacking. The weeks ahead promised to be interesting at the very least.

Both girls were tired by the time they got everything in place, but both were contented as well. Tempest followed Brittany to her room to share a few moments before she went to her own room. Brittany laughed as she took her pad and pencil from a nearby table.

This house needs a woman's touch, she wrote. *Perhaps we can at least make some curtains for the windows*.

Tempest nodded and responded, *I wonder if Aaron has something we can make them from?*

What about one of my old cotton dresses, in case he doesn't?

Excellent idea. Brittany, why were you angry with Aaron's friend?

I wasn't angry.

I may not be able to hear your voice, but I can see your eyes. You were angry.

Well, he was being so arrogant.

He was handsome. I wonder if they all look like him.

I hadn't noticed if he was handsome or not, Brittany wrote hastily. *We'd better get some sleep. We have an early start in the morning.*

Tempest watched as Brittany moved away and began to undress for bed. Her eyes still sparkled as they had when she'd confronted Night Walker. He was handsome, and whether Brittany would admit it or not, she was aware of it. From the doorway Tempest blew Brittany a kiss and left the room, closing the door behind her.

When Brittany blew out the lamp and climbed into bed, she was doing her best to keep her mind as far away from Night Walker as she could.

She began to consider the job she had come here to do, and a new determination took hold of her.

Night Walker had rejected the idea of a white woman teaching the Indian children, and had made it clear that he did not welcome her here. But she was as stubborn as he was. She knew the white world was closer than he would believe, and she intended to prepare as many children for it as she could. If she had to walk over him to do it, she darn well would. With this satisfying thought, she drifted into sleep.

Chapter Five

Brittany and Tempest were caught up in preparations for their new positions as teacher and assistant in the hospital. At the same time, both were trying to reassure their aunt and uncle that they were no longer needed as chaperones.

Within a few days, Aunt Claudia was already making plans to go back to Sioux Falls and then continue on to California, where she planned to visit her daughter. She promised Brittany she would write to James and assure him all was well. Of course, Brittany thought humorously, Aunt Claudia hadn't seen any Indians . . . especially not Night Walker. She wondered how close Aunt Claudia would come to a seizure if she saw him.

In the meanwhile Aaron was busy preparing to visit the Sioux village. Despite Night Walker's invitation to the two girls, Aaron now felt it would be best if he made this first trip alone. From Night Walker's reaction, he realized it might be difficult to convince the village council to accept a white woman as a teacher. Schoolmarms were so prevalent in his own society, he had never anticipated this problem when he'd convinced Brittany to accompany him.

"But, Aaron," Brittany argued, "if I am to have any chance of teaching the children in Flying Horse's village, wouldn't it be better if they saw me with you? Wouldn't they accept me more easily?"

"This is my first trip there since I've returned, Brittany, and I don't know if it is the appropriate time. Most certainly I will not take Tempest."

"What do you mean you don't know if it's appropriate? I thought that was why you brought me here? As for Tempest, it's best she remain here until we see how things go. At least I agree with you on that."

"Brittany," Aaron laughed, "you are most stubborn."

"I know." She smiled in response. "But I think that's the only way I can get what I think is right."

"What do you think you will accomplish? They will hardly listen to a demand from a woman."

"Aaron, I'm not . . . I'd like to try to establish some kind of relationship with the Sioux. At least open the door to talk."

"And you'd like to see the village . . . and the children."

"You've recognized my curiosity from the time we first met. I've come here with a goal. Give me a chance to fulfill it."

"I'll think about it, child, I'll think about it."

The following morning Brittany woke long before dawn, excitement drawing her up from pleasant dreams. Aaron had to decide today if he would let her go to the village with him. She knew he was already preparing things he meant to carry along and that he'd soon be on his way. She wanted to go so badly she could taste it.

They all ate breakfast early, and Aaron finally gave in as gracefully as he could manage. He'd decided that her enthusiasm might make a positive impression on Flying Horse and his council.

Aaron, Skinner and Brittany set out later that day with two packhorses loaded with gifts for his friends. Aaron had explained to both girls what great gift-givers the Indians were and that he usually tried to reciprocate when he could. He brought iron cooking kettles and other utensils the women loved. Aaron had also explained that these gifts were an entirely different thing from the supplies he brought, which usually consisted of salt, sugar and other necessities.

Brittany could see Aaron was excited. As they rode, he began to explain the unique situation in which Brittany was about to find herself.

"Brittany, you must control your questions and your opinions. The men will decide whether having a white woman teach their children is acceptable."

"The men? I thought the mothers taught the children, too. Mothers are women, too, or have they forgotten?"

"Well," Aaron said, "there is no doubt a woman can influence her husband or her children, and she does. But warriors . . . boys . . . are generally taught by their fathers."

"To read and write and—"

"No." Aaron drew his horse to a halt. "But if you are not going to abide by their beliefs and my wishes, then it's best you go back now. I won't have everything we've planned jeopardized because you don't agree with their culture."

There was no doubt in Brittany's mind that Aaron meant what he said. She swallowed any words she might have used to respond, and smiled.

"I'll be a good little girl and be as quiet as a mouse." One raised eyebrow made Brittany realize Aaron wasn't convinced. "I swear, Aaron. I'll be a docile young lady."

"I'm not trying to upset you, but this school is too important to be lost because we want everything our way. Look on us as peace negotiators as well as educators. Their entire culture is different from ours."

"I know. I'll do my best to follow your lead. I know how long you've needed a teacher and how difficult this might be. I'll do nothing to damage your plans if I can help it."

"Thank you, my dear. You won't regret it."

They rode on toward the village. Brittany contemplated her position, wondering for the first time what she'd gotten herself into.

After Brittany had gone, Tempest tidied up the house in her usual efficient manner. She went next to the infirmary, where she bathed and cared for Amy Carter, who watched her in awe. Thomas smiled and hastily wrote that there was little to do until later, and if she wanted to enjoy the day a bit she could.

Taking a book with her, Tempest started out for her habitual daily walk. It was warm out, so she wore one of her lightest dresses. She had tied her hair back carelessly with a green ribbon that matched the tiny flowers in her white dress. It was not long before the breeze blew wisps of her hair free of confinement.

Her skin was beginning to flush with a healthy glow and the beginnings of a tan; since she'd arrived at the mission she'd walked every day and had enjoyed the sun.

Tempest felt freer here than she had at home. Everyone seemed to accept her silence. She liked the immensity of this place. The blue canopy that covered the vast wide space made her feel anonymous somehow, as though her problems were not so significant after all.

She'd been warned by nearly everyone not to walk too far from the compound. There were no end of predators, she'd been told. But the day was too beautiful for her to worry about such things. She meant to enjoy it by finding a pretty spot to read the small book of poetry she had brought along.

After she passed beyond the thick stand of trees at the edge of the compound, she faced an undulating plain of waist-high grass that seemed to roll in the breeze like a mighty ocean.

She walked slowly until she felt surrounded by it, and enjoyed the exalting feeling that she was alone in a world of rare beauty and peace.

She moved slowly, enjoyed the almost sensual pleasure of warm sun, soft breezes and visual beauty. Caught up in all of this, she hardly realized how far she was drifting.

The tall grass grew shorter and shorter, and soon she walked out on a plain that looked as if a herd of cattle had grazed on it.

Across this field lay another dark green stand of trees. Tempest thought it would be the perfect spot to sit in the shade and read awhile before she started back.

When dawn broke, Soaring Eagle was already awake and preparing to hunt. His thoughts, however, were not on the weapons he was gathering, but on his brother. Night Walker usually shared almost everything with him, but Soaring Eagle knew there was some secret Night Walker was keeping to himself.

Soaring Eagle had a habit of hunting as a means of resolving problems in his mind and today was no exception. He would figure out what he should say to his brother and be prepared to confront him when the day was over.

By the time the day's glow was seeping through the early morning fog, Soaring Eagle was already riding away from the village.

Now he rode along the edge of the forest, enjoying what promised to be a beautiful day. As he rode he realized how long it had been since the great herds of buffalo had passed this way. The white man had preyed on them until it was difficult to find anything but small clusters. Always, when he began to hunt, he prayed to find the shaggy beasts that provided his people with so much. When he found one he gave thanks to the great spirit and spoke his thanks to the beast itself before he killed it.

From the edge of the tree line where he had paused, he looked out over a flat area of well-grazed grass. Surely some of the buffalo had passed this way. He was about to kick his horse into motion when he saw a movement on the opposite side of the clearing. He paused and sat motionless until he could discern someone walking across the field.

His eyes grew wide with shock when he saw the sun sparkle on hair the color of ripe wheat. A woman ! And even more surprising, a white woman! What was a white woman doing out here alone?

At first he thought to ride out to her, but he wasn't too sure how he would be received. Who knew what the white soldiers at the fort would do if she cried that he had attacked her? No, it was better to let her pass this way in peace and never know he'd been there. He remained still, watching her.

When she had nearly reached the center of the field, she paused for a moment. He watched her lift her face to the warmth of the sun.

Even from where he was he could see she was young. He smiled to himself at his own control. Had she been one of the women from his village, he would have ridden out to talk with her. Even now the temptation was great.

The smile froze on his face when a movement at the far end of the field drew his attention. Even from this great a distance he could recognize the huge, shaggy shape. It was a buffalo. It swayed its head back and forth, and in seconds Soaring Eagle realized it had seen the woman. Obviously she had not seen it. His experienced eye told him the buffalo was sick. Being herd animals, buffalo seldom went off alone. This one must be sick, and it was a threat to anyone in its path. It had to be killed—first to protect the woman and second to put it out of its misery.

There was no doubt in Soaring Eagle's mind that if she continued across the field, the beast would attack. He moved his horse out a few feet and called to her, but her attention remained ahead of her. He called out again, his voice deep and resonant. Surely she heard him. His worry began to change into anger. She had no business here anyway, wandering about alone.

The buffalo had lowered its head, and Soaring Eagle knew there was no question now of attack, and no question about what he must do. He kicked his horse into motion and raced to intercept the charging animal.

Tempest, totally unaware of the animal's threat and oblivious to Soaring Eagle's cries of warning, continued to drift slowly across the meadow.

Since Soaring Eagle was closer to her, it was his sudden movement that caught her attention. She turned abruptly and froze, her eyes widening with terror. Bearing down on her was the largest man she had ever seen, and he looked deadly. She could not run and she could not scream. To Tempest it appeared that she was being attacked by this fierce-looking person. Her legs trembled and her heart pounded so furiously she could barely breathe. He grew closer and closer.

He was almost upon her when Tempest flung up both hands in what would have been an ineffectual move had Soaring Eagle really been intent on harming her. She closed her eyes and prayed the end would be quick. She was startled when he rushed past her so close she could feel the brush of man and horse. She was so shocked she turned to follow his movement. Perhaps he was playing with her, tormenting her before he . . . Then she saw the charging buffalo.

Intent on its victim, the buffalo was confused by Soaring Eagle's attack. Illness and confusion brought the animal to a panting stop.

Because the buffalo was weakened, the ensuing

battle did not take long. Tempest watched as Soaring Eagle and the buffalo came together. Expertly he dispatched the animal, and when it lay dead, he turned his attention to the woman.

He dismounted and strode toward her. Relief that she was safe gave way to anger that she was alone and had not paid attention to his call of warning.

To Tempest he looked even more fierce, and she backed away from him.

"What are you doing here alone? Why did you ignore me? You could have been killed!" Soaring Eagle was now grateful that he had learned her language from Aaron. But despite his efforts at control, his voice was harsh.

Tempest made no sound, but her eyes welled with tears and she began to shake.

"Answer me, woman! Why did you not run when I told you to?"

Tempest was shaking her head. Thinking she was going to turn and run, he reached out and took hold of her shoulders. She gave a soft moaning cry, and he realized she was terrified of him.

Immediately he was contrite. He released her and backed up a step or two.

"I am sorry to frighten you," he said with a smile, "but you frightened me. Who are you?"

Tempest's face was white and he could see she was still trembling. Perhaps, he thought, because he was so well armed, she believed he might harm her. Slowly he took his knife from his belt. Her eyes flew from his face to the knife and back to his face. He'd been right. He laid the knife on the ground, and beside it he placed his bow and quiver of arrows. Then he stepped away from the weapons and extended both hands palm up to express his friendly intentions.

"I would not harm you. My name is Soaring Eagle and I am of Flying Horse's village. Who are you? What village are you from?"

She did not answer, and for a moment he was again annoyed. Then, like a flash of lightning on a black night, he realized she did not seem to understand . . . or to hear.

Perhaps . . . He moved toward her again. Since he had smiled and laid aside his weapons, she seemed less frightened. He went to her, placed his hands on her shoulders and turned her to stand with her back to him.

Lifting his head, he gave the cry of the coyote, and in seconds he knew. She could not hear him.

Tempest was certain she had no chance to get away from a man as powerful as this one, and she had recognized his laying aside his weapons and his gesture as one of friendship. When he turned her around to face him again, her eyes lifted to his.

For several seconds two uniquely different people simply stood and looked at each other. Soaring Eagle was bewildered. How could he talk to her? He pointed back toward his village, and Tempest shook her head no and pointed toward Aaron's home.

Soaring Eagle smiled a brilliant and relieved

smile. She was of Aaron's village, the only one that lay in that direction. Surely that made them friends. Still, how was he to convey this to her?

Along with his recognition of her condition came the realization of her beauty. She was unlike any woman he had known, flushed and golden as the morning sunrise.

He pointed to Aaron's village and pressed his closed fist against his chest. Then he pointed to his village, his horse, and then her. Tempest watched him closely. Once he'd pointed to her, he again tapped his own chest. Then again toward his village.

He could see the quick intelligence in her eyes and was overjoyed when she seemed to understand that he wanted her to accompany him to his village.

Tempest realized that his village was Aaron and Brittany's destination. Her decision, she knew, was risky but it was a chance she would take. This huge man had tried to express friendship and had rescued her from sure death. She smiled and nodded. Soaring Eagle decided at once that he was going to do all in his power to make her smile again.

He gestured for her to wait, then he turned, gathered his weapons and walked to his horse. As he led it back to her, his mind was searching for avenues of communication. Did she know the signs? When he reached her side he tried . . . but she only gazed at him. He sighed. He would have to try another way.

Had she been a woman of his village he would not have worried about her getting home. He could have gone on with his hunting. But this fragile-looking creature seemed so helpless. After the threat she had just faced, he didn't mean to take any chances. Besides, he had a good idea now that Night Walker already knew of the white woman, and he planned to watch his brother's face when he brought . . . he couldn't even ask her name. He shrugged away the obstacle. He meant to find a way.

His first problem would be to get her on his saddleless horse. Putting his hands on her was a problem. Aaron would certainly be angered if one of his women even thought she was harmed.

In one lithe movement he swung up on his horse. Then he reached down a hand, hoping she would agree to take it. He wasn't quite sure what he would do if she didn't.

But Tempest smiled up at him, no fear in her eyes, and took his hand. He swung her up before him.

For a brief moment the feel of her resting against him, the scent of her hair, almost took his mind from what had to be done. Then he kicked his horse into motion and rode toward his village.

Brittany didn't have to be reminded by Aaron how important their visit was, but she did have to keep his words of temperance in mind. She was fascinated by the number of tepees and the amount of activity she witnessed as they rode into the village. Color was her first impression, and peace was the next. A million questions clamored to be asked. Still, she kept Aaron's words in mind and did nothing but smile.

The entire village turned out to greet them, and did little to mask their curiosity. By the time Brittany stepped down from her horse, she was already surrounded, mostly by the young girls. Boys were much too self-important to reveal their curiosity. It was no surprise to Aaron that the first questioning voice was that of Never Quiet.

"Who are you?" Never Quiet asked immediately, knowing that once her father appeared none of her questions would get answers. She reached to touch the strange clothes Brittany was wearing. "So pretty. Are you Aaron's wife? Are you going to stay? If you are, I—"

"Never Quiet." The voice that brought a halt to Never Quiet's chattering was firm. Brittany turned to look at the man who now stood beside Aaron. "That is no way to greet our guests," he said. His face was stern, but Brittany was sure she saw a twinkle in his eyes.

Brittany came close to laughing as she witnessed the child's wordless rebellion. Never Quiet took a step away from her but refused to give more ground, and Brittany knew that at the first opportunity she would again be inundated with questions. As a matter of fact, she looked forward to it.

"Brittany, my dear, this is Sleeping Wolf."

"We welcome Aaron's friend to our village."

There was something familiar about Sleeping Wolf. Something she could not put her finger on.

"Perhaps Never Quiet can show you the village while Sleeping Wolf and I talk," Aaron suggested. This was obviously an immense pleasure to Never Quiet, but Brittany was aware that she was being relegated to "visitor" while Aaron and Sleeping Wolf discussed the future she planned to be part of.

Still, she had promised her cooperation, so she obediently went off with a proud Never Quiet and a cluster of young women and girls.

As they walked, Never Quiet kept up a steady stream of questions. Brittany did her best to answer some of them in hopes of stemming the flood so she could ask some questions of her own.

"My name is Brittany, and no, I'm not Aaron's wife, but I am his friend and I certainly hope I can stay. Your name is Never Quiet. Is Sleeping Wolf your father?"

"Yes." Her smile was quick and guileless. "He says I talk too much."

"Do you have brothers and sisters?"

"Oh yes," Never Quiet said. "Night Walker, Soaring Eagle, Laughing Thunder, Star Dancer and Running Cougar."

Night Walker! The huge, handsome man who had come to Aaron's house was this sweet child's brother. Brittany tried to push aside his image.

"Are they all older than you?"

"Yes." Her face, so easily read, displayed her annoyance at this. "If you are no one's wife, why did you come to live with Aaron?"

"I'm a teacher. I will teach in Aaron's school."

Never Quiet blinked in surprise. "Aaron has always taught us."

"I know, but he needs my help."

"You are not married and do not have any children?"

"No."

"If you are not married and have no children, then you have no one to teach."

"I teach any child that wants to learn."

"Learn what?" Never Quiet questioned.

Brittany was trying to control her smile. "Reading, writing, arithmetic and whatever else their curiosity leads them to. Wouldn't you like to learn to read and write?"

Never Quiet exchanged looks with the cluster of girls around her. "Aaron has been trying to teach me since I was a baby."

"Don't you enjoy it?"

"Sometimes . . . except when I do not want to go to school."

"What happens then?"

"I do not go," Never Quiet said innocently.

At that moment Brittany began to understand she might have more of a job cut out for her than she'd realized.

"That is not a good thing, Never Quiet."

"Why?" she questioned.

"Well . . . because . . ." Brittany began. But she realized there was no way to form a relationship in Never Quiet's mind between the world the child enjoyed now and the new, brighter world that could be in the future. Besides, she was doing exactly what Aaron had asked her not to do.

"It's difficult to explain," she said, feeling a retreat was in order. "Perhaps the next time I come, I can bring some books and read some stories to you."

"Grandmother tells us stories, but she doesn't have to read them. They are remembered stories of past times."

"I should like to hear some of them one day soon."

There was again a confusion of happy chatter, and the girls urged her to see as much as she could in the short time she would be with them.

Fascination with their daily life soon took hold. She was awed at the fine quill work with which the women decorated their clothes, especially the shirts of their husbands.

She tried to absorb as much as she could as she was taken from one tepee to the next and presented to one shy, dark-eyed mother after another.

Colorful woven baskets told stories of their own, as did the equally colorful blankets. Stories of ancestry so old there were few who knew all the tales.

She began to realize, as Aaron had intended her to, that these were people who did not need any sympathy from her or any of her race. What they needed was to be understood and respected on their own terms. Brittany was soon faced with the realization that she had, in reality, come here to change their way of living. That was no longer an acceptable goal.

The last place to which Never Quiet led Brittany was her own tepee. A pretty woman sat before it grinding grain for the evening meal. It was the same tepee she and Aaron had stopped at first. No doubt, Brittany thought, this was Never Quiet's mother . . . and also Night Walker's mother.

The woman smiled up at Brittany, and then rose to welcome her. "Welcome to our home," she said. "I am Night Bird." She was at least five inches shorter than Brittany, and very small. Brittany gazed at her, wondering that this almost delicate woman had given birth to a son as large and strong as Night Walker . . . in fact, had given birth to five other children besides her eldest.

Night Bird's eyes were like liquid amber, and Brittany knew they were assessing her very closely.

"You will join us for the evening meal?" Night Bird's voice was as soft and flowing as her eyes.

"I . . . I don't know. I shall have to ask Aaron."

"Oh"—Night Bird smiled—"I know Aaron will not leave without eating. My husband would not be pleased. Come, sit and speak with me." She glanced at her daughter, her eyes filled with love and a bit of determination. "And my chattering daughter will fill the water skins she forgot to fill this morning."

There was resistance in every line of Never Quiet's face and body. But it was never verbalized.

Instead she took up the water skins and started for the river. The sooner she finished the job, the sooner the million questions she had for Brittany could be answered.

Night Bird drew aside the flap and let Brittany step inside first. The tepee was much larger than she had expected, and looked surprisingly comfortable.

There were a great many buffalo skins folded against one corner. A large number of things Brittany could not yet name hung in various places.

The smoke hole at the top of the tepee was open so that the smoke from the fire could find its way out. Brittany was surprised to see a cast-iron pot, its contents bubbling away. She was reasonably certain this was among the many things supplied to the village by Aaron.

"Would you like a cool drink?"

"No, thank you."

Night Bird motioned for her to sit, and Brittany found that the buffalo robe she sat on was braced from underneath by a board against which she could rest her back. Night Bird sat across the fire from her.

"From what Never Quiet tells me, you have a large family."

"Yes." Night Bird's amber eyes glowed with pride. "I have four sons and two daughters. Never Quiet is my youngest."

"Yes, she has told me."

"It does not always please her to be the youngest. Perhaps that is why her tongue is never still. You have no children?"

"No, I am not married."

"You are far from your family."

"Actually my parents are dead. I have a sister and brother."

"Your sister has come here with you."

"I'm not surprised that you know that." Brittany smiled. "Aaron says it is impossible to cross this land without your people knowing it."

"Flying Horse and my husband take great care to know who crosses this land, who remains on it . . . and why they remain. And your brother, does he come with you?"

"No . . . he and his wife will remain in my parents' home."

Night Bird was about to ask another question when the sound of excited voices came to them. Both Night Bird and Brittany rose and went outside.

A rider was approaching, and in a minute an excited Never Quiet was at her mother's side. This was the most unique and exciting day that had ever occurred in Never Quiet's life.

"Soaring Eagle comes, Mother, and he brings someone with him!" She turned to face Brittany, her eyes glowing. "A woman with sun hair, like yours."

Brittany was shocked. There was, as far as she knew, only one other woman with hair the color of hers. How could Tempest have found her way into the company of Night Walker's brother, and what was she doing here? Had Tempest gotten lost? Was she afraid?

Brittany's heart began to pound as she watched the riders approach.

But the handsome young warrior on horseback was smiling and looked quite pleased at the furor he'd started as he came to a stop beside them. His smile wavered as he caught sight of Brittany.

He slid from his horse in a graceful motion and helped Tempest down. Brittany rushed to her sister's side, but Tempest's smile soon relieved her fears. Now she was full of questions and had no pencil or paper on which to convey them. She turned to look at the young man for her answers.

Chapter Six

Soaring Eagle was, for the first time in his life, a bit tongue-tied. It had been a shock to find a white woman in the wilderness, but to find another in his village was something else. For a minute he found it hard to focus on all he'd meant to say. But Brittany's questioning gaze had centered everyone's attention on him . . . especially his mother's.

"I found her," were his first words. It angered him that those three words made him sound a bit like a little boy who'd found some treasure he didn't want to share with anyone else. Stubbornly he set his jaw and told what had happened. In mid-story he was aware that Sleeping Wolf and Aaron had joined the group. He tried not to put too much emphasis on the fact that Tempest would be dead if he had not killed the buffalo. He didn't want to trip over his own pride.

"You've saved my sister's life," Brittany said. "I don't know why she was there, but I'm grateful that you were."

Soaring Eagle flushed both with discomfort and pride . . . and the pleasure he felt when Tempest's sunny smile returned to him.

"We owe you a great deal, Soaring Eagle. A life is a precious thing and it puts us in your debt." Brittany spoke softly. "I know of no way to repay you for what you've done."

"I ask no payment," he said stiffly. Brittany began to wonder if she had made a mistake. It seemed the warriors wore their pride on their sleeves.

"Then will our friendship begin to show you just how much we appreciate what you've done?"

This appealed to Soaring Eagle, who glanced again at Tempest. Her eyes had seldom left him since their arrival.

"Your sister cannot hear?"

"No. She suffered an accident as a child."

"And she cannot speak?"

"I . . . I don't know."

Soaring Eagle would have asked the questions that formed in his mind, but he read cautionary expressions on the faces of his father and Aaron.

Never Quiet was almost beside herself with the desire to know all about this pretty, silent woman and her sister. She was afraid that Aaron would remove them from the village before she could satisfy her curiosity.

But her worries were soon relieved. Sleeping Wolf had already extended an invitation for them to stay, and Aaron had agreed.

Soaring Eagle also felt relieved at this news. He tried studiously to keep his eyes from Tempest and to hide the pleasure her staying gave him. Although he had no idea how he would communicate with her, he didn't intend to let that daunt him. He had an overwhelming desire to see her smile again.

Although the others might have missed it, Brittany was not unaware that Tempest had been regarding Soaring Eagle with unusual intensity. What was worse was the admiring and warm glances Soaring Eagle was sending her way.

Brittany didn't want to start any kind of confrontation, but she was afraid things might be getting out of hand. Tempest needed to be protected from a relationship she could not possibly understand. Unaware of Aaron's astute gaze, Brittany moved a little closer to Tempest.

"Come, I will show you where you will sleep," Never Quiet said, quick to grasp the opportunity to again get Brittany alone. Brittany took Tempest's hand and motioned her to come with them. Soaring Eagle watched them walk away . . . and Aaron watched Soaring Eagle.

From a vantage point on a hill above the village, Night Walker watched the cluster of people before his father's tepee. Even from this distance he recognized Brittany. He watched her in animated conversation with his brother.

He watched as Never Quiet drew Brittany and Tempest away from the group. Only then did he urge his horse into motion and ride down toward the village.

By the time he arrived, Aaron and Sleeping Wolf stood alone talking. They had walked a short distance into the shade of a tree, where they stood together.

"Your son has done a fine thing, Sleeping Wolf."

"To rescue the girl from a suffering beast?" Sleeping Wolf shook his head at this.

"No, to be so considerate about the girl's affliction."

"He is much like his mother. His spirit is generous and his heart is always open to the weak among those he knows."

"I am glad he found her in time."

"Aaron . . . Why is the woman so frightened?"

"Frightened? Tempest? I don't think it is fear."

"Not the child Soaring Eagle found . . . her sister."

"What makes you think she is frightened?"

"She watches her young sister like the prairie mouse watches for the hawk. Does she not trust her?"

"You have sharp eyes, Sleeping Wolf. She trusts her sister, but she does fear. In fact, she fears more than her sister does. She protects her . . . from everything and anything. She would make the path her sister walks free of even the slightest pebble over which she might stumble. She watches for any sign of danger. She would stand between her and—"

"And living," Sleeping Wolf said softly.

"Yes, I'm afraid you are right. I had hoped that coming here would help to change that."

"Does she not know that the gods protect those like her sister? That they plan their lives no matter what others intend?"

"No, she does not believe that. She believes her sister's life is her responsibility."

"And what will happen when her sister takes her own life in her hands? I have looked closely and I see she will do so one day."

"Brittany will have to accept that and realize her own life is all she can answer for."

As Aaron spoke, Sleeping Wolf's gaze moved past him, and he smiled. "Night Walker comes."

"Ah," Aaron chuckled, "I am afraid your son also has some fears about this new situation."

"I have never seen him show fear of anything in his life."

"Fear of change perhaps."

"Of accepting the white man on our lands? That is not fear. Perhaps it is wisdom."

"Perhaps." Aaron smiled.

Neither man spoke again as they watched rider and horse approach. Night Walker dismounted in one easy gliding movement and, leading his horse, came to stand beside them. Before anyone could speak, Skinner hailed them from a short distance and came to join them. He had spent many days in the village in past years, and he and Night Walker were friends.

"Aaron"—Night Walker smiled as he turned to his friend—"it is good to see you among us again. And you, Skinner. You are welcome."

Skinner grinned his wide-faced grin.

"It is good to be here." Aaron spoke for both.

"I knew you meant to come soon, but you must have ridden with the sun this morning."

"We did. Brittany and I enjoyed the early morning ride."

"And her sister did not?"

"She didn't come with us. I am afraid she is more your brother's guest than mine."

"My brother?" Night Walker frowned.

"Let me explain," Aaron began. Rapidly he told Night Walker the tale of Tempest's rescue. Night Walker listened in silence, but he wasn't happy about the situation. His face revealed nothing of his thoughts. "Your father has asked us to stay tonight and we've agreed. It has been much too long since I have eaten your mother's cooking, and watched the young people gather to dance and sing."

"Yes . . . it has been much too long." Night Walker exhaled a ragged breath. "I must see to my horse. It has been a long ride." He led his horse away as Aaron and Sleeping Wolf watched— Aaron with a mild touch of amusement and Sleeping Wolf with a puzzled frown.

* * *

Night Walker sat across the fire from Brittany and watched her laugh at something Aaron had said. He fought the unwelcome desire to go to her and sit by her, where he could look into those green eyes. He wanted to . . . angrily he put his bowl down and stood up. His large frame drew everyone's attention as he left the tepee.

He breathed in a deep gulp of fresh, cool air. From the time he'd arrived until it was time for the evening meal, he had carefully remained out of Brittany's vicinity. But she had not remained out of his sight. He'd watched her laugh with the women and listen attentively to the chattering of the children. Effortlessly she was making friends with everyone she met . . . including most of his family.

He could happily have strangled his brother Laughing Thunder, who was amused by the situation. Soaring Eagle was worse, because he could not take his eyes away from the silent girl, who was obviously absorbing everything around her.

Star Dancer was fascinated with their hair and their mode of dress, for she had reached the age where being pretty and attracting the eyes of young braves was becoming important.

For Running Cougar their guests were a puzzle. He liked the two white women, but he had heard a rumor he didn't believe, that one was going to teach in place of Aaron. He was having a war between his warrior's pride and his avid curiosity.

Night Walker began to walk through the village to the nearby trees, where he could consider the arguments he meant to present to his father. Suddenly he froze in mid-stride as a soft voice came from behind him.

"Night Walker?"

He turned to look at her and felt his breath catch. In the dusky twilight she was like a dream . . . misty and golden. He fought for control of his senses, refusing to let them interfere with logic.

Brittany walked slowly toward him until she stood inches away.

"Are you angry with me for some reason?"

"Angry? No, I have no reason to be angry," he replied. But the tone of his voice told Brittany he was denying what he really felt.

"My sister and I come in friendship, Night Walker. Your village has greeted us as friends. Your family is generous and very kind."

"Have you told them why you are here?"

"Why do you think I'm . . . we're here?"

"You are here in our village for the same reason the whites are on our land. To take what belongs to us. Only you are worse, for you would change us. We are not white and you want us not to be ourselves. What would you have us be then? We would end up as nothing."

"You're unfair. You have decided before you understand. Why can't you give us a chance, give me a chance? Is it because I'm a woman? You think one white woman can make more changes than a man like Aaron?"

Her voice was like velvet, and she reached out to lay her hand on his arm. He could feel the cool-

106

ness of it as her touch sent a tingle through every nerve. He fought a surge of desire he was not prepared for. He was prepared to fight her . . . he wasn't prepared to want her. Yet he could feel his heart begin a deeper, stronger beat. His blood seemed to warm and flow through him like honey.

Brittany was equally aware of him. She could feel the hard muscle of his arm grow tense under her hand, and his flesh was warm and smooth to the touch.

"We *have* given the whites a chance. One chance after another. Always we have stepped back . . . and back . . . and back. Always our hands have been stretched out in friendship, and always the friendship has been betrayed and the treaties broken."

"Aaron is different than the others. So am I. I truly don't believe Aaron has ever broken your trust in him. From all the stories he has told me, he has lived with you in peace for many years. He's learned your language and doctored your village. So be honest. Is it Aaron you would drive away . . . or is it me?"

"You are right. Aaron has been a friend, but now I think he goes too far."

"Night Walker . . . you . . . your trust means a great deal to him. He would never betray it. He wants to give you a thing more valuable than you can imagine. The world you know is changing. The old may find it impossible to adapt, but the children can be taught. It's you . . . your brothers and sisters who will face the hardest changes. I want only to make it easier."

Brittany would never know the effect of her words on him. Night Walker's face was as unreadable as ever. But he felt the force of her words to his very core and somehow he knew they were true.

The evening shadows grew longer as the sun finally became a pale rim on a dark horizon. To Brittany now, Night Walker was a tall, dark and very formidable shadow. Still she stood and waited for his answer.

"What is it you want, Brittany Nelson?" He said the words softly, but they were like steel shards piercing her.

"Only for you to extend your hand of friendship one more time . . . to trust one more time. To let me walk in your world, learn from it, and let me show you mine. I want to be a friend as Aaron is a friend."

She waited quietly while he considered her words. No matter that she could not see his eyes, she could feel the heat of them. Still she stood.

His response caught in his throat. He forced himself to deny the effect she had on him. No woman had reached within him to that guarded place he had never shared before, and he didn't welcome this one.

Behind her the fires were being lit and he knew there would be dancing and celebration. The flames only enhanced her beauty, lighting her hair and silhouetting her form. He could feel desire for her well up in him like a dammed-up flood, a dam he had no intention of allowing to break. He fought for and kept control.

"I will do as Flying Horse and my father say, but I will keep my own council. We will have another truce . . . another treaty. We will see who breaks it first."

"Thank you," she said in a whisper.

Without another word he turned and vanished into the darkness. Brittany stood gazing out into the night for several minutes. She had a long, long way to go to win this fierce man to her side . . . but she meant to do it.

When a large fire had been built in the center of the village, Aaron took Brittany and Tempest to a place where they could observe the dancing, yet still be part of the celebration.

They watched Star Dancer move gracefully among the crowd, and Tempest and Brittany were as fascinated with her as she had been with them. If Star Dancer did not respond to the warm looks of the young men, it was partly her shyness and partly her knowledge that her parents' eyes were on her as well.

As for Laughing Thunder and Running Cougar, they were joyous and gave all their enthusiasm to the celebration.

Soaring Eagle watched carefully, considering how difficult it must be for Tempest, who could hear nothing that was going on about her. The drums beat out a low, throbbing beat and the young people began to dance to the rhythm. Tum-ta-tum, tum-tum, ta-tum. He felt the throbbing deep inside and the urge to move to the beat. Only then did an idea come to him.

He went to Tempest's side and knelt beside her. Aaron was seated between Tempest and Brittany, blocking Brittany's view of what he was doing.

Soaring Eagle took hold of Tempest's wrist, but his touch was not forceful, nor did it frighten her. Instead it piqued her curiosity and her interest. He wanted to show her something. She rose and moved with him.

"Tempest!" Brittany called out in alarm when she saw what had happened. She attempted to get up, but Aaron put out a restraining hand.

"Let them go, Brittany. Do you want to insult Soaring Eagle by showing that you don't trust him? He will do her no harm, I promise."

Brittany's worried gaze still followed Tempest and Soaring Eagle, and it took all her willpower not to follow.

Soaring Eagle walked around the fire with Tempest in tow until he reached the place where the drums were. He knelt down beside them and drew her down with him. Gently he took her hand and laid it against the side of the drum.

Her startled eyes lifted to his as the throb of the drums vibrated through her hand and into her senses. She could actually hear the drums through her hand. She smiled up at Soaring Eagle, and his return smile was filled with pleasure.

Pleased that he had been successful thus far, he

made the sign for *drum*. At first she didn't realize what he was doing, until he took her hand away from the drum, returned it and made the sign. Her bright mind grasped the idea . . . He was talking to her! He was talking to her! He knew she understood. With her free hand, she made the hand signal for *drum* and watched a smile light Soaring Eagle's eyes.

He drew her up beside him. Looking at the celebration going on all around them, he tried to decide what he could teach her next. But the confusion thwarted his plans. It was then that Never Quiet insinuated herself between them.

"What are you doing, Soaring Eagle? Why do you not dance with the others?"

"Go away, little one. Find your friends."

"Do you like her, Soaring Eagle?" Never Quiet grinned.

"Do you want your bottom smacked?" he growled.

Tempest was looking from one to the other, sure from Soaring Eagle's dark look that something was amiss. She withdrew her hand from his and walked back to where Brittany and Aaron were seated to rejoin them.

Soaring Eagle turned his anger and frustration on Never Quiet, who suddenly found it much safer to be out of her brother's vicinity. Still undaunted, he found a seat near Tempest. If he could not get her alone, at least he would be able to spend as much time close to her as he possibly could.

She looked up as he sat down near her. To prove

to him she understood what he was trying to do, she made the sign for drum . . . and smiled.

Brittany was certain she would not see Night Walker again that night, so she was surprised when she saw his broad-shouldered form join the merrymakers.

She was watching him when he became aware of it and turned his head quickly. Their eyes met, and something so alive and vital sparked between them that Brittany made an involuntary sound. For a long time their gazes remained locked.

She could not understand the tangled emotions that made her limbs seem weak and her blood warm. She felt overheated and breathless. Determinedly she tore her gaze from his. Tomorrow they would return to the mission. There she would be on safer ground. Safer! The thought shook her. Was she afraid of Night Walker? No! her mind screeched, but somewhere deep within her a small voice wondered.

"Brittany? . . . Brittany?" Aaron's voice seemed to come to her from a great distance.

"Huh . . . uh . . . what?" She turned to face him.

"Sleeping Wolf has asked us to stay until after the midday meal tomorrow. You don't mind, do you? I thought both you girls were getting along well. This would give you more time to get acquainted."

Mind? Of course she minded, Brittany wanted to say. She did not want to stay anywhere near Night Walker. But she smiled.

"No, Aaron, I don't mind."

"It seems Never Quiet wants to take Tempest for a walk in the morning to pick some berries. You know how Tempest likes to walk. . . . Brittany, are you all right?"

"Me? Of course, I'm fine. Why?"

"I thought that business with Soaring Eagle and the drum might have upset you. He meant well."

"Aaron . . . I . . . I know he meant well. But . . . Tempest has not . . . I mean . . . she has no defenses. She's so trusting."

"And you still believe Soaring Eagle would do her harm?" For the first time since she'd met him, Aaron displayed a spark of anger. "Don't you know that if he did her one bit of harm, it would shame and destroy him? Tempest is as safe with him as with any of the smiling gentlemen she might have run across back East. Are you setting a double standard, Brittany? Are Indians good enough to teach, but not good enough to . . ." He breathed in deeply as he saw her startled expression. "I'm sorry, I didn't mean to be cross with you. It's just that we're on the verge of realizing a dream and—"

"Don't worry, Aaron, I understand. It's just that Tempest is—"

"A woman," Aaron said. "One that does not really need the walls you've built around her. We'll be going home tomorrow afternoon. Even you will agree that Tempest will be safe there." Aaron walked away, leaving her filled with apprehension and guilt.

* * *

It was barely dawn. The night sky had not completely given way to the new day. The shadows between the tepees were deep enough to cover the movement of a solitary figure.

Soaring Eagle moved carefully. The last thing he wanted to do was waken his parents, who would be filled with a million questions. He lifted the flap of their tepee and slipped inside. He knew quite well which sleeping bundle was his sister Never Quiet.

He knelt beside her and laid one hand over her mouth while he shook her awake. Never Quiet was frightened, but she recognized her brother at once. Her curiosity, as usual, got the best of her. He motioned her to follow him, and they quietly left. Never Quiet could hardly contain her giggle. Soaring Eagle would be very nice to her. Obviously he wanted something from her. She loved him intensely, mostly because of his sensitive nature. He let her get away with much more than anyone else in her family.

Outside he drew her into the deeper shadows. For several minutes he was silent.

"Why do you wake me from my warm bed before it is even day, my brother?"

"Never Quiet, you must do something for me."

"Why?"

"What do you mean, why?" he asked sharply.

"You said that I *must* do something for you. Why *must*?"

"Maybe I have said the words wrong," he said

mildly, but she could tell he was gritting his teeth. "I am *asking* you to do something for me."

"What?"

"This morning you are to go with the white girl."

"The teacher?"

"No." He inhaled deeply. Never Quiet was playing with him and he had no intention of letting her get to him. "The silent one."

"Yes, we go to the hills to pick berries. Aaron and Father are going to be talking to Flying Horse and she wanted to walk."

"You know the high meadow where the big trees are?"

"Yes."

"If you were to go there to pick berries, I would be grateful."

"How grateful would you be?"

"What do you want, you little thief?" he growled.

"I am not a thief! I am going back to bed." She spun away from him, quite sure he wasn't going to let her get very far. She was right. He caught her arm and turned her back to face him.

"Wait. I didn't mean to call you any names, dear little sister. If there is something you want that I can give you, speak, tell me what it is."

"The little pony you caught . . . after you break him."

"What!"

"That little—"

"I heard what you said." Soaring Eagle glared at her for a minute and she could see his struggle between what he wanted and the desire to smack her. She wasn't surprised when what he wanted won out. "All right. You can have the pony." He smiled. "And if you meet anyone upon the meadow and make yourself scarce, I will see that you get a saddle to go with him."

"Oh, Soaring Eagle." Never Quiet laughed and threw herself in his arms, kissing his cheek over and over. "You are a wonderful brother."

"Just make sure no one else goes with you," he said as he hugged her and then held her away from him. "Especially not her sister."

"Do not worry. We will leave early. No one will be there." She giggled softly. "And I can find many things to do while you . . . show her where the best berries are."

"You are really wicked," he chuckled. "This is our secret?"

"Yes, it is our secret."

Never Quiet watched her brother walk a few steps away; then she called out softly to him. "Soaring Eagle."

"What?" He turned to face her.

"You really do not have to give me the pony. I would have done what you wanted me to do anyway."

She enjoyed his smile; then she went back inside to plot her strategy.

Brittany woke much later than she had planned. She could hear activity all about the tepee in which she and Tempest had slept.

116

But when she sat up and looked around, she was surprised to find Tempest already gone. She rose and dressed, then went outside. She would go to the river for water to wash, then join Aaron.

Actually she was anxious for Aaron to conclude their business at the village. She wanted to take Tempest back to the mission. There were so many things she felt Tempest did not know. They must talk, but there was no paper or pencil here for her to use. She thought of her brother and his fears for them. James had strongly opposed his sisters' adventurous plan to go West. What would he say if he knew they were in contact with men like Night Walker or Soaring Eagle? He would expect Brittany to give Tempest all the protection she could.

As she stepped outside, one of the young village women was passing by. Brittany remembered her name from the past evening.

"Wild Sage, good morning."

"Good morning," Wild Sage said shyly. She was a small-framed woman close to Brittany's age. Her eyes dominated her face. They were almond-shaped and black as a midnight sky. Her hair was ebony and gleamed in the morning sun. She stood silently waiting to see if there was something their guest might require.

"Have you seen my sister?"

"Yes. She went with Never Quiet this morning early to pick berries."

"Is that far from here?"

"I do not know exactly where they were going.

117

They will be back by the midday meal, I am sure," Wild Sage said confidently. "Would you like something to eat?"

"Yes, I would. Has Aaron gotten up yet?"

"Oh yes. He has been talking with Flying Horse for long hours."

"Great," Brittany said to herself, "everyone is doing something and I'm sleeping."

"What?"

"Nothing. I would like something to eat, though."

"Come, Night Bird has asked that you be brought to her when you were awake. She has prepared food and would speak to you."

A few minutes later, when Brittany had washed the night's sleep away and brushed her hair into some order, she found herself walking toward Night Bird's tepee.

She was welcomed inside, and the smell of food made her mouth water. Night Bird smiled and motioned Brittany to sit near her.

"I've enjoyed my stay here, Night Bird. I hope Flying Horse will understand the true reason why we came here, and allow the children to be taught by me."

"Perhaps," Night Bird said softly. "It would please me if Never Quiet could go to the school. I do not believe the warriors will agree to such a thing. Never Quiet is . . . is a girl who will always seek answers to many things. As for Running Cougar and Laughing Thunder . . . I do not know. Perhaps even Star Dancer will not wish to do this."

"You are a wise enough woman to know that only this schooling can provide the answers they'll need for the future. The world they'll one day live in will be very different from the one you know."

"I have a great fear," Night Bird admitted. "But changes cannot be made in a day. I am afraid it will be hard to show Flying Horse what you call your 'truth.' He has seen more of the white man's 'truth' than he wants."

"You've known Aaron a long time. Surely you know he is not like the others. He has lived among you."

"Yes, Aaron has made himself part of us in as many ways as he can. But . . . now he wants more than we can give."

"Do all your people feel this way?"

Night Bird cast Brittany an assessing look. She, too, had observed Soaring Eagle with Tempest, and she knew more by reading Night Walker's actions than even he realized. Both of her older sons worried her, and the presence of the two beautiful white girls worried her, as well.

"Why do you ask this thing?"

"Because, as you know, all your people do not think or act alike; neither do white people think and act alike."

Before Night Bird could speak again, the flap was drawn aside and Laughing Thunder entered. His smile was quick, warm and welcoming, and to Brittany proved the words she had spoken were true.

"Laughing Thunder, where is your sister? Never

Quiet has gone without filling the water sacks again. She is going to get a taste of the switch if she does not mend her careless ways."

"Do not be upset, Mother. She is just excited over our visitors. I am sure she forgot only because she had promised the white girl to take her berry-picking this morning."

"Where have they gone?"

"To the high meadow, I think. I saw them going that way," Laughing Thunder replied as he took up a bowl and squatted down beside the low-burning fire to dish himself up some of the thick stew.

"Usually they go berry-picking in larger groups. Are they safe there?"

"Mother, do not worry, I saw Soaring Eagle riding that way just after dawn. I'm sure he will be nearby should they have any problems." He said the words nonchalantly, without observing that Brittany's face paled a bit and her hands clenched in her lap.

But Night Bird had read the expression on Brittany's face. She was upset about something that involved her son and Brittany's sister. Was Brittany like the rest of the whites, using words that only meant something when she was not involved on a more personal level?

Night Bird was proud of all her children, but the one closest to her heart was Soaring Eagle. He was the gentle one. The one who felt for others often before himself. Soaring Eagle would be the one to see in the silent girl a creature in need and extend his hand.

She hoped that what he felt for the white girl was that and only that, for she feared there would be a much larger problem should it be more.

Chapter Seven

When Brittany left Night Bird's tepee she was both unsure and uncomfortable with her emotions. She had come West in the hope of finding real purpose in her life—she wanted to be useful. She had brought Tempest along because she thought Aaron, his school and hospital, would give Tempest a chance to be self-sufficient, to realize new self-esteem.

But she had not planned on someone like Soaring Eagle walking into Tempest's life. Nor for that matter did she expect to come face to face with a man like Night Walker, who had an effect on her that could upset all her plans.

She knew Tempest's vulnerability, and now, in fact, she also recognized her own. She walked slowly toward the tepee she had shared with Tempest, her head down. Deep in thought, she did not sense Night Walker's presence until she was almost upon him.

"Good morning." His voice was deep and vibrant.

She looked up abruptly. It was obvious he had come fresh from the river. His hair was still damp and a few silvery drops of water lingered on his skin. His whole body seemed so . . . so vitally alive that it set her teeth on edge. She did not like the fact that he strummed her senses like the strings of a guitar. His smile was warm and open, and this above all things made her wary. She remembered the words of their last meeting. Was she going to have another battle with him? They had made, at least as far as she was concerned, a compromise.

"Good morning." She tried to match his smile. "You've been swimming."

"The water was warm, and the day is good. You have eaten?"

"Yes, I had breakfast with your mother."

"Ah." He chuckled softly and Brittany could feel the warmth of deep affection. "She is where my sister gets all her questions. My mother has learned to contain them; Never Quiet has not." He moved to stand closer to her. "I have come to ask you to ride with me. I have many things I would like to show you. It might make it easier for you to understand."

"What must I understand?" She was hesitant to be alone in the wilderness with him.

"I cannot say it in words, I must show you. I have a horse ready for you." There was a challenge in his eyes, and she refused to be intimidated by it.

"All right, let's go."

"Can you ride in those—" He motioned with a frown at her long skirts with the layers of petticoats beneath.

"No. If you will wait, I'll change."

"I will wait," he said complacently.

It took Brittany only minutes to change into a riding skirt and to tell Wild Sage that she would return soon. Then she rejoined Night Walker, who said nothing. But his eyes revealed his appreciation of her slim form in the more revealing apparel.

Brittany enjoyed riding, and it took Night Walker very little time to see that she could handle herself quite well. He had no idea why this pleased him and refused to take the time to dwell on it.

They left the sparse stand of trees that lay near the village and crossed a shallow river. Before them now lay a vast rolling plain that, in the distance, gave way to range land and then the Black Hills.

These hills ran for almost 125 miles in length and were over 60 miles wide. To those living on the plains before them, they were both a guard and a barrier. A sentry that watched silently over their lives.

"Why are we going into the hills?"

"Because what you must see and hear cannot be told to you."

"Why?"

"Why?" He laughed softly. "Because you will not believe me if I tell you." *I only hope, he thought, that you believe me once I show you.*

Brittany remained silent, enjoying the scene before her and the pleasure and freedom of this ride in such an open and, in its own way, beautiful place.

Night Walker rode close to her and occasionally she let her eyes drift to him. No matter how she tried to deny it, when she compared him to the men she had known, they came up lacking.

The sun glistened against his smooth skin, and long, limber muscles rippled as he held his stallion in complete control.

His black hair was held back by a red band, and the color accentuated the depth of his dark eyes and the whiteness of his quick smile as his gaze met hers.

She watched his hands, one resting on his thigh, the other holding the reins. They were large and long-fingered, and very capable looking. She brushed away the thought of how it would feel to touch them . . . to feel them touch her.

Her cheeks heated with the unwelcome thoughts and she struggled to regain her control. She was being ridiculous, she thought angrily, and how he would laugh had he known where her thoughts had drifted.

But laughter was far from Night Walker's mind.

He was aware of everything about her, from the way the sun caught her hair to the cool look of her flawless skin. He had thought long into the night about his plans for this day. He had considered that there was much about him, his people and his land that she did not know or understand. Perhaps if he tried to make her see through his eyes, he would be able to convince her what kind of an intrusion the white man really was.

As they approached the hills, even Brittany, who was not in the least superstitious, sensed a change. After a while she realized the change was more in Night Walker than in the hills about them.

She wanted to question him, but decided to wait until he had shown her what he had in mind. Before too long he drew his horse to a halt before a rough and craggy hill. He dismounted, so Brittany did the same.

"Do you mind a short climb?" he questioned.

"No. Where are we going?"

"Up there." He motioned to the peak of the hill.

"Lead on," she said with a smile.

He paused to look closely at her; then he, too, smiled and began to walk. Brittany followed but as the way grew steeper and more difficult, she began to wonder if this trek was a good idea.

The narrow path was rough, and soon she found that his hand was always there. When she thought she might slip and fall, she was silently grateful to feel his hand on hers and his strength take the weight and the danger from her.

At the moment that she felt she surely could not go a step further, she realized he had stopped. She stood beside him on a craggy ledge and looked out over a breathtaking panorama.

The Black Hills rolled away in high, rough peaks and shadowed valleys. In a way it was a brutal view, yet Brittany sensed a serenity, a majesty about the place that defied description.

"These hills have stood here since the first day *Wakan Tanka* created them. A day so long ago that even the ancient ones cannot tell the beginning."

"*Wakan Tanka?*"

"He lives on the tops of the mountains in the sacred Paha Sapa, the Black Hills. You cannot see him, for he wraps himself in the robes of the dark clouds, but you can feel his presence. I have often felt it. During my vision quest he drew close enough to make me understand."

"God," Brittany whispered.

"That is a word of the *wasichu*. There is much difference between the God you worship and ours. You have a house where you go to worship. You would not have it defiled by the presence of nonbelievers who would destroy it." Night Walker extended his hand to encompass all about him. "Here is where we come to worship *Wakan Tanka*. These hills are as sacred to us as the house in which your God dwells. The *wasichu* come to us and want to change the place and the way we worship. They come to change all that we know and love from our way to theirs. It is not just the taking of our land, it is the taking of our hearts and the

127

taking of our life's blood . . . our children."

His gaze was intent on hers. He wanted her to see why it was impossible to greet the encroaching white man with open arms any longer. "Below us, on the plain, roam the buffalo. The buffalo is sacred to us as well. But does the *wasichu* care that the buffalo carries our lives? No, he slaughters at will and takes only the hide, leaving the meat to spoil on the plains. Meat that belongs in the bellies of our children."

She could hear in his voice an anger and pain that stirred her emotions. She understood what he was saying, and realized he placed all the *wasichu* in one category. His fear was for *all* his people from *all* of hers. This could mean they would turn their backs on the only thing that could save them from total obliteration.

"I understand what you are saying, Night Walker, but you judge unfairly. You told me you would abide by what the council said. But your heart will never accept anything unless you truly understand that all whites are not alike. I would love to know all of your ways, if you would teach me. But only if you will be fair and listen to me, as you want me to listen to you."

He inhaled deeply and turned from her to look out over the rugged hills. Brittany could not take her eyes from him. He was as much a part of this land as the air about them and the tall cedar trees that grew here.

She wanted desperately to be a bridge between her people and his. How could she explain that to this tall man who was so sensitive to the earth around him? She felt the urge to touch him, to somehow console him, to convince him that she was not motivated by greed, but by a desire to help. She reached out and laid her hand against his back. She could feel his muscles tense and would have drawn her hand away and stepped back, had he not turned to face her abruptly.

They stood a breath apart. Her hand was still raised and he gently reached out to enfold it in his. Brittany drew in a deep breath as her awareness of her surroundings became even more sensitive. She could smell the mingled scents of the breeze, the cedar trees, and the leather and pine that lingered and blended with the warm smell of the earth. Night Walker's hand was warm and strong as it entwined with hers.

His gaze held hers, watching her green eyes darken and widen as something awakened in her. Brittany was suddenly still, as if she could not draw her next breath.

Very slowly he reached with his other hand to touch her hair, catching it in his fingers.

He drank in her beauty like a man who has thirsted for a long time. The sun kissed her skin to gold and her mouth to lush pink. Her lips were half parted as if she awaited his touch.

Very slowly he bent forward and touched his mouth to hers. Her lips were soft and moist, as he'd known they would be, and they resisted only for a moment before they parted and accepted his with a sigh.

It was new, and yet it was as ancient as time itself. When they ended the kiss, both were a bit disoriented and breathless. Both were shaken by what they had shared. Neither wanted it, and both knew it made an unsolved problem even worse. But neither could deny that something with immense power held them.

"Does this anger you, *wasichu*?" he said softly.

"No, it does not anger me. It does not make me afraid, either. Did you think it would?"

"Perhaps."

"I am not a child to be afraid of a pretended threat when I know the man who threatens would not betray his own honor, nor destroy mine." Her gaze held his, steady and clear.

Night Walker smiled and shook his head. She had read his thoughts. She did not frighten easily, and for an unaccountable reason this pleased him.

"You are very proud."

"That is not a good thing?" Brittany finally smiled. "You are very proud as well. It is good to be proud, but even better to be able to bend and to learn of new ways and new things."

"So . . . you will tell me of your ways and I will tell you mine. What will that change?"

"Maybe nothing, maybe everything."

"Let us go down. There is still much I would like to show you."

"Night Walker, the sun is getting high and Aaron will be looking for me. He said he wanted to leave by the midday meal."

"We will be back in time," he said confidently. Then he took her hand and they began the descent.

When the reached the bottom they looked again across the rolling plain. They stood side by side, enjoying the breeze.

"This, too, was a gift to us from *Wakan Tanka*. Here the buffalo came in mighty herds. Now we must search for them. The hills, the plains, the buffalo, all gifts to keep us alive. Our gods, to keep our spirits on the right path. What else would you take from us, *wasichu*?"

"I take nothing from you, Night Walker. That is what you do not seem to understand. I only want to give you—"

"Give us?" He laughed again. "Your language and your words on paper? Your people and their treaties have brought us many things. *Wicocuye*—sickness; *wawoya*—hate; *wawuagle*—prejudice; *waunshilapsne*—pitilessness. We have a legend that speaks of you."

"A legend? Tell it to me."

"Come." He motioned her to the shade of a nearby tree. "I will tell you of how we knew of your coming long before we first saw you."

Brittany knew she had promised Aaron she would be ready to leave by midday, but she could not draw herself away from Night Walker. She walked to the tree with him and they sat together.

"Many generations ago," he began, "*Iktome*, the bringer of bad news, went from village to village and from tribe to tribe. Because he was a messen-

131

ger, he spoke all languages so all tribes understood. There is a new generation coming, a new nation, a new kind of man who is going to run over everything. He is a liar. He will appear from someplace across the great waters, and he comes to steal all four directions of the world. This new man is not wise, but he is clever. He has legs of knowledge, and wherever these legs step they will make a track of lies, and wherever he looks his looks will be all lies. At this time, *ecohan*, you must try to know and to understand this new kind of man and pass the understanding from generation to generation.

"The white long legs will take all the things you can look around you and see—the grass, the trees, the animals. The *Iktome Hu-Hanska-sh* will take them all. He will steal the air and give you a new and different life. He will give you many new things, but hold onto your old ways; mind what *Tunkashila*, the grandfather spirit, taught you." He turned to look at Brittany. "He will bring you a new faith. He will come; whether you want him or not, he is coming from the east. He will try to tame you, try to make you after himself. This man will lie . . . he cannot speak the truth."

Night Walker grew quiet and his gaze held Brittany's for a long time before she could put into words the thoughts that had been twisting in her mind since he began to talk.

"I know the legend is truth. There have been many lies. But there are words in the legend that you have ignored."

"What words?"

"Let me see if I can repeat the words of *Iktome*, because I think, amid all the bad news, he has given you the answer and it is the answer I believe in. He said"—she closed her eyes, trying to remember accurately—"you must try to understand this new kind of man and pass the understanding from generation to generation." Brittany leaned close to Night Walker and laid her hand on his. "And that is what I offer you, a means of understanding. One you can pass on."

She had no doubt that Night Walker had never given this part of the legend a thought, especially not the way she presented it. She could see that this was a whole new train of thought and it had shaken him.

"I would only give you, your children and their children a way to understand so that you cannot be fooled by words you don't understand, by writing on treaties that you can't read, and by numbers that can cheat you." She removed her hand from his and stood up. "It is best I get back before Aaron begins to worry."

Night Walker stood up and took a step that brought him very close to her. As it had been the first night when she opened the door and found him, he suddenly seemed to fill her whole vision. Their gazes locked, and Brittany felt as if she could not move.

"You speak well of what you must believe."

"I not only speak and believe, but I will prove to

you that I mean my words, if you give me half a chance."

"It is not my decision."

"But your words mean a lot, especially to your family and to the young braves, who must admire you."

His lips formed a half smile. "Must?"

"I . . . I mean—" Her cheeks flushed, but she was too stubborn to back down. "I know you are much admired, Night Walker. Even Aaron thinks you are a very special person."

"And you?" he questioned softly as he slowly reached to touch strands of her hair that had come loose.

"Me?" She felt something coil tightly within her.

"Would you teach me these things you believe I should know?"

"If you choose."

"What I would choose is to learn how your people think. I would choose to have my questions answered, and I would choose to find out why you cannot be satisfied with what your own gods have given you and feel you must take what the gods have given others."

"You might find we're not so far apart after all."

His hand had released her hair and moved gently to her cheek, tracing a downward path until he touched the pulse at her throat, which had begun to beat rapidly.

"Have you been told how beautiful you are, Brittany Nelson?" His fingers slid gently along her collar bone. "Your hair is like the first morning sun."

He lightly touched her shoulder, then moved his hand to the back of her head and slowly drew her to him.

Brittany felt as if a force bigger than the land around them drew her into a vortex. She could no more fight it than she could have stopped breathing. Perhaps her flustered reaction to the first kiss had held some fear, because she was all alone with Night Walker in this vast wilderness. But this one was different. The first kiss had been tentative, had been discovery, had been just the beginning of awareness.

This kiss was explosive. Brittany found herself in his arms without realizing either of them had moved.

Night Walker felt her slim form mold to his and her soft, giving mouth accept his, and every sense he had came to life. For this moment both forgot the barriers that stood between them.

But it could not last and both knew it. Brittany stepped back from him, forcing herself to move away. In her eyes he read denial. He believed that she wanted to step away from all that he was. He smiled a humorless smile.

"Come," he said gently, "The other things I wished to show you will wait for another day. I will take you back." He turned and walked away from her, toward the horses. In a few moments Brittany followed.

Never Quiet and Tempest had seemed to understand each other almost at once. From the moment Never Quiet had come into their tepee and shaken her awake, Tempest had felt comfortable with her. She had been looking forward to spending this day alone with Never Quiet, whose quick, innocent smile promised a day of adventure with no pressure involved.

She'd been pleased when Never Quiet offered her moccasins and a buckskin shirt and tunic to wear. When they'd walked from the village, Never Quiet had done her best to point out things and make the signs for them.

Tempest had tried to pay attention to Never Quiet, but as usual Never Quiet was so enthusiastic that she rushed from one thing to another until Tempest was confused.

It was quite a trek to the place where the berries seemed to grow the best. Never Quiet had handed one of the two baskets she carried to Tempest, who'd needed no instructions when she saw the weighted limbs of the berry bushes.

An hour had passed in leisurely picking, and now Tempest paused to pop a berry into her mouth to taste its rich sweetness. She watched Never Quiet drift away from her and realized that she could savor this time to relax. It was good to know no one was hovering over her, protecting her from every imaginary thing until she felt as if she were being smothered. A part of her exulted in this new freedom, and she concentrated on filling her basket so she could set it aside and truly enjoy this precious time.

Finally her basket was full and she set it aside.

Then she stood and simply gave herself over to enjoying the day. She had learned that even picking berries was part of a day's work, for they would be crushed and mixed with lean parts of beef or buffalo meat and dried in the form of cakes for the long winter months. Never Quiet had slowly and laboriously shown her how this was done before they had gone for the berries, and Tempest had understood how important it was.

She closed her eyes and raised her face to the sun; then she lifted her thick hair and let the air cool her skin. After a moment she opened her eyes to again absorb the view.

A short distance away, Soaring Eagle sat on his horse and watched her in fascination. He wanted to join her and yet he wanted to continue to watch her. He felt a constriction in his breathing and his hands trembled a bit. The shock of his feelings was enough to make him hesitate. He had never felt this way before in his life and just wasn't sure what to do.

Slowly he edged his horse forward until he was less than fifty yards from her, but still she was not aware of his presence. He looked around for Never Quiet, and then smiled. She was nowhere in sight. All he had to do was go to Tempest. Why then did he hesitate? What was he afraid of? He knew the answer. He was uncertain, and that alone was a novelty for him.

Finally he could not wait any longer. He dismounted, tied his horse and walked toward her.

Her gaze was so intent on the landscape before

her that Tempest did not note his presence until he stood beside her. She was startled and gave a soft sound of surprise before she recognized him. Then, to Soaring Eagle's immense relief, she smiled a warm and welcoming smile. There was no doubt or fear in her eyes. He answered her smile. Gently he opened his hand and extended it to her. She did not hesitate to place her hand in his.

Aaron and Sleeping Wolf left Flying Horse's tepee after a long, relatively productive conversation. Aaron had tried to explain to Flying Horse that Brittany was a much better teacher than he would ever be, and that going to a formal school would give his young warriors better medicine to face the oncoming whites than they had now.

Of course he had not gotten an enthusiastic agreement. But Flying Horse had not been angry either, and that was a good sign. There would be many more conversations before any agreements were made, but Aaron was hopeful.

"Well, I guess I'd best start making preparations for the trip home. I'm sure Never Quiet will be back with Tempest soon. I wonder if Brittany is getting ready. I'd best go and see."

Aaron walked through the center of the village toward the tepee Tempest and Brittany had shared. But when he stopped there, Wild Sage informed him that Tempest had gone berry-picking with Never Quiet, and Brittany had ridden out early.

"Ridden out?" Aaron was puzzled. "Did she say where she was going?"

"No. She only asked me to tell you that she would be back in time to return home with you."

"But I can't understand this. She is a stranger here. She may get lost or—"

"No, Aaron," she laughed, "she will not get lost. She is with Night Walker. There is no way for her to get lost."

"Night Walker? Are you sure?"

"Yes. I am sure. He was waiting for her by her tepee when she returned to it. They left together."

"Well . . . my goodness." Aaron smiled to himself. "This is a novel turn of events. I wonder what brought this about."

Aaron returned to his own sleeping quarters, where he began the preparations for the journey home. Once everything was ready, he went outside. He found Skinner and discussed packing the horses.

"We'll leave when the girls return," Aaron said.

"Do you want me to go and get their things and pack up?"

"Yes, I think that might be a good idea."

Skinner left and Aaron again gazed about him, looking for a sign of the girls. An hour or so later he received a surprise. Down the path that led from the woods, Never Quiet drifted toward home with two baskets of berries. There was no sign of Tempest.

As Aaron walked toward her, Never Quiet paused, and then kept walking toward him.

"Never Quiet, where is Tempest?"

"In the high meadow. She filled her basket of berries and I filled mine. I am bringing them back."

"But you can't leave her up there alone! It's too dangerous. You know what happened the last time she was alone—it nearly cost her her life."

"But . . . she is not alone."

"She's not? But I thought Brittany rode with Night Walker this morning?"

"I do not know about that."

"Never Quiet—" Aaron had reached the end of his patience—"if Tempest is not up there alone, who is with her? One of the women from the village?"

"No . . . not exactly."

"Never Quiet!"

"Soaring Eagle is there. They are together. He . . . he just happened to be riding there this day and saw her." Never Quiet was studiously avoiding Aaron's gaze.

"Is that the truth?" he asked gently. Never Quiet licked her lips and struggled for words that would not be lies. She should have done as Soaring Eagle had told her to do when they first made their plans. She should have remained with the baskets of berries until he and Tempest had returned from their walk. Now she was not only in trouble with Aaron, but her parents and Soaring Eagle would all be angry.

"No," she said softly.

"And what is the truth?"

Reluctantly she told Aaron of the bargain she had made with Soaring Eagle. She was a bit surprised when he displayed no anger.

"Never Quiet, I will keep your secret. But you must promise not to do this again."

"Do you want me to go and—"

"No. Leave them for a while. Perhaps it is good for both of them to find the limits of their relationship. They have to recognize their problems." Aaron was talking more to himself than to Never Quiet, who had no intention of interrupting his thoughts. Then his attention returned to her. "Go and play with the other children. I shall watch for Tempest's return."

Never Quiet left, more than reluctant. She wondered what Soaring Eagle would do to her after he came back and had to face Aaron with what he had done.

But it was still another two hours before he saw Tempest and Soaring Eagle walking toward the village. Walking! Both of them! Aaron had to contain a grin. It was unheard of for a warrior to walk so and to lead his horse. This was proof that Soaring Eagle was beginning to care about Tempest. It pleased Aaron and yet it worried him. Worried him because he was pretty certain what Brittany's reaction would be.

To make the matter more complicated, he saw two riders approaching from the opposite direction. Brittany reined her horse to a stop when she saw Tempest with Soaring Eagle. She exchanged a word with Night Walker, and then rode out to meet Tempest.

Tempest saw Brittany approaching. She waved and smiled. It was Soaring Eagle who sensed that Brittany was not much pleased with the situation.

He'd done a very unseemly thing, but the two hours he had spent with Tempest were worth any censure he might face now. He had no intention of running from the consequences of his actions, no matter what they were.

"I didn't know my sister was to be with you this morning, Soaring Eagle," Brittany began. "I was told she would be with Never Quiet, picking berries."

"The baskets are full," he said. "We only spent a little time talking."

"Talking?"

"It might surprise you to learn that Tempest has mastered many signs this day. Your sister is a very smart woman. Soon, she will be able to talk freely to anyone in this village."

Aaron had now stopped beside them. Though he listened to what Soaring Eagle said, he was watching Brittany's face. He was certain that the emotion that moved fleetingly across it was . . . jealousy.

He was startled by this realization; he was sure Brittany had not recognized the emotion herself.

"It's good for her to learn the signs," Aaron said enthusiastically. "If any of the young children who have not yet learned English are brought to us for medical treatment, she can ease their fears. She already has a way with them, and now she'll be able to talk to them."

Tempest, too, had been watching Brittany. She had no idea why Brittany should be upset, but obviously she was. But Tempest's heart was too light to let anything spoil her happiness. She had enjoyed the morning more than she could ever explain to anyone.

"I think it is time we got on our way home," Aaron was saying as Night Walker rode up beside them.

"Yes," Brittany agreed. "It's time to go."

"Aaron," Night Walker said. "I would come and speak with you soon. There are many things I must know."

"Come any time. You are welcome."

Night Walker was well aware that Brittany did not as yet share Aaron's feeling. Later, as the visitors began their journey home, Night Walker and Soaring Eagle watched in silence. Each was engrossed in thoughts that might have surprised the other.

Chapter Eight

Daniel Nixon had spent the weeks after his meeting with Senator Gifford making arrangements. He had told his father and stepmother nothing. There would be time enough for talk when he was rich.

He'd telegraphed Fort Pierre and received a reply from Colonel Brady. Daniel now had official standing as a government agent; as such, he'd been invited to come out and report on the relations between fort, village and mission.

"I'll send word when I've arrived and am settled," Daniel had told his cohorts when he'd met with Robert Preston and Major Cline.

"Whom will you meet there?" Robert had questioned.

"A Lieutenant Cole Young." He'd turned to face

Lee. "Do you know anything about him? Can he be bought? Does he have any . . . secrets that can be effectively used?"

"I've checked his record clear back to his childhood," Lee had grumbled. "The man has no secrets, no really bad vices that I can find. He's a dedicated soldier and as loyal as Job. I wish I could say otherwise, but I can't."

"Well, then we will have to convince him that we are in the right and that his continued loyalty is expected."

"How do you propose to do that?"

"I'll cross that bridge when I come to it. There is no human alive that does not have a price. With enough time I'll find his. Gentlemen, I must be on my way. Expect my first contact as soon as I arrive."

"Good luck, Daniel."

"Don't worry. I don't intend to leave all that gold buried out there. I'll see to it our plans are carried out."

"Wonderful. When do you leave?"

"In the morning."

"I've already sent a message to your contact there. Don't worry about finding him, he'll find you."

"He has a name?"

"Yes, Jethro Bodine."

"What do you know about him?"

"Enough to get him hanged several times over. Don't worry. He's been in the territory several years. He's worked among the Indians, and knows both them and their language."

"How many men does he have?"

"He'll get as many as you need when you need them."

"Well then, it sounds like we're ready to move," Daniel had said. "Within a year, I predict we'll have all the wealth we want."

"With our plans, who knows. We might just have an empire . . . a very lucrative empire."

"Yes," Daniel had said softly, "an empire."

Now, as he was about to leave the train at Sioux Falls, Daniel recalled that he had not felt it necessary on that night weeks ago to tell his cohorts that an empire only needed one emporer. Ultimately, he would be the one to rule this golden empire.

When he stepped onto the train platform, Cole Young was there to greet him.

"Mr. Nixon." Cole clasped his hand, "Welcome to Sioux Falls. I'm Lieutenant Cole Young. I'm here to escort you to Fort Pierre."

"Thank you, Lieutenant. It's been a long trip and I'm a bit tired and dusty."

"Then why don't I stand you to a drink tonight?"

"Fine, and maybe you can fill me in on the conditions in this territory."

"Very good. Come with me and I'll take you to the hotel. My orderly will see to your luggage."

They walked to the hotel together. Later that evening Daniel came downstairs and met Cole in the lobby and the two went to dinner.

Over drinks Cole answered Daniel's questions about the fort and the Indian villages beyond. As he did, Cole tried to divine Daniel's purpose in being there.

"So, you consider these people a lot more civilized than most Easterners think?" Daniel was asking.

"Lord, yes," Cole said, "and a lot more intelligent than they're given credit for."

"I take it you're friendly with them?"

"Hardly. I don't see much of them. I'm out here to keep peace, and as long as they're peaceful, I try not to bother them. I do know a man who is very friendly with them, though."

"Oh, and who is this?"

"His name is Aaron Abbott. He's a missionary and he teaches a bit. He's got a mission between us and the village."

"He's not afraid?"

"No, I guess not. He's been there for several years. Speaks their language well. I guess he's pretty close to them; so close he's got a school going."

"A school! For Indians! I can hardly believe that. I was told they were mostly ignorant."

Cole ignored this. "Aaron even brought out a teacher. A young and pretty teacher, I might add. Miss Brittany Nelson, and her sister, Tempest."

"Seems this is an unlikely place for a white woman, especially a pretty one."

"A lot of people thought that when they arrived. Matter of fact, the train you were on brought quite

147

a bit of luggage for Brittany and Tempest, sent by their brother."

"Perhaps when you take the baggage to the mission, you would not mind if I accompanied you?"

"No, no, of course not." Cole tossed down the last of his drink. "Mind if I ask just what you are doing way out here?"

"I've been given a position in the Bureau of Indian Affairs. Sort of a liaison between the Indians and Washington. I'm to see to all the legal technicalities of land ownership, problems of any sort that might arise."

"I don't understand. There has been no question about land ownership. The Sioux live on their own land, and if they cause no problem, why should we interfere?"

"There is an immense westward movement. More settlers will be coming, either to homestead here or passing through. I am here to see there are no problems. Actually, I'm sort of an observer, here to make recommendations."

"And if there are problems?"

"Then . . . I must consider recommending the removal of the Indians to a reservation."

"The Sioux leave the Black Hills?" Cole laughed softly. "That will never happen. Those hills are sacred to these people. And Aaron Abbott would never allow it."

"Since their welfare is my concern as well, I think Mr. Abbott and I will get along well." Daniel stood up. "I do think it's about time I retire. This has been a long and tiring trip."

"We'll be leaving for the fort early tomorrow."

"I'll be ready. Good night, Lieutenant."

"Good night." Cole watched him walk away and wondered if he was carrying trouble in Aaron's direction.

Daniel went to his room and prepared for bed. He was considering Cole's words. He didn't like the idea of a man like Aaron Abbott among the Indians. Nor did he like the idea of a teacher. It was much easier to deal with a man who could not read or write. Even if he convinced the Indians to trust him, he would not be able to manipulate them if they could read and understand any papers he might lay before them. No, he did not like the idea of a teacher at all.

When Daniel and Cole rode through the open gates of the fort, they were dusty, tired and hungry. They had more than the usual number of wagons following them. In addition to supplies for the fort and the mission, there were all the things James had sent his sisters.

Cole was not surprised to hear that Aaron had come the day before and was waiting for him.

"Now you will have your chance to meet Aaron," he said to Daniel. "He's here."

"Excellent."

"I'll have an orderly show you to your quarters, while I report to Colonel Brady. Once you've cleaned off some of the trail dust, come to my office. Aaron will most likely be there."

"Very good. It won't take me long. I'm anxious to meet him."

Cole rode on to his own quarters, where he dismounted and went inside. It was less than fifteen minutes later that he heard a knock on his door. He answered it quickly.

"Aaron, good to see you again."

"Thank you, Cole. I think you have some supplies for me?"

"A lot for you, and even more for Brittany and Tempest. How are they doing, by the way?"

"Wonderfully. They have taken to the mission like ducks to water."

"There's someone I want you to meet, Aaron. He came in with me today."

"Oh?"

"Man named Daniel Nixon."

"What's he doing out here? Military?"

"No, government. Something to do with Indian land and settlers. It's a general inspection, I'd say."

"Government?" Aaron was puzzled. "The Sioux have a treaty. Any time the government comes nosing around, it almost always means trouble. I'm not going to tolerate them pushing these people one more time."

"Take it easy. He seems like a level-headed man and I don't think he's looking for a problem." Cole smiled. "By the way, how's your school coming along?"

"Well, since Brittany and Tempest visited the village, more children have been showing up every day. I don't have all the children of Flying Horse's village yet. Some of the young warriors are afraid of what they don't know, and proud. But I have a feeling Brittany will eventually win them all over."

"Aaron . . . I'd like to go to that village sometime. I'm sure Mr. Nixon will want to, too. I hated to tell him I don't have any contact. I feel like a damn fool."

"I don't suppose I'll get away with arguing with the government, but I intend to hold out as long as I can. I'm sorry, Cole."

"It will come."

"I know. But not with my help."

"Oh, Aaron, there's to be a little celebration here. Lieutenant Murphy has been transferred back East and we want to give him a good send-off. Do you suppose Brittany . . . and Tempest might like to come?"

"I'm sure they would. They've been working hard, especially Tempest."

"Why especially Tempest?"

"It seems that many in Flying Horse's village took a special liking to her. You'd be amazed at the number of bruises, minor cuts and make-believe injuries that have shown up." Aaron laughed. "She smiles and treats them. She's been learning to talk with her hands and has become pretty good at it really. I still can't fathom how she learned so much in such a short time. Course, she's still kind of solitary."

"Well, getting back here and having some fun might be good for them both." Cole rose to his feet. "I expect Mr. Nixon. He'll probably have a lot of questions for you."

"Maybe some answers, too," Aaron replied as he and Cole relaxed and waited for Daniel's arrival.

A short time later, Daniel was announced. After the introductions he shook hands with Aaron.

"So, you are the man who runs the mission."

"Yes."

"You've been out here for some time?"

"A number of years."

"Cole tells me you are friendly with the Indians out near the Black Hills."

"That would be Flying Horse's village. Yes, I'm proud to say I am."

"I should like very much to meet them."

"Well," Aaron said quietly, "I suppose you could get Cole to take you for a ride."

"And that's just what it would be—a ride," Cole said. "Mr. Nixon, I'll tell you the truth. The military's role here is to try to keep peace. The Indians don't cause us any problems, so we've never pushed to see them. Matter of fact, I don't exactly know where they are."

"How can you keep peace if—"

"By not raising an alarm when there isn't any trouble."

"And the whites already here—what about their protection?"

"Most of them have made their peace with the Indians long before this. They don't seem to be having any problems."

"And what of this mission?" Daniel asked.

"From what I hear, the Indians have no religion. How do they take to your preaching?"

"You're wrong about them not having a religion. They have a very profound faith in *Wakan Tanka*, their God. I am not here to force my God or my faith on them; I'm here to try to better their lives any way I can. Through medicine and education."

"Education?"

"Yes. I have built a school for which I already have an excellent teacher."

"You have taken this upon yourself without asking the permission of the government?"

"Permission? Why should the government be asked permission to teach elementary things to these people? I don't need to request permission should I care to share my knowledge with another."

"I'm afraid you are wrong, Mr. Abbott. The Bureau of Indian Affairs takes an active interest in such things. I have the honor of representing our government in this territory. I have come to study the situation and report my findings to the Bureau of Indian Affairs."

"And when was this decided?"

"Most recently," Daniel replied.

"Mr. Nixon . . . what were you before you were chosen for this position?"

"A lawyer. Why?"

"I might have guessed that. We need to discuss this. You'll find you are not really needed here. The last thing these people need is more of the white man's law . . . or more of the white man's government. Having to put up with a military fort on their land is insult enough. But they have been both gracious and tolerant about it."

"You are right, Mr. Abbott," Daniel said quietly, "we will have to discuss this."

There was a moment of silence while Aaron adjusted to the idea that Daniel was not a man who was going to do anything less than what he planned to do.

Cole wanted to defuse the situation, so he spoke enthusiastically. "It might be a good idea if you met the people who work with Aaron. Especially his teacher. I was just telling him that we have a party planned in a couple weeks. It will give you an opportunity to meet most everyone in the territory."

"Sounds like an excellent idea. I'll look forward to it." Daniel turned to Aaron. "And to seeing this school of yours, not to mention a woman who has the courage to come here to teach."

Aaron added nothing more, and Cole chose to be silent on the subject. Somehow he'd begun to dislike Daniel Nixon.

"I think it's time we got something to eat. That was a long trip and I'm hungry," Cole said to break the uneasy silence.

The meal seemed a bit strained to Aaron, but both Cole and Daniel tried to be as amenable as possible.

The situation was one Aaron had to think over. He did not know yet how far Daniel's authority went, or for that matter, what Daniel had in mind.

Still, all his instincts told him this was a situation that was not going to benefit his school, his workers . . . or his friends in Flying Horse's village.

After they ate, Aaron excused himself, telling Daniel and Cole he had to make arrangements to get his supplies back to the mission. He'd not planned to leave so quickly. Now he wanted to be away from this man who pretended friendliness, while every sense Aaron had screamed danger.

Danger, but why, and from where?

The next morning Aaron left early. It was hardly day, but when he and the packhorses were ready to leave the fort, Cole was there to say good-bye.

"Aaron . . . you're leaving pretty fast, aren't you? Does it have anything to do with our guest?"

"What do you really know about him, Cole?"

"All that I can know. He turned his credentials over to the colonel and they seem to be in order. He has been sent by Washington. What trouble do you think one man can cause?"

"Cole"—Aaron grinned—"Samson was only one man, but he managed to pull down a temple."

"Ah, but he had the power."

"Power is a strange thing. This man has a power, too. I wonder what he intends to do with it."

"You're too cautious. What can he do if Flying Horse and his people cause no problems? Where they are is their land by treaty. I plan on keeping as much distance between it and Mr. Nixon as I can. Will that ease your mind a bit?"

"Yes. Thanks, Cole. I'll see you in two weeks. Perhaps I'm jumping at shadows. I'm sure all of us will be looking forward to this party. Who knows, Brittany and Tempest might be the ones to convince our man here that all is well and Washington's meddling is not needed."

"I'll see you sooner than that. I'll be escorting Mr. Nixon out to the mission as soon as he's ready to travel."

Aaron rode away from the fort, and Cole stood and watched until he disappeared, trying to rid himself of the feeling that Aaron might be right. He, too, felt there was some kind of trouble brewing.

From the doorway of his quarters Daniel also watched Aaron ride away. This man and his ideas were a thorn in his side. He must arrange to have Aaron and his school destroyed as soon as possible. He considered all the plans he had made and knew he was not going to let anything or anyone stand in his way.

Soaring Eagle sat on a fallen tree and with a sharp stick drew in the earth. He had to concentrate to remember the letters Never Quiet had so patiently tried to show him. A . . . B . . . C . . . D . . .

Flying Horse had agreed to let the children come to the school, even the young braves. Though some of the boys had been a bit insulted that they had to attend, Flying Horse's word was the final one.

Star Dancer was happy to go to school; it was easier than doing all her daily chores. But Running Cougar was incensed, and at first adamantly refused to go. Soaring Eagle was the one who convinced his younger brothers to go, but still Running Cougar went only when he felt like it. Soaring Eagle, of course, had an ulterior motive for wanting the children to attend. He wanted to learn and he could not go to the school. He was a warrior! But he was a warrior with a thirst for learning, and an even deeper one for being with the sun-haired Tempest.

Never Quiet had teased him unmercifully, but she had displayed a great deal of patience teaching him the rudiments of the alphabet.

What got between him and his concentration was Tempest. Never Quiet had ridden back and forth between the village and the mission, often with Laughing Thunder and Running Cougar, but sometimes alone. Her thirst to know the magic of the stories Brittany had told her had taken wing when Brittany began to teach her the letters she would need to learn to read.

He had ridden there with Never Quiet the first few times, until he discovered that Tempest took a walk every afternoon. He followed her and they met again as they had done on the high meadow.

She was not afraid of him and always welcomed him with a smile. She also welcomed the knowledge he brought, for he continued to teach her signs. She would point to something and he would show her the sign. Every day she got better and better at it until they could communicate almost in sentences.

He had no sign for what he was beginning to feel for her. No sign that she would understand. Would she understand that he longed to hear her say his name, that he would give anything to have her reach out to touch him? Sometimes the feelings got so out of control that he had to leave her before he did something that would bring disgrace on his whole family.

He had read Brittany's eyes and was sure his feelings for Tempest would be unwelcome.

Tempest was so beautiful, so fragile, like the small golden butterfly that flitted from flower to flower. He wanted her with desperation, for he knew that his village and her sister would not approve.

Who could he turn to for answers? All his life it had been either his father or Night Walker. But Night Walker had changed since that morning in the village when Aaron had visited and brought his guests. Night Walker had frequently been gone from the village. Even when he was there he seemed withdrawn and thoughtful.

Soaring Eagle sighed and tried again to form the strange letters that made the white man's language. He'd been told by Never Quiet that once he learned them all, he could understand the writing of the whites. Maybe it would make things between him and Tempest easier if he knew her ways and her language.

He moved the stick slowly, so immersed in what

he was doing that he did not hear anyone approaching.

"Are you well, brother?" The voice was so unexpected that Soaring Eagle dropped the stick and stood abruptly, scuffing his moccasins in the dirt so that it would no longer reveal what he was doing. Night Walker dismounted and walked toward him.

"I am fine," Soaring Eagle replied. For a moment he was frustrated that he could think of nothing else to say. "Why do you ask?"

"It was merely an echo of our mother's question this morning." Night Walker shrugged. "She believes you are deeply troubled by something." He sat on the log and stretched his legs before him. "She says that you are eating little. Every day you have gone hunting, yet you come home with no meat." He looked up at Soaring Eagle and his gaze held his. Soaring Eagle refused to look away. "Is it for the reasons I think?" he asked quietly. "Do you ride to Aaron's?"

There had never been a lie between them and Soaring Eagle would not allow one now. "Yes. I have ridden there. Why? Is it wrong?"

"I did not say that."

"Am I a child that I must ask to ride where I choose?"

"No, Soaring Eagle, you are not a child. You are a man. And a man must know and understand that what he wants sometimes is the wrong thing."

"Why, Night Walker? Tell me why it is wrong. What do you fear?"

159

"There is no fear in my heart, just caution. Aaron should not have brought these two white women among us. Would you turn our children over to them so that all we know and believe can be washed from their minds?"

"I don't believe that is their plan." Soaring Eagle sat down beside him. "Tell me what you truly believe. Tell me that I am wrong and maybe then I can try to understand."

Night Walker was shaken. How could he tell his brother he was wrong when at least Soaring Eagle had had the courage to do what Night Walker wanted to do?

Night Walker knew he had cheated. He had told Brittany he would listen, but he hadn't. He had only tried to force her to see his way.

How could he decry what Soaring Eagle felt, when his dreams had been filled with Brittany? He could still feel the length of her slim body pressed to his and still taste the sweetness of her kiss.

Of course, he had sensed that Brittany was not happy that day in the village, that somehow she had thought it wrong for Soaring Eagle to look at her sister. He had resented her attitude as much for his sake as Soaring Eagle's.

But he could not turn and meet his brother's eyes, because he knew Soaring Eagle had only done what he himself longed to do.

"Night Walker?"

"I do not know what I believe. I cannot tell you what to do or to think. I can only warn you to be

160

cautious, to prepare yourself to be rejected. They are different and they cannot change. They expect us to change . . . and we will not."

"Perhaps," Soaring Eagle said gently, "change can be a good thing."

"No one has discovered the fact that the two of you are meeting. I would only warn you, brother; that is all. This woman, she is . . . special. Even if the whites approved, it would not be easy."

"But you are not telling me not to go."

Night Walker was quiet for a moment; then he spoke softly. "No, I am not."

"Never Quiet has found Brittany and Tempest to be patient and kind to her. She has told me that—"

"Never Quiet is another story," Night Walker laughed. "She will find the answers to her questions no matter where she has to go to find them."

"But she teaches them as much as she learns. She has said the white teacher is trying very hard to learn our language. And Never Quiet is not always one to sit and patiently learn."

Night Walker fought the pleasing idea that Brittany was trying to learn his language. He could hear her smooth voice speaking his tongue, saying words . . . He controlled his thoughts and stood up.

"You can sit and dream all day if you choose, lazy one; I have things to do. I need more arrows." He looked down at his brother. "Soaring Eagle . . ."

"Yes?" Soaring Eagle waited expectantly.

161

"Never mind. Just be careful."

As Night Walker walked to his horse and mounted, Soaring Eagle's puzzled gaze followed him. There was an unspoken thing between them, and Night Walker seemed to be very troubled by it.

Finally, after he had decided he would speak to Night Walker again about this, he settled back on the log and picked up the stick. He was anxious to learn all the letters so that when he saw Tempest again he could show her. A . . . B . . . C . . . D . . .

Night Walker rode slowly, his mind on Brittany. He knew he could not put her from his thoughts; he had tried day after day. Perhaps it was because he felt guilty that he had not honored the truce that had been proposed between them.

It might be easier if he listened to what she wanted to say. At least he would know the boundaries.

He was not a boy, not a dreamer; he knew quite well he wanted to see her again. When he finally reached the boundaries of Aaron's land, he drew his horse to a halt.

He considered what would be the best way of seeing Brittany alone. There was too much activity around the mission to make it easy. Still, he waited and watched.

The building Aaron called a school sat some distance away from the rest of the mission. From his vantage point Night Walker could see that the door stood open, and that someone must be inside. That someone was most likely Brittany.

Hoping he was right, he urged his horse into motion and rode slowly down through the shadows of the trees to the back of the building.

Chapter Nine

Brittany was working on her lesson plan for the next day. Sunlight streamed through the windows of the schoolhouse as she pored over her books. Though she was delighted that the children were beginning to come, she was not as happy at the mission as she'd expected.

It had something to do with Tempest, she realized. Brittany felt a kind of lonely desolation, as if some part of herself was gone. She had felt the subtle shift of Tempest's attention away from her and all she had provided, to something else. Provided? Yes, she had done her best to provide for Tempest since the day of the accident. Hadn't she always been beside her? Hadn't she always tried to shield Tempest in every way she could? Along with James, Brittany had been Tempest's sole source of . . . well, most everything in her world. She had spent hours, days, weeks at Tempest's side. Of course, she didn't mind, she valued Tempest's love and would have done anything necessary to care for her.

She meant to see that Tempest never suffered again if she could help it.

She knew her response to Tempest and Soaring Eagle being together was irrational, but she could not fight the strange, unwelcome fear she'd felt when she'd seen the two of them that day in the village. Soaring Eagle was a young, strong and very handsome man. Something about the way Tempest had looked at him had shaken Brittany completely.

Nothing could be allowed to develop between those two, she'd decided. Not because Soaring Eagle was an Indian—that problem had not occurred to Brittany—but because she was afraid that Tempest was only a novelty that had caught Soaring Eagle's interest. A novelty that would one day become boring. When he found other things to interest him, where would Tempest be? No, Brittany would not allow it. She would not let her sister be hurt again. No one could provide for Tempest the way she could.

She was overprotective of Tempest and knew it, yet she couldn't let go. Tempest needed her, could not go on without her. Soaring Eagle was just a passing threat. Tempest would not do anything that would cause Brittany a problem.

Brittany put down the book she was looking

through and tried to examine her deepest thoughts. What was she suddenly so afraid of?

She didn't want to know . . . but she did. Her fear was of a dark-eyed man with a devastating smile. Whatever she was, she was honest. The kiss they had shared had reached a place she had protected for a long time.

As if he were with her, she could feel the warmth of Night Walker's skin and the strength of his arms. Her mouth could still feel the pressure of his, and even though she struggled, she could not deny that she had enjoyed his kiss, had wanted it.

She knew Night Walker did not want her here. He had never given her a chance to present arguments from her point of view. He had told her what he felt, and expected her to blindly agree. Well, he was wrong and she was right. She meant to push the emotions he had aroused in her aside and prove to his village, and to him, that she had something of value to offer his people.

When Night Walker appeared in the back entrance of the school, Brittany did not see him. His moccasins made no sound as he stepped inside. But after a step or two he halted.

Brittany was seated at the desk with a ray of sunlight bathing her in its glow. He couldn't move, or even breathe. The sight of her stirred a vague memory within him.

She must have sensed his presence, for she suddenly lifted her head and turned to look in his direction. Their eyes met, and both stilled, as if a breathless hush had fallen over them. Then Brittany rose, and as she did the misty glow of sunlight made her seem a vague and ethereal form, and only then did the reality of his memory spark to life. His vision. The woman whose face he had not seen. He knew with every sense he had that she was Brittany. He couldn't understand what it meant, or why she had been shown to him that way. She was to have some effect on his life and his future. Still, he had no way of knowing if it was good or bad.

"Night Walker," she said softly. "I haven't seen you for almost two weeks. I know you've visited Aaron often before. I hope your friendship isn't suffering because of me."

"I have had much to do."

"Then"—she smiled and took another step toward him—"it is not Aaron you have come to see?"

"No," he honestly replied. "I have come to see you."

"I hope you're not still angry that Flying Horse decided to allow the children to come to school?"

"He has made the decision, but do you know how hard it will be for the young warriors to be taught by—"

"A woman?"

"Yes."

"Pride is not an excuse for not getting what you need to face a new way of life. I hope that all of them will realize this. Until then, I will fight for each mind I can get."

"This problem is not my reason for being here, either."

"Then why . . ." She watched him as he approached her and she could not read the look in his eyes.

She looked up into eyes that suddenly seemed puzzled and uncertain.

"I would talk to you again." He smiled to ease his peremptory words. "Or . . . I would rather hear you talk. The last time, perhaps I was not as ready to hear as I was to make you hear."

"No." Brittany's lips formed a half smile. "You were not in a listening mood."

"Your sister is not with you to help with the work?"

"She worked late at the infirmary last night and went in early this morning. Then I suppose she will go on one of her walks. I'll never understand this need for solitude. She has suddenly decided she must be alone, and she enjoys walking."

Night Walker turned his head so that their eyes no longer met. He could not tell Brittany that he knew where her sister went. Not until he knew how she would react. He had to find that out without causing Soaring Eagle and Tempest any problem. He hated subterfuge, and it made him slightly angry that Brittany's worry over her sister might increase because of her relationship with his brother. Soaring Eagle was a man of honor and would not hurt Tempest in any way. Still Night Walker wondered if Brittany would believe this.

If it angered her or frightened her that Soaring Eagle was interested in her sister, how did she truly feel about him? He didn't like the idea that he cared. He had caught the eye of the shy, smiling girls in his village and could have his choice among them. It annoyed him that he was so uncertain. He meant to find his answers.

"Maybe she finds much beauty here."

"I'm sure she does. I think this is one of the most beautiful places I have ever seen. But . . . Tempest . . . well, she needs to be protected, sometimes even from herself. She . . . she's . . . vulnerable."

"Vulnerable?" The word was new to him.

"She's gentle, and sweet, and trusting, and she can easily be hurt. I don't want her ever to be hurt again. You can't imagine what she went through as a child."

"All of our lives are built on trust, and there is no one who has not been hurt. Perhaps it has made her stronger. Stronger than you know. Besides, you cannot be a shield all her life, and you cannot stop her from being hurt any more than you can stop her from searching for her own happiness. What if you choose to marry?"

"I do not choose to marry."

"Now?"

"Never."

Night Walker paused. He found this hard to believe. In his world all women married, if possible, and all men knew the value of a good wife.

"You choose to live always alone?" His eyes met hers steadily. "Never to have children? . . . Never to share your old age with a husband?"

Brittany was surprised at the emotions his questions brought forth. She was half angry at her own reaction, and at him for causing it. It was none of his business what she chose to do with her personal life.

She turned from him and walked to the back entrance. Sunlight sparkled across a meadow that vanished into a stand of trees. She watched it glisten on the creek that skirted the meadow and vanished into the woods.

Night Walker had watched her in silence, realizing she did not mean to answer his question and had closed a door between them. Despite all his denials, he didn't want that door to close. He walked silently up to stand behind her.

"It's so different here," Brittany said quietly, without turning around. "I'm trying to adjust to the differences. I'm trying to understand all you've told me. . . . Are you going to try as hard?"

"That is the reason I came." His voice matched hers in quietness and gentleness. "To hear your words. Will you walk with me?"

"Yes."

He moved to her side and they walked together across the gentle rolling ground of the meadow to the edge of the creek. There they walked side by side for some time without speaking.

Soon the mission was out of sight and they were alone. Night Walker waited patiently for her to speak. Finally she turned to face him.

"Night Walker, I have thought about all you told

me, and I can understand how you feel. But your reasoning only holds true if your world goes on as it has in the past, and that's not going to be possible. You cannot just think about here and now. If you don't think of tomorrow, then you only have today. Nothing will ever change and . . . you will not survive what the new days will bring.

"There is a reality you refuse to face. Already there is a fort that is close to you, even though you choose to ignore it. Already there are settlers . . . farmers . . . here, and whether you want it to happen or not, there will be more and more, until you have to face them.

"You have choices. To run, which I know you cannot do. To fight a battle that you cannot win. Or you can learn to meet the whites on their own terms, with more of an understanding of their world than they have of yours. Aaron . . . and I can give you that. We can help your children so that they can be prepared for a future that will be different from anything you or they have known before. It will be hard. But it would be harder if someone like Aaron didn't care so much."

"And you care, as he does?"

"Yes, I care."

"Why?"

"Why?" Brittany smiled. "I cannot say. Perhaps because I want to make amends, or perhaps it is a challenge to me. I want you to see and share some of the wonderful things I have to give."

He liked her smile and even enjoyed the light of

excitement in her eyes. She truly felt deeply about her reasons for being here.

He moved closer and watched her eyes register her awareness of him. Within inches of her he stopped, and held her gaze with his.

"You speak words that are an echo of Aaron's. But what is in your heart, Brittany? Do you see us as a people with outstretched hands, or do you see us as children to be taught to obey? Do you see us as part of a game you play?"

"A game!" Her eyes sparkled with anger. "You are so arrogant that you believe I would leave my world, and a very comfortable world it was, to come out here and face God only knows what dangers, to play a game! I don't need to do this. I did it because in my heart I thought I could make a difference!" Brittany was angry now, and she struggled against a desire to strike him violently.

He remained still, waiting for her gaze to meet his. "I have thought your heart deceiving, Brittany Nelson," he said quietly. "I have tried hard to believe that all you have said has been false. Words can lie; they can cover over what is really felt."

Brittany had no words either to deny what he said or to convince him that she could not allow his disbelief to end what both she and Aaron wanted to provide his people.

"You have to understand, I can't allow anything to interfere in the plans Aaron has made. He wants so much for you and your people, and he expects so much from me. I can't disappoint him.

He brought us here for a purpose, and this battle between us is not it."

Night Walker came up beside her and reached out to turn her to face him. He tried to search her face for an answer to something he could not put words to but felt more deeply than he had ever felt anything before.

"There is more than this small battle between us, do you deny this?"

"That would be like denying an earthquake. I cannot deny it, but I cannot let it take command. It is too fast and . . . maybe I'm too scared. You give me no time to think rationally."

"Perhaps it is not good to let you think too much." He smiled. "Then you will go back to being a teacher. I asked you a question before, and you never gave me an answer."

"A question? What question?"

"I asked if you choose to live always alone. Never to have children. . . . Never to share your old age with a husband."

"A . . . hus . . . husband?" Her voice shook. She could feel something deep inside her tremble, and she struggled for an answer.

"There is much I must do before I consider marriage." She finally turned to look at him. "I suppose that, like any other woman, I would one day like to have a husband and children. But not now. Now, I have the responsibility of my sister, my promise to Aaron . . . and my own dreams." Again she turned from him. She heard him move and was, for a breathless moment, afraid. He came up behind her but didn't touch her.

"I did not trust you, *wasichu*," he said softly, "and I did not seek this feeling that fills me. I want you, Brittany Nelson, and I don't want to want you. I want to hold onto my anger and distrust, but when you are near, they melt away. The great spirit makes our lives as he chooses them to be. Perhaps the circles of our lives are joined. I will tell you now that I will no longer fight you. It has already been decided that our children will learn your ways and your words, and I will go on wanting you. . . . But I will not allow what I want to hold me prisoner. You must choose what you want and where your life leads. Remember, no matter how much we love, or wish to protect someone, we are only responsible for our own lives. It is all the great spirit freely gives us."

Brittany heard his words and inhaled deeply, closing her eyes as she tried to form a response. But there was a silence behind her that told her Night Walker was already gone.

She was right, she argued with herself. She didn't want to feel what he made her feel. She knew her promise to Aaron, and her need to keep Tempest safe and happy, had to be her first priority.

When she married, it would be when Aaron's work was complete. Then she would go home and choose a man who belonged in her world as she belonged in his.

She didn't want to remember that Night Walker's touch could set her on fire. She didn't want to hear his words echo in her mind. He wanted her . . . and she had wanted him.

Slowly she walked back toward the mission. With each step she promised herself that she would wash the memory of Night Walker's touch from her mind if it was the last thing she did.

For a long while, it didn't occur to her that she hadn't seen Tempest for hours, nor had she seen much of Aaron since he had returned. She had thrown herself into work and into forgetting Night Walker's fiery touch, and the words he'd spoken, which stubbornly lingered in her mind despite every effort to wipe them away.

To keep her mind occupied she decided to find Tempest. But when she walked by the infirmary, Tempest was not there. Nor was she at their house. Brittany was beginning to worry now.

Where in the world was Tempest?

Soaring Eagle had found Tempest by the stream that lay on the far side of the meadow where they had first met. They had walked beside it for a while. Tempest was quite unaware of the turmoil that swirled in the mind and heart of the young man who walked beside her.

He enjoyed being with her, just walking beside her, and looking at her when he thought she wasn't looking at him. He enjoyed pointing things out and showing her the signs and he delighted in the way she grasped every new thing immediately.

He had come to meet her today determined to

tell her what was in his heart, but walking beside her, he struggled for the right way to tell her what he felt. How could he put into sign language the way his heart skipped a beat every time she smiled at him? The way her soft laugh and occasional gentle touch set his blood coursing through him? The way she could look at him with her eyes sparkling and set his whole day right?

Tempest had knelt by the shallow, rippling stream and dipped her hand into the water and smiled up at him as she made the correct sign for water, then for river, then for stream.

He smiled and knelt beside her. She was eager to please . . . and beautiful. She was intelligent and quick . . . and she was beautiful. She was proud and sweet . . . and she was beautiful. By all the gods he knew, she was the most beautiful thing he had ever seen.

Soaring Eagle caught her hand with his and watched to see if he frightened her. But obviously he didn't. Now was the moment! Now he had to make her understand . . . but how? How!

Her eyes were questioning him. Not with fear or resentment, just questions.

Holding her hand, he pressed his other hand against his heart, then slowly he pointed to her. He repeated the gesture very slowly. The last thing he wanted was for her to misunderstand. But he watched her face, especially her amazing blue eyes, and knew she did not misunderstand at all.

Her lips parted slightly and he waited with his breath caught somewhere in his chest.

Tempest had reached out one delicate, small hand and traced the firm line of his jaw, then gently let her fingers trail down until her hand lay against his chest. She could feel the thunder of his rapid heartbeat.

She knew without words. Every line of his face, the half smile on his firm, wide mouth, the humming tension of his lean, muscular body, spoke a language that left no doubt in her mind.

Very slowly she cupped his face between her hands and drew his head down to her. Their lips met in a kiss as delicate as the touch of butterfly wings and as explosive as a thunderstorm.

He wanted her! By all the gods, how he wanted her. It took every ounce of restraint he had not to pull her down to the sweet-smelling grass, to remove the interfering clothes and feel the warmth of her flesh next to his.

This he wouldn't do, because he knew that the look he would see in her eyes would forever damn him.

For a minute they could only look at each other, somewhat stunned by the magnitude of this feeling they shared.

He reached to take the ribbon from her hair and thread his fingers through the soft strands. He'd wanted to do that for weeks.

He laughed in exultation, and her laughter blended with his. For now, the discovery was enough. He knew the barriers as well as she did and knew they needed time.

But the morning was theirs, and as other couples had done since the beginning of time, they found joy in just being together.

He found a bed of wildflowers, plucked one and tucked it behind her ear . . . and kissed her. He walked through the meadow in the warm sunshine . . . and kissed her. In fact he took every excuse to taste her sweet lips.

He knew one thing for certain, he would go on teaching her until she mastered the sign language, but he would also go on learning to read and write her language. He would have to if they were to find a way out of the dilemma they found themselves in. But he would find a way, because he did not intend to let anything or anyone stand between them.

Chapter Ten

When Daniel first caught sight of Brittany Nelson
as he and Cole arrived at the mission, his spirits
lifted. She was much prettier than he had thought
she would be. She did not fit his idea of a teacher,
especially one who would leave the comforts of a
civilized home for a place as primitive as the mission.

Confidence filled him. She would be easy to
drive away. One confrontation with a hostile
would put her on the first means of transportation
home.

When she joined them, looking a little flustered,
both Cole and Aaron greeted her warmly. Then
Aaron introduced her to Daniel, explaining that he
had come to observe the interaction between
whites and Indians.

"I must say it is a bit surprising to find a girl as lovely as yourself so willing to bury herself in the wilderness," Daniel said.

"Bury?" Brittany smiled, but Daniel could see at once he had trod on dangerous territory. "I don't look at it that way. I'm not buried here, I choose to be here. There are so many things to be done. If you're here to work on behalf of the Indians, I guess that makes us companions in the same boat."

"Touché," Daniel laughed. "I'm sorry if I spoke out of line. Your pretty face destroyed my caution. I'll be more careful in the future."

"Cole," Brittany said, smiling at him, "it's nice to see you again."

"You're looking well, Brittany. How are you adjusting to life out here? A bit different from back East." His smile was refreshingly open and Brittany returned it.

"Actually I like it."

"You're getting tanned. It looks good on you. Your hair is lighter, too. Most becoming."

"Your compliments will turn my head," she protested with a laugh.

"Where is that pretty sister of yours?" he asked. "Is she taking to this territory as well as you are obviously doing?"

"I was just looking for her, as a matter of fact. Have you seen her Aaron?"

"No, but don't worry about her. She can be amazing sometimes. She seems to have a way of communicating with everyone."

"Yes, she does," Brittany answered with a smile. "I'm trying to master some of the sign the Sioux use, and surprisingly Tempest is much better at it than I will ever be. She has the people of Flying Horse's village coming to her with all the imaginary illnesses in the world, from a splinter to unaccountable fevers! The children adore her."

"I would say that the young men come pretty close to adoration as well." Aaron chuckled.

It was Daniel who noticed Brittany's frown. Ah, he thought, at least I've found one fly in the ointment.

"There's Tempest now," Aaron said.

The group turned to see Tempest walking from the shade of the trees. She walked slowly, as gracefully as if she were dancing, and it was obvious that her mind was elsewhere.

When she finally saw Brittany, she smiled and waved, and started in their direction. Brittany frowned. Had Tempest's hair been loose and free when she'd left the house this morning? She was uncertain. But she was certain that she had not left with a flower tucked behind her ear like that. Where had she been all this time?

As Tempest grew closer, Brittany could well see that her eyes literally glowed and she exuded happiness like a child on Christmas morning.

"My Lord," Daniel said softly. "What a lovely creature she is."

"It's easy to see this country agrees with her," Cole said.

Brittany remained still. There was something

181

very different about Tempest. But it was so elusive that she could not put her finger on it. She felt something stir within her that she could not name or recognize.

When Tempest stopped beside Brittany, she smiled warmly and rested her hand on Brittany's arm for a moment.

Brittany took out the small pad and pencil she always carried in her pocket.

Tempest, where have you been?

Walking. Did you know there is a waterfall not far from here? It's beautiful.

You worry me dreadfully.

Don't worry, I'm very cautious.

Tempest smiled at Cole and extended her hand in welcome. Cole took it and held it for a long moment. Then Tempest turned her gaze toward Daniel. Her smile faltered for a brief second, and she turned a questioning gaze toward Brittany.

His name is Daniel Nixon, Brittany wrote. *He is here as a representative of the government to make a study of Indian affairs.*

Tempest nodded and smiled again at Daniel, who seemed as captivated as Cole had been.

"Daniel, this is my sister, Tempest. I'm afraid she cannot hear you, nor can she speak. But I'm sure I speak for her when I welcome you here."

Daniel bowed slightly and smiled at Tempest.

He seemed captivated by Tempest's beauty, and Cole was shaken by the feeling of resistance that the realization caused in him. He felt protective of Tempest, he argued with himself, but he knew that was certainly not the complete truth.

He decided it was because he didn't quite like or understand Daniel Nixon's presence . . . or rather, the need for his presence. He felt a confusion of emotions that kept him from speaking again.

The group was attracted by someone calling Brittany's name. Daniel watched both Brittany and Tempest smile warmly as a young Indian girl approached.

"Never Quiet," Brittany said as the girl grew close enough for her voice to be heard. "Are you alone?" She looked beyond Never Quiet hopefully for a second before she caught herself. She seemed to be looking for him in every person, every shadow.

"No, I have come with Laughing Thunder. We have brought one of the others to the healer."

"Dr. Hammond?" Brittany asked. But Never Quiet shook her head.

"No, he would see the silent healer."

Both Brittany and Aaron were surprised. The silent healer. It seemed Tempest was making deeper inroads into the faith of these people than she and Aaron ever hoped to do.

Aaron was about to speak when he observed that Never Quiet had ceased to smile. Her eyes were on Daniel. To both his and Brittany's surprise, she turned to Tempest and her hands flew in sign too quick for even Aaron to follow, at first.

Who is the white one with the cold eyes? Never Quiet signed.

His name is Daniel Nixon. He comes from the great white father in the East, Tempest replied quickly. She knew Brittany was looking at her in surprise. There would be a lot of questions later, but she no longer cared what anyone's reaction was. She was happier than she had been in a long, long time, and neither she nor Soaring Eagle had done anything but spend time together while he taught her sign and the magic beauty of the place where they lived.

Does he speak with the voice of the white father?
I don't know.
I hope not.
Why?
Because I do not like him. He looks like a hungry wolf . . . with a smile.

At this Tempest, to the curiosity and surprise of everyone, laughed.

"I have a feeling they were talking about me," Daniel said. "I'm curious. Not only about what she said, but about the efficient way she said it . . . and that your sister understood so well."

"It is the sign language Never Quiet has been teaching her since we arrived. I must admit I didn't realize Tempest was as proficient at it as this. I'll ask Tempest what she said."

Brittany wrote quickly.

What did she say that was so amusing, Tempest?
Only that there must be many handsome men from the East.

Tempest was a bit surprised to find herself lying so easily, but she felt it was more diplomatic than telling Brittany that she, too, thought Daniel Nixon had very cold eyes . . . and the smile of a wolf.

But as Brittany repeated her words to Daniel and Cole, Tempest's gaze locked with Aaron's. The look in his eyes told her Aaron had understood at least some of Never Quiet's communication. He took a long look at Never Quiet and realized that although she was a chatterbox, she was very clever as well. Children often had finely tuned instincts, and Aaron decided to keep his own counsel and not open his thoughts to Daniel Nixon . . . the man who smiled like a wolf.

"Daniel, will you join us for lunch and let Brittany and me show you our school?" Aaron said.

"I'd be delighted," Daniel said agreeably.

Tempest wrote hastily that she would see to whomever needed her medical care and join them later. Brittany watched her and Never Quiet walk away, conversing rapidly with their hands. She had the uncomfortable feeling that there was a gulf growing between herself and Tempest, and an even worse feeling that Never Quiet and the villagers were filling it for Tempest.

Dinner that night was relaxed. Daniel had been given a thorough tour with an accompanying lecture on Aaron's plans and hopes for the mission, its school and infirmary.

The more he saw, the more Daniel's thoughts became resolve. It was obvious to him that Aaron, his mission, his school, and Tempest and Brittany

Nelson were going to be bigger thorns in his side than he had bargained on. He meant to observe more and make his plans in good time. For now he was certain of at least one thing: He had to rid himself of the problem Brittany Nelson presented. There would be no more school, no teacher. Not if he could put a stop to it . . . and he could, of this he was certain.

The next day both Tempest and Brittany were extremely busy and had little time to be with Aaron, Cole or Daniel, who discussed the mission and its purpose and backing at length.

Of course, Aaron recognized at once that Daniel asked a multitude of questions but contributed no information about himself or his plans. Finally Aaron asked him point blank.

"Well, I do have many things to take into consideration," Daniel said. "But I think one of the first things the Indians need here, maybe not too far from your mission, is a place to trade and to get the benefits of white civilization. We can provide them with a great many necessities that would make their lives better."

"But that has always been part of my plan," Aaron said.

"A government post," Daniel emphasized. "I'm sure the Bureau of Indian Affairs will want to decide what the natives require . . . and what's traded to them. No offense meant, Aaron, but ungoverned trading out here could turn a handsome profit for an enterprising, unscrupulous person."

"You're not implying that that is my motive for being here, are you?"

"Hardly, no, hardly. I'm saying you can't govern the whole area. Only the United States government can do that. I'm taking a trading post into consideration, and while I'm here, I'll look about for a proper site."

"And what will you trade? You and I both know there are some influences best not brought into their world."

"Of course. I only intend to trade what I feel they really need."

Aaron sensed a double meaning, but he could not be sure. He intended to keep a close eye on whatever plans Daniel Nixon suggested.

Brittany and Tempest, exhausted from an afternoon of hard but rewarding work, walked together toward their small house to prepare for dinner.

Brittany was well aware that Tempest had been unusually withdrawn and she'd decided not to intrude. Tempest would tell her what her thoughts were when she was ready. There had never been any secrets between them.

Brittany was secure in the knowledge that the love she and her sister shared would overcome any problem . . . and Tempest was trying to find the words that would make her sister understand . . . understand, and not be hurt. She sat in the small sitting room brushing her hair and remembering what had led to this moment.

At first she had thought the meetings with Soaring Eagle were accidental. Then she had realized that for some reason he was keeping watch, guarding her, and she had felt protected. Protected and safe.

Then she began to realize that the meetings were far from accidental, but well planned by him. She should have ceased her random walks and their meetings then, but she didn't want to.

He was unique, different in a thousand ways from every other young man she had ever known. From the night he had put her hand against a throbbing drum and given her the sign for it, he had opened one door after another.

Tempest hated to deceive, either her sister and Aaron, or the others at the mission, but she knew in her heart that none of them would understand. How could they when she hadn't understood herself . . . until yesterday.

Could she share with Brittany this new and vital thing she had discovered? Could she make Brittany understand? Uncertainty kept her still. She would wait, wait until she could find a way for Brittany to know Soaring Eagle better.

Tempest watched the conversation about her as dinner proceeded. Sometimes, she thought, it was best to be in her silent world. Since she did not have to converse, she had an opportunity to watch people closely. Often her presence was forgotten.

"Oh, by the way, Brittany," Cole was saying, "there is to be a dance at the fort. You and Tempest have been invited. Would you like to go?"

"It sounds like fun. But I shall have to ask Tempest." Brittany turned to Tempest and withdrew her reliable pad from her pocket. When she pushed her hastily written note before Tempest, Brittany was surprised that at first there was no reaction. Then Tempest looked up at Brittany and slowly shook her head negatively.

Why? Brittany questioned at once. *It might be fun.*

Please go, Brittany. I want you to. But I really don't want to go. I'll be perfectly all right here.

I won't go without you.

That's not fair. You want to go, I don't. It seems pretty silly for us not to compromise. You go. There is so much to be done in the infirmary. Thomas and I have several patients now.

Brittany still looked doubtful, but Tempest reached out and laid her hand over Brittany's and smiled.

Aaron, who had been observing closely, figured out what the problem was.

"Tempest doesn't want to go?" he questioned.

"No, but she insists I do."

"Brittany, if you're worried, don't be. She is perfectly safe here. It might be good for you both," Cole interjected.

"Cole, how can you say that? I would never forgive myself if something happened while I was gone."

"Like what? You are not leaving a six-year-old

child. She'll be among a number of friends who respect and care for her," Aaron said.

"Of course," Daniel agreed. "And perhaps she will feel more comfortable here than with the crowd of military men at the fort."

Brittany was certain there was something about Tempest's resistance that was unusual. But she couldn't put her finger on it. Perhaps when they were alone she could get to the bottom of it and convince Tempest to go with her.

Tempest knew, even when Brittany acquiesced, that the battle was far from over. More than ever, she wished she could explain her feelings for Soaring Eagle.

As dinner went on, Daniel's feeling of satisfaction grew. He had a sense that shy little Tempest was hiding something, and he meant to find out what.

After dinner Tempest and Brittany walked back across the compound to their house. Aaron had some work to do and he made his guest comfortable before he went off to do it.

Despite Tempest's desire to confide her feelings to Brittany, she could not seem to take the first step. If Brittany did not understand, if she fought the idea of Tempest's relationship with Soaring Eagle, she might effectively put an end to it. Brittany would talk to Aaron, and Aaron would go to the village as he often did, and it would bring an end to everything. Tempest felt a wave of despair at this thought. She didn't know what she would do if Soaring Eagle were gone from her life.

The night grew deeper and both women went to bed still puzzled by their individual problems. Finally the entire mission slept. Only then did Daniel leave the grounds stealthily and find his way to an appointed meeting place. He had gotten a message in Sioux Falls, and with it had come a roughly drawn map. Roughly drawn, but accurate. Two men were already there waiting for him. One was a dark-haired, bearded man with dead brown eyes, as if he could commit murder with little compunction.

The second man was tall and lean. He was the cleaner of the two, but his eyes were no warmer. Deep in their green depths lingered a leashed rage. Daniel held his hand out to this one first.

"I take it you're Jethro Bodine." Daniel smiled.

"I am. This is Charlie," Jethro replied in a deep yet quiet voice. "I think I've gotten everything arranged. Major Cline's letter was pretty clear."

"You have the maps?"

"Yes. They're pretty good, too. I checked them out personally before you arrived."

Daniel waited expectantly for Jethro's mask to slip, so he could get a good look at the man behind it. But it didn't. Daniel only sensed that he had been educated, had once led a better life. Jethro kept intruders away from his past and let no man reach into his soul.

Daniel turned his attention now to Charlie. "I have a couple of problems," he stated coldly. "One is this damnable Aaron Abbott and his mission,

SYLVIE SOMMERFIELD

and the second is the white teacher he has brought here to teach the Indian children."

Charlie laughed a cold, brutal laugh. "Throats can be easily cut."

"Don't be a fool. The last thing I want is to stir up the military. I want all my plans working before the military gets involved. It might be necessary to throw a scare into her, though."

"Her?" Charlie questioned.

"The teacher, Brittany Nelson. Her sister will not be a problem. She can't hear or speak. No, it's the teacher I want to get rid of. I'll send you word when the time is right. For now, Charlie, I want you to keep a close eye on the mission."

He went on to explain his suspicions about Tempest. "I don't want her hurt, nor do I want her to know you are even around. I want to know everything she does, who she sees, and if she has any contact with the village. I will be going back to the fort with Aaron and some of the others for a couple of days." His eyes held Charlie's. "Remember, I want information, no games and no chances. I don't want any of them at the mission to see or hear any sign of you. Is that clearly understood, Charlie?"

"Yeah, I understand."

"Good."

Charlie started to move quietly away, and only Daniel's gentle touch on Jethro's arm told him to remain.

When Charlie had faded into the darkness,

192

Jethro moved closer to Daniel so their voices would not carry.

"You made good use of the other map you were sent?" Daniel asked.

"Yes. The map and the instructions. Did it all by myself so no one would know, like you ordered."

"And you found exactly what they thought you would find?"

"Yeah. No one can trace me and no one has any idea where the samples came from, and I have all the men lined up that we might need."

"We knew we were right. We knew it!"

"If word of this had gotten to the fort, Brady would have squelched it, and that Cole Young is just as bad. If word had gotten back to anyone else, there would have been a stampede."

"Well, the word isn't out, and I don't intend for it to get out."

"This mission sure as hell sank its roots in the wrong place."

"Don't worry, they won't cause us any problems. They're bleeding hearts and only want to do good. We're smart enough to keep them here as cover for as long as we need them. When my plans are complete, they'll be expendable."

"I'd better get going," Jethro said.

"The map, Jethro."

"Oh, yeah." He removed a packet of folded papers wrapped in rawhide from inside his shirt and handed them to Daniel. "They're all marked real careful"—Jethro grinned—"except for the markings that show where the lode is."

193

"Don't you trust me?" Daniel asked with amusement.

"About as far as you trust me . . . partner. When the time comes, we'll go there together."

"All right," Daniel said quietly. Those two words and his tone of voice told a very astute Jethro that he had been right to keep something back. "Oh . . . Jethro . . . you have more samples?"

"Yeah." Jethro reached inside his shirt again and pulled out a leather pouch, which he put in Daniel's hand. "I dug this less than a mile from that mission. Take a good look."

Daniel returned to the mission. Only when he was safely inside his own quarters and away from prying eyes did he open the pouch and pour the contents out into his hand.

In the glow of lamplight the glitter of gold made him inhale deeply. The nuggets were almost pure. He nodded. In his hand he held the key to a fortune, and he did not intend to let anything or anyone stand between him and it . . . not anyone.

Chapter Eleven

Chapter Eleven

Daniel used the role of observer carefully. He became aware of the tangled emotions that existed not only at the mission, but among the Indians who came to see Aaron and to see the silent healer.

He had told Aaron that he would be staying for several months, and had offered to pay Aaron's people to help him build a small cabin. In the meanwhile, he watched and listened and realized that although Tempest seemed happy and at peace, Brittany seemed tense and wary of something. Daniel would catch her watching her sister with a puzzled frown.

Time was his enemy. Every day that Brittany taught, the Indians learned more of the white man's ways. Now young warriors, as well as children, were beginning to attend the school. The days were warm and scented, and the magic of summer covered the territory. By the end of the season he wanted Brittany and all the mission done away with.

Daniel was never aware that Night Walker watched him as closely as he watched the others.

It took over two weeks, with help, for Daniel to erect his cabin. He had made sure it sat some distance from the mission. Far enough for Daniel to move around freely and to have visitors no one would see.

Night Walker was disturbed to see how often Brittany and Daniel walked together and talked. He would see her laugh at something amusing Daniel had said, and Night Walker would clench his teeth. But he could not interfere. He had no hold on Brittany. He refused to acknowledge that he wished he had. It would have given him great pleasure to drive this one white man from his land.

As much as he wished to deny it, Night Walker knew he longed to be with Brittany again. He wanted to look into her eyes and understand her feelings for this white intruder. They were of the same culture and obviously had a lot in common. Certainly much more than he and Brittany had. Yet a slow, fierce anger was growing in him. Anger at himself for being weak and not at least trying to lay claim to what he wanted.

He made up his mind to ride into their midst and find the answers he needed. But another thing now drew his attention and puzzled him. He had been watching the mission closely, yet he was always aware of what was going on around him. He soon discovered he was not the only one watching. He decided it would be best to discover who the intruders were. On one occasion, he followed one of the observers to a nearby stream and watched, puzzled, as the man went about a strange activity Night Walker did not understand.

He watched the man dig stones from the stream, wash them clean and then put them in his pocket. It was very odd. After the man had gone, Night Walker went to the stream and knelt beside it. He could easily see that some of the stones glittered and were pretty . . . but they were still stones. He gathered a handful and put them in a small leather pouch he wore at his waist. At the right time he would ask Aaron what they were and what effect they might have on his people.

For three days he watched the observers' every move, finding out where they camped and often coming close enough to hear parts of their conversations. Something else at the mission besides the glittering stones drew them, and he worried that a golden-haired, green-eyed woman was part of it.

He could wait no longer. He rode down toward the mission just as the sun was casting its final red glow.

Tempest wondered if she had ever felt so good in her life. For the past weeks she had realized that for the first time in a long time she was truly happy. She stood up and dusted off her hands, half smiling at her own feeling of satisfaction. She had put away the medical supplies she had used to treat a wide-eyed, adoring little Indian girl who stood nearby.

Not only had Tempest made the girl feel better, but she had spoken sign to her and they had laughed together. In the little girl's mind, Tempest seemed like one of the mysterious angels Aaron had told them stories about.

Tempest signed that she would be fine now and dropped two small pieces of the cook's home-made candy into her hand.

The child scampered away to tell all her friends. Day by day Tempest realized that the people at the mission were going out of their way to help her. Yet they never acted as though she were incapable of managing on her own.

The women had made it obvious that they trusted her, and this gave her self-esteem a tremendous lift. They shared their smiles and warm looks of acceptance, and Tempest blossomed like a flower in the warm sun.

Thomas, most of all, had given her complete trust and often used his note pad to question her on a treatment, asking her opinion and taking her suggestions under consideration. She felt useful and productive.

The child had been the last of her few patients of the day, and the early afternoon sun was still warm and bright. She had time . . . and she knew

Soaring Eagle would wait for her until the sun set if he had to.

The thought of him sent a shiver of pleasure through her. How handsome he was, and how kind, and gentle and giving. She sighed. And how difficult it was going to be to tell Brittany.

But now was not the time to consider that. She rolled down her sleeves and buttoned the cuffs, then took her shawl and left through the back door.

She reached the edge of the woods, and slowed her steps. She had thought of a million ways to tell Brittany and discarded them all. The last thing in the world she would ever do would be to hurt her sister, and Brittany would be hurt. She would think Tempest had lied. Tempest knew Brittany's protectiveness was love, but it was a love that was smothering her. She loved her sister with her whole heart and was scared to death to see anger, pain or worse . . . disappointment in her eyes.

She walked, engrossed in her thoughts and worries about her sister. Soaring Eagle stood some distance away and watched her. He could have revealed his presence, but he wanted to enjoy looking at her for a few minutes. He was always afraid that each time he saw her might be the last.

But within minutes she sensed his presence and looked directly at him. He didn't know how she could do it without hearing, but she always sensed he was there.

Tempest watched Soaring Eagle as he walked toward her. How tall and beautiful he was. He

seemed as one with the panorama that surrounded them. His ebony hair caught the sunlight, and his black eyes appraised her with a
warmth that made her feel so very alive and so
very special . . . something she had not felt since
. . . she still could not face the old and bitter memories. It was better to think of the man who was
slowly erasing the nightmares and replacing the
pain with a feeling of wholeness and purpose.

He came to her and took the hand she reached
toward him. Slowly he drew her into his arms.
Tempest raised her lips willingly for his kiss, and
with a sigh of contentment she nestled against
him.

"Golden one," he whispered against her hair,
knowing she could not hear. How he wished she
would say his name. If she spoke, and Aaron had
said he thought she could, he wanted it to be his
name she spoke.

He took her hand and they walked together. He
wanted to show her so much. First, that he could
print the words she had taught him. He knew all
the letters, but he didn't know why they were of
value, or what help they would ever be to him.

They found a quiet place and sat close to each
other. He was pleased to hear her soft laugh when
he wrote both letters and words.

Suddenly he gripped her arm and she looked at
him in surprise, but he was pointing toward the
sky. There an eagle was soaring in lazy circles. He
smiled and tapped his chest to show the relation-

ship. She responded by picking up the stick and printing *Soaring Eagle* in the dirt.

Soaring Eagle gazed at the letters with some awe. They represented . . . HIM! Suddenly the full import of what she was teaching him became crystal clear.

He looked at her with revelation brilliant in his eyes, and Tempest could not help laughing from sheer joy. He understood! How smart he was, how wonderful, and how handsome . . . and kind . . . and handsome . . . and clever . . . and how much she loved him.

Soaring Eagle was excited. He pointed to her, and then to his name scratched in the dirt. *Make your name*, he signed. Tempest obediently took the stick and printed her name, only to be confused by his puzzled frown.

What is wrong? she signed.

I do not understand.

What?

What does it mean, this . . . he motioned to her name. *Tempest?* He had no sign for her name. It was a new word for him.

Tempest? It means a fierce storm.

He gazed at her for a dumbfounded moment, then he threw back his head and laughed.

You, a fierce storm? You are as gentle and calm as a summer breeze. Whoever gave you such a name?

My mother, and I'll have you know, warrior, that I can be fierce if I need to be.

Can you now, little flower? His eyes were teas-

201

ing, and she nodded with a quick smile. *That I do not believe.*

You do not? Why?

He took her hand in his and turned it over to brush his fingers across the palm. Then he raised it to his lips and kissed it gently.

Because, he signed, *your heart is like the rainbow after the rain, and your spirit is like the white dove. I shall call you White Dove.* His gaze met hers. *And you are the most beautiful creature I have ever seen, White Dove. I have a great love for you.*

He remained very still, hoping, praying and for the first time in his life completely uncertain. No one knew the barriers that stood between them better than he, but he didn't care anymore. The only thing that was important now was the answer she might give.

Tempest rose slowly to her knees and reached to gently lay her hand against his cheek. Her eyes filled with tears, and an agony flowed over him like a dark cloud. She meant to tell him she would never meet him again.

But her smile was tremulous as she slowly made the sign he desperately wanted to see.

I, too, have a great love for you.

The flame she had ignited within him burned low. It had been waiting like a pulsing entity to be stirred to life. Now it no longer let him deny its existence. His blood seemed to flow faster and hotter within him, and his skin felt too tight to contain this building, explosive thing. Every nerve he had was alive with her. Now, there was a ques-

tion he had to ask, because everything depended
upon it.

Tempest, he signed, *will you join with me? Will
you be my woman?*

Did he see her smile? Did she sign the word he
wanted to see? His breath seemed to go still, and
his heart began to pound.

Yes! . . . Her answer was yes!

Tempest, he signed in his excitement, *say my
name. Let me hear you say my name.*

Tempest jerked back from him and he was
alarmed at the fear he saw in her eyes. Old memories that he knew nothing about crowded her
mind, and Soaring Eagle was severely shaken. He
would never have brought that look into her eyes
if he could have prevented it.

*What have I said? What have I done? It was only
a foolish desire to hear you speak my name! I am
sorry, please forgive me!*

He was frightened that he had destroyed the
fragile trust growing between them, and even
more frightened that in some way he had hurt her
terribly.

Tempest was doing battle with the memories of
the train wreck, the last time she had spoken. She
backed away from him and saw the agony in his
eyes. He didn't know what he had done, she argued with herself. He had offered her nothing but
love. But he wanted something from her she didn't
think it was in her power to give, and she didn't
know how to make him understand her fears.

He looked at her with anguish clearly written

on his face. But he could only wait. He could not force her to do what she was incapable of doing.

He was furious with himself. Aaron had warned him that she was of delicate spirit, and that her heart was wounded . . . that it needed time to heal. He had thought only of himself, and now maybe he had driven her out of his life with his foolish demand. He extended his hands to her, palms up, but he could not cross the distance between them. That she would have to do . . . or he must go.

A long moment passed, crushing his heart with every second. Defeat was something he found hard to accept. He wanted to beg . . . to plead with her to forget his stupid request. The look in her eyes was destroying him. He turned his back . . . and waited.

"Soaring Eagle." The words were spoken so softly that at first he thought he heard them only in his mind. "Soaring Eagle." No! She had spoken his name. He turned and saw the sunshine through her tears. He knew her sacrifice was a tribute to the love they shared. He walked slowly to her, dropped to his knees before her, and gently put his arms about her waist. He rested his head against her breast.

For a moment he could only hold her and thank every god he knew that he had not driven her from him. He vowed silently that she would never have another moment's pain that he could prevent.

Tempest remained still, and now Soaring Eagle rose to look down into the depths of her blue eyes to share the truth that lay between them. It took no words, no sign, for each to know what the other was promising.

Gently he took her hand and led her with him to the soft grass beneath the shade of a huge tree, where they stood together. To him she seemed so amazingly sweet. He reached out and gently touched her cheek. Her face turned toward his hand to press a kiss there, and to feel the warmth of his palm.

Tempest gazed up into Soaring Eagle's intense dark eyes, wanting to hold this rare and beautiful moment forever. He put his arms about her and drew her against him. Their bodies touched and the flame of mutual need leapt between them. He took her mouth lightly, tasting, touching, blending until both were lost to the magic.

Tempest clung to him, her eyes closed, eager to feel more of this unique and beautiful thing. He held her with one arm and slid his other hand down the curve of her hip to hold her more firmly against him. With her arms about him, she rested against his hard, muscular frame. She was unaware of anything but the seeking mouth that possessed hers completely and the need to be held closer and closer.

When the kiss ended, he gazed down into her eyes for several minutes; then he again bent his head to brush her lips with his. Softly, like butterfly wings he kissed her again and again, until he heard her soft sound of total surrender.

Tempest was oblivious to her surroundings

now. Nothing existed in her world but the hands that gently caressed her and the mouth that ravaged hers.

He loosened her hair from the restraining ribbon and threaded his fingers through it. Its golden beauty was like satin. When her hair hung loose and free, his fingers moved to the buttons of her dress, to slowly release them. In a few minutes the dress lay in a pool at her feet. She dipped her head shyly, frightened now to meet his gaze. His fingers lifted her chin gently, and she gazed up into a reflection of her own emotions. His warm touch on her sensitive skin brought an involuntary gasp of pleasure. He drew her down with him to the soft grass, where his lips began to discover more sensitive places.

Her breasts were soft to his touch, but the nipples, as pink and as delicate as flower petals, hardened as his tongue traced a heated path from one to the other. She moaned in exquisite pleasure and pressed him closer to her, closing her eyes in complete abandonment to these new and powerful sensations.

When Soaring Eagle left her arms for a minute, she opened her eyes to find the reason for this momentary emptiness. He moved away from her slightly, long enough to remove his clothes, and then he quickly returned to her side. But not before a startled and wide-eyed Tempest gasped in surprise.

He was a magnificent masculine creature. His bronzed body was long and lean and well proportioned, with taut, sinewy muscle. Complete symmetry of movement gave him a lithe grace. The sight of his manhood roused and throbbing shattered her equilibrium momentarily, but then he was beside her, gathering her body close to him. He soothed and eased her fears with gentle kisses and caresses, until she forgot her fear.

Her slim body was cool to his touch and his hands sought to memorize every line and curve. A slim hip, a long slender thigh, the soft, flat plane of her belly, which curved into a warmer place that drew him like a magnet. To touch searchingly, to hear her soft sounds of pleasure thrilled him.

Aware that this first time would be difficult for her, he forced himself to go slowly. She was so slim and small, and he was well endowed. But his heart sang as she became the aggressor, seeking the unknown and promised pleasure. She came to vibrant life beneath him. All that had meaning for her now was Soaring Eagle. The magic of his love was consuming every rational thought she had.

They blended, moving together, giving and taking in wildly shared abandon. She held nothing from him, but gave herself to him body and soul. He filled her completely, and the fiery culmination of their love left them both weak and clinging to each other as their world slowly righted itself.

He lay beside her and drew her against him. She curved her body to his and rested her head on his shoulder, content. Soaring Eagle smiled. At this moment he felt many emotions . . . but regret was certainly not one of them.

They would face their problems with courage and determination. He knew he would have to be dead before he would ever let her go.

Tempest thought in the same vein. Soon they would discuss their plans . . . soon. But not now. For now there was only the two of them in a world full of love.

SYLVIE SOMMERFIELD

Chapter Twelve

When Night Walker rode down onto the mission grounds, he was aware that there was a bustle of activity. Someone was preparing for a journey.

He found Aaron, who was supervising the loading of some bundles on a wagon. Aaron smiled his welcome.

"Night Walker, good to see you."

"I have wanted to speak to you."

"Oh? Something important?"

"I believe so. I must speak to you alone."

Aaron drew Night Walker aside, out of the hearing and the view of others. "There is something wrong, Night Walker. I can see it in your eyes."

"There are two men watching the mission. I do not trust their purpose." He watched Aaron's face go pale.

"What could they want with us?"

"I do not know, but I thought I should tell you of their presence."

"Unfortunately, I have to leave for the fort tomorrow morning. When I return I will look into this matter."

"You must go to the fort?"

"Not just me, my friend. I am taking Brittany along. There is to be a dance at the fort and she's decided to go."

This news should not have bothered Night Walker at all . . . but it did. "How long will you be gone?"

"A few days. I'm sure Brittany will not want to leave her school longer than that. She is a girl who takes her responsibilities very seriously."

"And her sister will go as well?"

"No, Tempest has decided she does not want to go. She will remain at the mission."

"Is Brittany close by?"

"Why, yes, I believe I saw her over at the school."

"I would speak with her."

"Well, go on over," Aaron replied. He paused and looked closely at Night Walker, who seemed to want to say something else. "Night Walker . . . you will—"

"I will keep watching the mission."

"I appreciate that."

"The others are watching, as well."

"I know. But we can do little. While I'm at the

fort perhaps I can persuade Cole to prohibit strangers here."

"I do not know who they are or what plans they might have, but they are keeping a close watch on you. There are three that I see . . . so far. I have a feeling there are more."

"Do you think we are in danger?"

"If they meant to harm you, they could have done so some time ago. I will continue to watch them. Maybe I can learn their purpose."

"Now I worry about Tempest staying here."

"I can give you my word, and the word of Soaring Eagle, that no harm will come to her."

Again Aaron looked closely at Night Walker, and he knew Night Walker had not told him everything that was on his mind. But he knew he was not going to hear everything until Night Walker was ready to tell him. Aaron was certain there was a great deal between Tempest and Soaring Eagle, but he also knew Night Walker would say nothing about his brother if his life depended upon it.

"I will go and see Brittany. There is something I must say to her," Night Walker said. He paused, and then looked directly at Aaron. "Aaron . . . who is the white one that has joined you here?"

Ah, Aaron thought, the green-eyed monster has reared its ugly head. "His name is Daniel Nixon, and he has been sent here by the government to make a study."

"A study? What is this thing . . . a study?"

"My government has sent him to observe and see what is occurring between you, me and the fort. I can do little but cooperate with him. I have to answer to my government as you have to answer to your people. You can see, I have little choice."

"What do you think of him?"

"It is hard for me to say yet. I haven't seen how he will deal with your people, and I do not know him well enough to judge."

Night Walker smiled. "I will judge for myself."

Aaron watched him walk away, and was pretty sure Night Walker was not going to find anything acceptable in Daniel Nixon . . . especially if Brittany smiled upon him in Night Walker's presence. He hoped there was not going to be any trouble.

Night Walker paused by the door of the school, and then pushed it open. Brittany was seated at her desk with an open book before her from which she had been reading. He looked about at the still, awed faces of the children and felt something stir within him. With words from her precious books she was capturing their thoughts and opening vistas they had never imagined before. Even Laughing Thunder and Running Cougar seemed to be entranced.

Brittany never felt so satisfied as she did when she saw the evidence of young minds struggling with new thoughts. But when she sensed another presence, she stopped reading and turned to the door. There was a rustle of movement as if the children did not approve of the interruption. Night Walker took a great deal of pleasure in Brittany's brightening eyes and her quick smile when she saw him.

"Night Walker. I'm glad you are here. I wanted to see you before I left." She turned, dismissed the class, and then walked to stand near him.

"Aaron has said you are going back to the soldier fort."

"It's only for a celebration. I'll be back in a few days."

"I have come to ask you to walk with me. I have something I would speak to you about."

When they left the schoolroom they walked for a while in silence. Brittany knew that whatever was on Night Walker's mind would not be said until he'd considered his words.

"You have something to celebrate at the soldier fort?" he asked casually.

"Yes, it's a dance of celebration for Lieutenant Murphy."

"They dance for one man . . . why?"

"Just for fun," she laughed. "Night Walker, you said you had something to talk to me about."

He looked at her and wanted to tell her he did not want her to go, that he especially didn't want her to go with this man Nixon. He could no more tell her that than he could tell her about Tempest and his brother.

"I have come to warn all of you that there are people watching what goes on here, and to ask if you would know why."

"I didn't know anyone was watching, but what harm can they do? Maybe it is only curiosity."

"They are white."

"White? I don't understand that at all. I didn't think there were any other whites but those who work with Aaron and the homesteaders."

"They do not work with Aaron."

"How do you know?"

"Because Aaron knows nothing about them. You will go to the fort, and I will continue to watch and look for answers."

"You think we are not safe here?"

"You are safe from my people." He smiled. "I am not so sure of yours." They paused to stand beneath the branches of a tree, and were effectively shielded from the mission compound. Night Walker looked down into her eyes, and words and thoughts were frozen as a sweeter memory took over.

Brittany watched his eyes grow warm, and she felt again that shaky, melting feeling and had to struggle for control.

"I will miss you," he said quietly. "I have found that I think of you as part of this place."

"Thank you, I believe that's one of the nicest compliments I have ever had. Night Walker?"

"Yes?"

"When you rode in, did you see Tempest anywhere?"

"No, I did not." A new thought occurred to him. He must warn Soaring Eagle about these men, for he and Tempest spent much time alone and he would not want something to happen . . . not to the silent one, and especially not if she was with his brother.

"I know Aaron says she will be safe here and I know she doesn't want to go to the fort, but I feel as if I am deserting her."

"If it will ease your mind, I will see she is taken care of."

"I would be grateful."

"If you want, I will see she is invited to spend some time with us in our village. My family, especially Never Quiet, thinks she is magic. She would be most welcome."

"I . . . I would prefer she stay here, at least until I get back."

"What do you think you are protecting her from? There is no one in my village who would see harm come to her in any way."

"I did not say that," she protested, but she turned from him.

"Do you know how honored she would be?"

"That's not the point."

"What is this . . . point?"

"I don't know," she said helplessly.

Night Walker wanted desperately to take her in his arms and hold her, to ease the doubts he saw in her eyes, and to tell her that no matter how it hurt, one day she must let her sister make her own decisions. One day she must let her go.

"Perhaps," he said gently, "you think that because Tempest cannot hear, she needs to be protected. Perhaps . . . you protect her too much."

"You don't know how it was when we lost our

parents, when Tempest lost her hearing. It was terrible for her. James would not let her out of his sight, and I had to protect her. She depends on me!"

"And you think that is the best way to protect her? To always let her depend on you?" He felt her resistance. "Or is it that you need her to depend on you?"

He watched defensive rage leap into her eyes. "I don't care to hear your thoughts on the matter. I have told Tempest, and I will tell Aaron and you. I want Tempest to remain close to the mission while I am gone, or I will insist she come with me."

"I think, even though she is the quiet one, your sister is much like you. I do not think you can be told where you must go or not go. I do not think you would let someone else command your life, and I do not think she will, either. You are stronger than you think . . . and she is stronger than you think. I would not see you hurt."

"What are you trying to tell me, Night Walker?"

"Only that you must see that everyone is in command of his or her own life, and that no one can speak or act for another."

"That is your belief, and I won't say it's wrong. But it's not mine. You do not know how helpless Tempest can be. The episode with that buffalo should have been proof enough. I cannot turn away and let her go into danger when I know she is helpless against it. I can't and I won't. Is that all you came to tell me?"

"No."

"What then?"

The breeze had blown strands of her hair across her cheeks, and he reached to brush them aside, letting his hand linger on the soft skin. "I did not come to speak of your sister at all. I came because . . . because you linger in my mind, Morning Sun, and I cannot erase the thoughts of you. I said I have missed you, but it is more than that. I would tell you—"

"Brittany!"

Both Brittany and Night Walker turned at the sound of another voice. Daniel stood a short distance away. He had approached Aaron to ask Brittany's whereabouts, and had sensed that Aaron had been reluctant to tell him. But he had, and Daniel had gone to find her.

He had come upon the two standing beneath the shade of the tree, and had instantly been enraged. The Indian was actually touching Brittany. Daniel contained his rage and studied Night Walker. He didn't like what he saw. This savage was going to put his hands on a white woman! It was unthinkable.

Worse yet, Brittany seemed fascinated by him. What was between these two? The Indian was a tall and very strong-looking man, and Daniel sensed that he posed a threat to his own plans. He watched for a minute, gauging Night Walker. Dangerous. He saw Brittany as she could not see herself, and knew she reacted strongly to this man. Any man who elicited a strong reaction in a woman like Brittany was indeed a threat to him.

He watched as Night Walker bent closer to Brittany. Did he mean to . . . ?

"Brittany!" Daniel said her name more to stop Night Walker than to get her attention. He smiled when he saw them both turn toward him, for Night Walker looked anything but pleased with the interruption. There could never be anything between these two. One Indian, one white. No self-respecting white man would tolerate it.

Night Walker watched Daniel walk toward them, and a wall of caution erected itself in his mind. He watched Brittany smile, and the wall grew higher and stronger. He understood the threat represented by Daniel Nixon.

"I've been looking for you." Daniel smiled at Brittany, ignoring Night Walker. "Aaron has just about gotten everything packed, and wants to know if you have anything else to put in the wagon."

He might have been ignoring Night Walker, but Night Walker was certainly not ignoring him. Daniel tried to keep his attention on Brittany, but he became acutely aware of the dark and piercing gaze of this powerful-looking warrior.

"Daniel," Brittany said. She could not help but be aware of the way Night Walker's body had stiffened, and the way his face had gone expressionless. "Night Walker, this is Daniel Nixon."

"Aaron has spoken of you," Night Walker said. He smiled, and the smile Daniel returned was just as cold. "I do not understand."

"Understand what?" Daniel questioned. *You damned savage, of course you don't understand,* he thought.

"Why you would build here or what you want to . . . observe. Aaron is the one we wish to trade with. We have worked together for long years."

"But Aaron does not have the authority to trade. He is here to minister to the Indians and bring them to God. I hate to distress Brittany, but I do not think Aaron has the authority to have a school here either. However, I will contact the right authorities on that matter as soon as I can."

Brittany was shocked at this, but she looked toward Night Walker, who was smiling now. With Nixon's few words he knew and understood Daniel Nixon as if he had known him for years . . . yes, he knew this man, and all the men like him who had preceded him and come for profit. He did not know where the profit would be made, yet. But he meant to find out.

There were no other words or arguments that could have drawn Night Walker to Brittany and the cause of her school as those words did. If Daniel fought the school, it must be a threat, and now Night Walker needed to find out why.

Before another word could be said, Night Walker's attention was drawn to another man walking toward them. This man wore the uniform of the soldiers at the fort.

Brittany's gaze followed Night Walker's, and Daniel's followed hers. Here was another man

SYLVIE SOMMERFIELD

who might interfere. Daniel had to make sure these two did not develop a friendship.

Cole was looking at Night Walker as he came toward them. Aaron had told him a great deal about this man, and Cole had wanted to meet the warriors from Flying Horse's village for a long time.

"Aaron told me I could find you here," he said to Brittany. "He also said one of the men from the village was here as well." He spoke directly to Night Walker now. "I have wanted to meet you. I'm Lieutenant Cole Young. You have no idea how many stories Aaron has told about you at the fort. It's gotten my interest."

Night Walker smiled. "I am Night Walker, and Aaron has told me much of you as well."

"I have asked Aaron to bring me to the village a number of times, but each time he has claimed it was not the right time. I've no idea what he meant by that. I think it's time we meet and talk with each other, don't you?"

"I am sure Aaron has his reasons," Night Walker said. "It has not always been a good thing for our people to meet. It seems there is usually something your people want when we do."

"I want nothing," Cole said firmly. "I think we have to live on the same land together, and peacefully is the better way."

There was nothing Brittany wanted more than for Night Walker and Cole to go on talking. But she didn't want Daniel involved. She knew she seemed abrupt, but she wanted to get Daniel away.

"And I think it is time for me to join Aaron," Brittany said. "I have taken time from my duties long enough. Daniel, will you walk back with me?"

Daniel agreed, and Night Walker watched them go with a glint in his eyes that might have shaken both of them. It shook Cole, who did not have time to say anything before Night Walker turned to look at him again. The look was gone, but Cole wondered if he was ever going to forget it.

"I must go too," Night Walker announced abruptly.

He had no time to talk idly with this white man when he considered the threat that Daniel Nixon posed. He knew that greed had brought Daniel Nixon here, and trading would not satisfy it. He meant to remove Daniel Nixon from Brittany's life, one way or another.

Later that night, when Brittany was walking from the school toward home, she heard her name softly called. Night Walker stood just at the edge of the trees. Not in the least afraid, she walked to him.

"Night Walker?"

"You leave for the fort tomorrow. I wanted to give you a gift before you go."

"A gift?" Her smile was quick and he liked the pleased look in her eyes. But when he held out his hand, what lay in it made her draw in a deep breath. It was a unique necklace made of colorful beads. Three strands on each side of a circular silver piece, from which three slender white feathers hung. "Oh, Night Walker, it is so beautiful. Thank you." She reached for it, but he smiled and took her hand, drawing her closer to him and deeper into the shadows.

"I would put it on," he said.

Brittany turned her back and lifted the weight of her hair. She felt the warmth of his hands as he fastened the necklace about her throat. Then she let her hair fall. But before she could turn back to face him, Night Walker slid his arms about her and drew her against him.

He buried his face in her hair and inhaled the scent of it. "You go far, Brittany. I would have you remember that there is one here who desires your return above all others. I would not have you forget." Slowly he turned her to face him.

In the moon-touched shadows she could barely make out his lean features, but every sense she possessed knew every line, every plane of his face . . . and every long, muscular line of his hard body. Catching both sides of her face in his two hands, he tipped it up to his. Gently his lips brushed hers, and it was with satisfaction that he heard her ragged indrawn breath.

A bolt of swirling pleasure shot through Brittany's body at the first touch of his mouth against hers, and when his tongue parted her lips, she shivered and clung to him.

Deep inside her a sensation of radiant heat flamed into life. His large, hard hands were gentle now as he caressed her back and hips and drew her tighter to him, deepening the kiss they shared.

Brittany tightened her arms about him: for this moment she was lost in the emotions his kiss and his warm touch were bringing to life. His near nakedness made his body more accessible than hers, and he was exhilarated when he felt her soft hands move over him.

He loosened the buttons of her dress and opened the bodice. He heard her gasp of shock as he bent to capture a hardened nipple and suckle it hungrily. Every rational thought he had was slipping away. He could not take her here . . . but he wanted to, and he knew she wanted him as well. Would he build or destroy this perfect thing if he fulfilled his need for her?

He had wanted her, but even he was not prepared for the intensity of pleasure he felt at the thought of plunging himself deep within her and making love to her until he wiped out all thought of any other man.

He buried his face between her breasts and felt her clasp him to her. He savored the clean, sweet scent of her and let his hands roam her body, pushing up her skirt until he felt the warmth of her thigh.

"Oh . . . Night Walker . . ." Her voice was a soft, sighing moan but it shook him back to reality. He knew her hatred tomorrow would match her passion tonight. Slowly he stood. He wanted to release her . . . but he could not. He needed more . . . so much more. Night Walker was saved from ruining everything by the sound of Brittany's name being called from a distance. It seemed to shake Brittany into reality as well. She looked up at him and realized she did not regret what they'd done. Her cheeks flushed, and she was glad he could not see that her desire had far from died.

"I must go," she whispered. But her arms were still around him.

"And I must let you. But it is not in my heart to do this thing." Again he bent his head and caught her mouth in a deep, drugging kiss; then he murmured against her lips, "Come back soon, Morning Sun. I will think of you and miss you until you do."

Then he was gone, and Brittany was dizzy with wanting. She stood for a moment wishing she knew how and where she could follow him, for at this moment she would have . . . shamelessly. She touched the necklace at her throat, then turned and walked toward home.

In the darkness Night Walker watched, his body afire with the agony of need. Then he, too, turned and left.

Chapter Thirteen

Although Brittany didn't see him, Night Walker sat his horse on the ridge overlooking the mission when the group left for the fort the next morning. He watched until they were lost to sight, and then turned his horse toward home.

When he arrived in the village, he was in no mood for conversation. He found his lodge empty, and he was grateful for that. He threw himself down before the fire and allowed the black mood to hold him.

He, who had always faced the truth the best he could, was overwhelmed with its revelation now. He had fought it for a long time, and had even begun to doubt his earlier certainty that what existed between his brother and the white girl was wrong. He had said nothing to put a barrier in their way. Perhaps he envied his brother a bit, for Soaring Eagle seemed to have pushed all the barriers aside. Still, Night Walker knew, even if Soaring Eagle did not, that the barriers could not be pushed aside so easily.

"They are dreamers," he muttered to himself . . . and he wished he were the same sort of dreamer. One who could say what was in his heart and know that Brittany would return his dream, and say it was hers as well.

He found no comfort in seclusion. Finally he rose from his bed and left the lodge. He would concentrate on the intruders who watched the mission with such interest. He strode to his horse, but before he could mount, his name was called and Never Quiet was running toward him.

He could see she was in her usual condition, excited about something he could be certain was none of her business. Still he could not help smiling, for he had a love for this small sister of his who sometimes surprised him, especially when he had to retrieve her from some mischief she had been in.

"Night Walker! Night Walker!"

"Never Quiet, what has you so excited?"

"Night Walker, can I ask something of you? Don't be angry with me."

"I have no reason to be angry with you, unless, of course, you have forgotten to help our mother with the firewood and the water skins this day . . . as usual."

"No, you are wrong. I have done everything

Mother has asked." Never Quiet giggled. "In fact, she is so surprised that when I asked her—"

"What? What is so important today?"

"I would ask if I can have the bridle you were to give me . . . the one you promised me. Soaring Eagle has tamed my pony and I would ride with him."

"But it was not promised until the celebration of your birthday."

"I know, but that is only a few days away, and today . . . I need it today."

"Why?"

"Night Walker . . ." she whined.

"Tell me why it is so important today," he insisted.

"I would ride with Soaring Eagle," she replied. She did not look at him, and was certain now he would refuse her.

"Why must it be today, and where do you go?"

"To the mission."

"But Aaron is no longer there. Why do you not wait until he and the teacher return from the fort? And . . . why does Soaring Eagle ride there today?" He said the words, but he knew the answer. Hadn't Brittany told him that Tempest was not going to the fort with Aaron and her?

"Soaring Eagle rides to get White Dove."

"White Dove?" His brows came together in a puzzled frown.

"That is the name he has given the white girl . . . Tempest."

227

"It is not right that he be there with her when Aaron is gone."

"Oh, he will not be there, he brings her here."

"Never Quiet—"

"But he does. She wants to come, and he has said he will bring her. I want to go with him. Please, Night Walker, let me have the bridle now."

"Where is Soaring Eagle?"

"He is bathing in the river, and he wears his best shirt. I think he likes White Dove."

"Wait here," Night Walker commanded, and one look at his face told Never Quiet that if she wanted the bridle she had best obey. She watched him stride toward the river.

He arrived at the river bank in time to see his brother walk from the water. He paused to look at him. Soaring Eagle was a strong and able warrior, and Night Walker knew the women of the village had found him more than acceptable. Night Walker didn't want to see his hopes dashed.

"Night Walker." Soaring Eagle smiled at his brother's approach. He shook the water from his dark hair and reached to draw on his shirt. It was a buckskin that his mother had softened and cured until it was almost white. She had also done some of her finest beadwork on it until it was a thing of beauty.

"You are like a feathered bird this morning," Night Walker said. "Where do you go that you must look so fine?"

Soaring Eagle had never told a lie in his life, and

228

especially to the brother he loved and admired more than anyone else in the world.

"I go to the mission."

"Aaron is not there, and he will not be there for several days," Night Walker said. "But I think you already know that."

"Yes, I know that," Soaring Eagle replied. "I do not seek Aaron."

They looked at each other, and Soaring Eagle lifted his chin in stubborn determination. He loved Night Walker . . . but he loved White Dove also, and he was not going to deny it.

"This will cause a great deal of trouble with the whites, I think," Night Walker said softly. He did not want to cause Soaring Eagle a problem, but he felt he had to make him see where his actions might lead.

"Why? I have asked you this question before, and you had no answer. I am not afraid of the whites. Not those at the mission, or those at the fort. I am not going to give up White Dove without a battle." He looked closely at his brother's troubled face. "And you do not want to surrender, either. Night Walker . . . if you can tell me my love for her is wrong, if you can tell me I should give her up even though White Dove wants to come with me, if you can tell me you would not do what I am doing, then I will not go."

Night Walker wanted to form the words, he wanted to stop Soaring Eagle, but in all honesty he knew the truth. If Brittany had said yes, that

229

SYLVIE SOMMERFIELD

she wanted him, all the whites at the fort could not have beaten him away.

"No, I cannot say that."

"Then I will back away for no man."

"This may bring more trouble than you bargain for. And the trouble will not be so much yours as it will be hers. They—these whites—look with scorn upon a woman who would love one of us. Can you face her and know you caused her such grief?"

It was easy to see that Soaring Eagle had not thought of it that way. His gaze was piercing as he studied Night Walker. "Is that the reason you will not speak to her sister? You have gone to her, haven't you? You want her as I want White Dove?"

"Yes, I do. But I will not make her choices for her. She will understand when she goes back to the fort how hard it would be for her. She will make her own decisions."

"And you have little faith that she will choose you?"

"Very little."

"Then I am luckier than you. I think White Dove's life has been hard for her. I think she has found peace here, and will not turn away in the face of their rage. I do not think the white teacher has had to suffer. Maybe that will make it hard for her."

"And you still intend to go?"

"Do you intend to stop me?"

"No, I am not one to judge anyone else. I wish you happiness, Soaring Eagle . . . and your White

230

Dove." He watched Soaring Eagle's quick smile, and his gaze followed him as he walked toward the village. He meant to give Never Quiet the bridle, and he would welcome White Dove among them . . . and he would watch for Brittany's return, for he felt it best she hear the words from him. Perhaps he could battle on Soaring Eagle's behalf . . . before their world exploded.

Brittany arrived at the fort with cheers and happy shouts in her ears. Colonel Brady waited on the porch of his office, and beside him stood Esther Brady, who was impatient to ask Brittany and her sister a million questions.

They greeted the newcomers with enthusiasm, and Esther looked about the group.

"Where is that pretty sister of yours?"

"Tempest wanted to stay at the mission," Brittany said. "She insisted she had a lot of work to do. She is a very conscientious girl."

"I'm sure she is . . . and she does not relish parties."

"No," Brittany admitted. "Since she cannot hear the music, she hasn't found parties very . . . interesting." But she was thinking of the night in the village when Soaring Eagle had placed her hand against the drum and how she had found the rhythm of the music and enjoyed it.

There were several letters waiting for Brittany. Three from James, and several from Tempest and Brittany's friends.

Brittany read them that night, and was delighted to hear that James was finally engaged to be married. It was as if life back in Philadelphia had gone on quite well without her and Tempest.

She waited for the feelings of regret or loneliness to overcome her, but they didn't. Instead an unexpected vision presented itself. She could see the mission . . . the school, and Night Walker. See them as if they were more *home* than Philadelphia ever was, or could be again. She had changed, and the change was a surprise.

Esther came to visit, and Brittany made tea for them to drink while they sat and talked.

"I must say the mission certainly does agree with you," Esther said brightly. "Why, you're just blooming. Come, tell me all about it."

"I am enjoying myself, and everyone at the mission is so devoted."

"What about those Indians you're working with? I've heard some tales."

"Don't believe a thing you hear, Esther. They are not painted devils, and I've found them very hospitable."

"Hospitable? You mean you've been to their village?"

"Yes, and found myself treated with respect and consideration." She went on to explain about her trip to the village, and to describe everyone she'd met there. Esther watched her in fascination, and when Brittany was finished, she smiled.

"I wish there were more of you out here and less of the military."

"Esther!"

"Well, that's what I think. I love my husband, but like all military men, he has to be in command or he has to pick up a gun. Our Aaron has the right idea. Meet the Sioux on their own ground and talk; it does more good than a gun will ever do. Tell me more."

Esther seemed insatiable when it came to hearing about the people Brittany taught.

"I think, if I could get just a few to go on to college, to go back East, to work to bring our cultures together, there would be no need for a fort out here," Brittany added.

"Do you think you can accomplish such a thing?"

"With the older ones, no. But, Esther, there is a girl, Night Walker's sister, Never Quiet. She is so bright and so interested. Why, if given a chance, there is no telling how far she will go. She could be a teacher too, one her people would accept more willingly than me."

"Night Walker. A very interesting name."

"A very interesting man."

"Tell me about him."

Brittany began with a description of Night Walker, and she soon warmed to her subject. She described the first time she had seen him, and how frightened she had been and how resistant he had been. She went on to tell how well respected he was among those in his village and how much she wished she could wipe out all the barriers that stood between them.

"He is so impressive, Esther, and so intelligent.

I would like to be able to . . . to discuss . . . things with him. I would like . . ." She paused, realizing Esther was watching her closely with a Mona Lisa smile on her face. "What?"

"This man sounds exciting. Is he really as handsome as you say?"

"Did I say he was handsome?" Brittany asked, but she felt her cheeks go pink.

"In about a hundred different ways. I would like to meet him. Why don't you and Aaron arrange a meeting between some of Flying Horse's people and some of the folks from the fort?"

"Aaron says . . . they do not want to come here, and they do not want the soldiers there. There have been too many problems, and Flying Horse believes separation is better."

"Then our problems will never be solved."

"In time—"

"No, Brittany, time will never heal these wounds. We need people like you, Aaron and your Night Walker to create change."

"He is not 'my' Night Walker."

"Isn't he?" Esther said softly.

"Esther . . ."

"I wouldn't say a word to anyone. Your life is your own. Don't you listen to anything but your heart, either. Life is short and uncertain. Don't let anything or anyone govern yours, but you."

"Esther . . . what would happen? I mean, what would people do . . ."

"Have a conniption," Esther laughed. "Most likely these boys out here would be put out, and the women would be arrogant and unforgiving. Most likely, if he looks like you say, they'd be pea green with envy, too. None of which means a hill of beans next to what you feel and what you want. If you let them decide your life . . . you might never get to live it. You'll go through the motions and stick to the rules . . . and never know if you would have found happiness or not."

"You're wonderful, Esther."

"Oh, pish tosh. I'm a woman. I had to run away with Steven, did you know that?"

"No."

"My parents thought he wasn't good enough for me. He was poor, for one thing, and he was from . . . the wrong side of the tracks, you might say. Anyway, they had my very safe and secure husband already picked for me. Steven was, in the eyes of most everyone in our town, a go-nowhere person. But I knew better. He's carving himself a nice career. Do you know, when this tour of duty is over, he is to go to Washington?"

"How exciting. He could do so much."

"Yes . . . it's you and your Night Walker who might just make that happen out here, though. I know Cole has begun to think as Aaron does, that among us all something might work out. Cole would be a wonderful intermediary, if he was given a chance."

"Do you think so?"

"I think Cole is a good man and that he's interested in making a difference."

"You don't think Daniel feels that way?"

"I don't know him well enough to judge."

"Esther . . . do you think the government really needs that trading post with Aaron there already?"

"Now, if you knew the government like I do, you'd know they always want a piece of things, and they always want to be boss. They can't have Aaron doing it all, can they? Why, a half dozen senators and congressmen would have fits. Profit, my girl . . . there has to be some profit. Look to see what they have to gain. Somebody, somewhere has a profit to make."

"I don't see what . . . unless it's just land."

"Maybe that land has more value than you know. You'll have to look and see."

"What do I look for?"

"Whatever the government is looking for. I don't know. All I know is that it's Aaron and his kind that go out there to do good. You stick with him."

"I will."

The conversation turned to dances and fashions, and when Esther left, Brittany had a great deal to consider.

The night of the dance was warm and the full moon lit the fort compound like midday. Brittany walked across the compound with Daniel, and they could hear the music as they approached.

Brittany wore the best gown she had brought. It was a deep blue, with a voluminous skirt consisting of layer after layer of lace-edged ruffles. Cut low to show off her smooth, creamy skin, it held the attention of everyone who looked at her.

The men were filled with a lusty desire to meet and dance with this lovely creature, and the women with a silent regret that this beauty had ever come to the fort.

Brittany was besieged by men wishing to dance with her, and she felt cosseted and a bit excited . . . but she also felt as if each man would have liked to set her on a pedestal and pamper her like a child. She didn't like the feeling that she was to be treated as if she were not intelligent enough to do more than look pretty.

"You look very beautiful tonight, Brittany," Daniel observed when he finally found the opportunity to dance with her.

"Thank you, Daniel."

"Are you enjoying yourself?"

"Yes, I am. I don't often have the opportunity to dance."

"Don't you miss civilization?"

"Civilization?" she questioned. "I find life at the mission perfectly civilized."

"I know how . . . important you consider that mission of Aaron's, but you have to admit, the Indians have a long way to go to reach our level of civilization."

"I don't see the situation that way. When I visited them, they were warm and very welcoming. I couldn't have been treated with more consideration in my father's house. I don't think there is anything holding the Sioux back but education, and I want to see if I can help give them that."

"Brittany, that is a commendable attitude, but

you do not really know them as I and several of my people do. Under certain circumstances they can become bloodthirsty. Why, they would kill you and your helpless sister as quickly as they would steal a horse, and with as much consideration."

Brittany felt a sense of annoyance. She could not envision Night Walker painted and full of enough violence that he would kill someone like Tempest.

She remembered the day he had taken her from his village to the sacred hills and tried to explain his faith to her. She remembered his laugh, and the pride that seemed to govern every move or thought he made. She remembered his obvious love for his family and the close bond that held them together. And she remembered more . . . much more.

"I find that hard to believe. Flying Horse's people have been peaceful for a long time. Cole has said that he doesn't even know they are there. They have caused him and those at the fort no trouble."

"They have been peaceful because Aaron is lenient with them and is giving them everything they demand. I am to see to it that the trading is done more equably, and that the government gets all it is due. We cannot let a bunch of savages stand in the way of progress."

"Aaron is not a fool. He has tried to give as much as he has received."

"I didn't mean to make you angry. I'm sure"—

his voice was so condescending that Brittany wanted to scream—"that Aaron is doing his best. But, you see, religion has no place in government. Our constitution says that distinctly. So it would be better if Aaron stayed out of the trading business."

Aaron had been conversing with Cole and Colonel Brady, but he could see Daniel and Brittany. He watched her face and smiled to himself. He had thought Brittany found the handsome man interesting, but what he saw now was politely controlled anger.

When the dance finished, Brittany and Daniel rejoined them.

"Well, I've enjoyed our visit, Steven, but I believe I am ready to start back to the mission in the morning," Aaron said. "I have pressing business there that I must attend to."

"Aaron, must you really leave so soon? And how is your school doing?" Steven asked, as if he had strong doubts it could possibly succeed.

"It's doing very well," Aaron replied.

"I still think the military should have had some say in that. I do not want trouble stirred up."

"I don't think there will be any trouble." It was Cole who spoke, and Brittany was a bit surprised that he should be the one to come to Aaron's defense. "We have had no trouble with Flying Horse's village, and I think both Aaron and Brittany can be considered good judges of the welfare of both Indian and white. From where they are, they command a better view of the situation and the people."

"I may privately agree with you, Cole," Daniel said. "But the education of the Indians is a controversial goal. They are ignorant, and need more contact with whites if they are going to step into our century."

"And you consider your trading post the right contact?" Brittany questioned.

"Yes, a trading post will provide contact with our ways and our culture. Then we can consider training them."

"Training them?" Brittany said softly, and it was only Cole and Aaron who saw the rising storm. "You make them sound like animals . . . like dogs you can train to fetch."

"Perhaps, for a time, that is all their limited mental capacities will be able to handle," Daniel responded. "I have learned a great deal about them, and they are not the most responsible people in creation."

"How many languages do you speak?" Brittany inquired.

"My own, of course. Why?"

"There is a girl in the village, Never Quiet. She is clever and she is intelligent. She not only speaks her own language, but she has also learned French from the traders and trappers, and she speaks English as well. Besides all that, she can speak with her hands as fluently as she can with her voice. This does not sound like limited mental capacities to me, but extreme intelligence. And, she is the most hospitable creature God ever created. She welcomes the knowledge we bring her. Can we do any less?"

Daniel flushed, but retained his equilibrium. "That does not prove the validity of setting up a school at the mission for the Indians. The children should be taken from their parents and taught our ways so they'll learn to live with the whites."

"Separate children from their families, their roots, their culture? That is a barbaric idea." Brittany's temper was seething.

The discussion was growing into a heated argument, and for Brittany's benefit, Aaron felt it was time to bring it to a halt.

"I'm sure there is a lot of time to resolve these problems. For tonight, we are guests of the colonel and I do not think we should disrupt his party."

Brittany knew she had made a mistake, and restrained herself from making any more remarks. She meant to do what she knew needed to be done, no matter what Daniel had to say. She would change his mind . . . she had to.

Daniel watched her dance away in another soldier's arms, and walked to stand beside Steven Brady.

"That girl is too trusting. I have heard rumors that she and one of the men from the village are rather friendly. I think Aaron is taking advantage of two innocent girls to forward his own plans. He has his school . . . and he intends for it to continue. He has been a friend of the Indians and sees

241

things their way . . . even to delivering those two girls into the hands of savages."

Steven looked at him in shock. "He would not let such a thing happen."

"Wouldn't he? His mission means more to him than they do. Besides, they come from a wealthy family, and keeping them here will ensure a steady supply of books for the school and medicine for the infirmary."

They were interrupted then, and Daniel was glad. It left Steven with a great deal to think about. When Daniel got back to the mission, he would see what he could do to force Steven to act. No doubt, he would soon contact someone back East and request the removal of Aaron and his mission. Then his own plans could move forward.

Brittany felt relieved when the party ended. She had thought to relive the pleasures of her former life. Now, she realized, she only felt out of place. She wanted to return to the mission.

She was thinking of Tempest, and wishing she had not left her behind. She worried that Tempest would need her and she would not be there.

Feeling warm and a bit uncomfortable, she decided to walk outside. The air was pleasantly cool and she looked up to see the midnight sky lit with a million stars. It never ceased to amaze her how much closer the heavens looked out here in this vastness than they did back home.

"A penny for your thoughts." The voice came from behind her and she turned to see Cole walking toward her. She smiled as he drew closer.

"I was thinking of how close the stars seem to be."

"Yes, remarkable, isn't it?"

"I don't remember them being so intense back East."

"Do you miss home?" he asked as they continued to walk.

"I thought I would miss it more than I do. Cole, how long have you been out here?"

"A couple of years."

"And you've never been to the village?"

"No. I have coaxed Aaron many times. But he thinks the military and the Indians don't mix. Maybe he is right. I'm glad I met Night Walker, though. He is . . . not quite what I expected. But I don't suppose that will make a difference."

"Why do you say that?"

"There has been one confrontation too many. I don't think either side will trust the other."

"But why do there have to be sides? Aaron has found peace with the Sioux."

"I don't know. Maybe because we are so different."

"And being different is reason enough to be intolerant?"

"No, I didn't say that. It's not enough reason, but it is a fact. I don't know if red and white can mix . . . in any way."

"What is that supposed to mean?"

"Nothing. I am not going to discuss cultural differences with a pretty girl on a night like this." He smiled, but she knew he was deliberately dodging the issue. "I wish you wouldn't go back so soon."

"I did not come to the Dakotas to dance at the fort and to remain useless. I came here to teach and I intend to do that. Maybe I can visit the fort occasionally, when work and weather permit, and you can visit us again soon."

"I would be delighted. Actually, I have been looking for another excuse to go to the mission."

"Then consider this an open invitation. Come any time you choose."

"Thank you, I will. Brittany?"

"Yes?"

"Is . . . is there someone special at home who is impatiently awaiting your return?"

"There is no one impatiently or patiently waiting for me. I'm afraid I have few ties there except my brother."

"What is the matter with the men back East? Have they lost their eyesight and their good sense?"

"Thank you for that lovely compliment," she laughed, "but they're not to blame. I'm afraid I have a one-track mind, and I was too busy getting my education and taking care of my sister."

"That must have been very difficult for you."

"Not as difficult as it has been for Tempest. She suffered a great deal. Both James and I have tried to protect her from any more suffering."

"And you brought her out here."

"I didn't intend to bring her; she just demanded to come. Yet she has been happier here than she has been for years."

As she said the words, she realized the deeper truth in them. The real change in Tempest had come at the time of their visit to the village. She was happy . . . truly happy, and it frightened Brittany to think of the reason for her sister's happiness.

Suddenly she wanted to run back to the mission. She had the overpowering feeling that something was going to happen to Tempest, and she would not be there to stand between her and whatever it might be.

"And you have been happy, too."

"Yes, I guess I have. My work is challenging, and I feel as if I am doing something worthwhile. Besides, I like it at the mission. It's so—" She shrugged and laughed again. "I don't know. I just like it."

"Aaron was lucky to get you. But is that a future for you?"

"What do you mean?"

"I mean, don't you want a husband and children of your own one day?"

"Yes, I do."

"Brittany, would you mind if I came to the mission once in a while? Just to check on your progress, of course. But, perhaps we could get to know each other better, and—"

"I would really like that, Cole. It would be good for the mission, too, to have the military aware of what we're trying to do."

"Then I shall come at the first opportunity." He was far from satisfied with her answer, but he would accept it for now. There would be plenty of time to court her. After all, he practically had her to himself. There was no real competition at the mission, and she would soon get tired of all work and no play. Yes, he would have all the time in the world to win her.

"I think it best we go in now. We would not want to start rumors," Brittany said. She knew that Cole was interested in courting her, and she did not want to tell him that as she had heard his words, she had seen Night Walker in front of her eyes as clearly as if he were standing there.

She had to rid herself of this infatuation, and put thoughts of Night Walker in their proper place. She and Tempest had not come here to cause more difficulties than they could cure. There was no room for romantic fancies, and she had to make that clear to her sister, as well. There was no room for impossible dreams . . . no room at all. She tucked her hand under Cole's arm and they went back inside together.

The next morning the group left the fort early. Each of them was caught up in his own thoughts.

Aaron felt satisfied, for he had seen evidence that Brittany was putting down roots at the mission and the school. It was clear she had found immense satisfaction in her work, and she had fought for the rights of the Indians even if she had not realized it. She had learned to love, and he knew that given enough time, she would choose to stay here forever.

For Brittany leaving the fort brought assorted feelings. She was woman enough to have enjoyed the attention she had received, and to feel the excitement of dressing in pretty clothes and having a handsome man tell her she was beautiful.

She remembered the day Night Walker had taken her to the hills . . . "Has anyone told you how beautiful you are, Brittany Nelson?" he had asked her. She remembered his gentle touch and the feel of his arms about her. And she remembered Cole's words . . . "I don't know if red and white can mix . . . in any way."

Confusion held her for a long while, for she remembered Esther's advice as well . . . "Follow your heart, Brittany."

Well, she thought, right now her heart led her to the children she could help and the vistas she could open for them. If she sought approval in a pair of dark and smoldering eyes, she pushed the thought aside.

When they reached the mission land, Brittany was even more excited than she had thought she would be. As they crested the hill and looked down the rough trail that led to the cluster of buildings, Brittany had the distinct feeling she was coming home.

A shout and excited voices told them they had been seen. She craned her neck to spot Tempest, and waved vigorously when she did. When the wagons pulled to a stop, Brittany was the first to climb down. She went to Tempest and embraced her. Her sister returned the embrace, and smiled her delight at Brittany's return.

As they walked to the small house she and Tempest shared, Brittany could feel the excitement that filled her sister, and she vowed she would not leave her behind again.

Once inside, Brittany paused. She sensed rather than saw a change. When she looked around, she saw several objects that had not been there before.

The floor was now covered with a fur rug, which Brittany recognized as buffalo. On one wall there was a carved piece of thin wood, shaped in a circle. It was covered with a piece of buckskin that had been tanned and whitened, then painted in a colorful pattern. It was unlike anything she had seen before, and it was pleasant to the eye.

She took out her pad and pencil and questioned Tempest about the objects.

They are gifts from the village, Tempest replied.

Brittany paused before responding. She did not want to upset Tempest, but she did not want her to accept gifts that might cause a misunderstanding.

It's easy to see how much they appreciate all you do, she answered.

Brittany, I have not really told you how glad I am that you made all of this possible for me. I would have missed something very special if I had not come here with you.

Brittany smiled and embraced her sister fiercely. Then she wrote on her pad, *I've missed you.*

I have missed you as well.

What have you done while I was gone?

I spent most of my days at the hospital. And of course I have walked and written letters. I hope Aaron can spare someone to take them to the fort to see they are posted.

Speaking of letters, there are several from James. You can read them as soon as I dig them out of my baggage. One thing exciting, though. James is engaged to be married.

Brittany watched Tempest's face as a smile appeared and her eyes glowed.

How wonderful!

Perhaps you would like to go home for the wedding?

She watched the smile fade.

No, Brittany, I do not want to go home. I have begun to feel as if this place is home. I don't want to leave. Do you?

No, I don't.

Tempest was smiling again. *I am so glad to see you back. Come, let's dig out those letters. I'm anxious to read them.*

Tempest turned to leave the room, and Brittany followed with a feeling that, somehow, Tempest had grown in the time she had been gone. And Brittany realized she didn't like the feeling.

Chapter Fourteen

Instead of returning to the mission right away, Daniel had ridden on to Sioux Falls. There was someone waiting for him there, and a report to be made.

"You . . . you mean to wipe the mission out completely?" Robert Preston asked in shock. He was the only one of the conspirators to make the trip and would report to Major Cline and Senator Gifford when he returned. "What will—"

"You needn't worry. To get that much gold, they'll overlook the methods I have to use."

"The end justifies the means."

"Yes. When you have your share to spend, you'll soon forget how it was gotten, too."

"I . . . I suppose."

"Don't grow weak and foolish. These people

mean nothing to us, and we have too much to gain to feel sympathy for people who shouldn't be where they are in the first place! You go back and tell our friends that I have everything in hand. The papers will be full of the 'bloody massacre' the Indians have committed. That will put an end to any interference in my plans."

Robert agreed, for he recognized that the cold brutality of this man would not be stopped . . . and his desire for his share of the gold overpowered his conscience.

When Daniel returned from his swift and rewarding trip to Sioux Falls, he went immediately to meet with Jethro. The news he received was more than welcome to him, for he knew exactly how to use it.

"I'm telling you, it was her sister," Jethro said. "Her and that buck must have been meeting out there in those woods for a long time. They were pretty cozy. I got a feeling there's a lot going on there that's going to come as a surprise to the old man at the fort."

"It's going to come as a surprise to her sister, too," Daniel chuckled. "It's just the thing we needed."

"You going to tell her?"

"I think it's my duty, don't you? We have to protect her, don't we?"

"It's going to get someone pretty angry at those Indians."

"Yes, isn't it?" Daniel said. "I wouldn't be surprised if this news . . . and you boys pushing the teacher around a bit is all it takes to get Aaron out of the mission. Our government isn't going to be happy about his carelessness when it comes to a pretty white girl."

"Her sister doesn't ever go far enough from the mission for any of the boys to get hold of her."

"But she will, my friend, she will. Give me a little time, and you'll find her right where I want her. Be patient . . . and watch."

Jethro watched silently as a very satisfied Daniel walked to his horse and rode toward the mission.

Brittany was aware that something about her sister had changed, but she could not put her finger on it. She would catch her daydreaming, smiling to herself as if she possessed a wonderful secret.

If anything, the Indians who came to the mission with assorted ills seemed even more friendly with Tempest, and Brittany felt left out when their hands flew in sign so fast she could not follow.

For Tempest, the knowledge that she was deceiving her sister pressed hard on her mind. She knew better than anyone else how protective Brittany was, and how betrayed she would feel when she learned the truth. Still, she did not know how to tell her sister about Soaring Eagle and her decision to spend time with him in his village.

It only made matters worse when Brittany told her about the conversations she had had at the fort, and the way most of the whites felt.

But it is so unfair, Tempest wrote.

252

I know. There is little we can do but go on with Aaron's plans and hope time will prove we are right.

Brittany, I must confess something to you.

What?

While you were gone—

"Brittany . . . ?" Daniel's voice interrupted them, and Brittany turned toward him. Doing so, she did not see the look on her sister's face, but Daniel did. Tempest tried to keep her face expressionless, but Daniel had already seen her dismay. She did not like or trust him, and he knew it. "Can I speak to you for a minute?"

"Of course," Brittany replied.

"Will you walk with me for a while?"

Brittany was surprised, but she agreed. Hastily she jotted a note to apologize to Tempest, who simply nodded, then stood and watched them walk away with a frown furrowing her brow.

As they walked Daniel remained silent, as if he were trying to put bad news in a form that would not upset her.

"What is it, Daniel? What's wrong?"

"I hate to be the one to carry tales. It's only that I am worried about what might happen . . ."

"Daniel, for heaven's sake, if something is wrong, please tell me."

"It is about Tempest. I have been given word of her . . . relationship with the Indians."

"Is that all? I know how she cares for them. I—" Brittany was ready to do battle with Daniel's prejudice. She wasn't prepared for what he said next.

"Wait, Brittany, it is not that she cares for

'them,' it's that she cares for one. In fact, she has been slipping away from the mission for a long time to meet him."

Brittany stopped in her tracks and looked up at him, her face filled with shock. For a moment she couldn't speak.

"Slipping away to meet him? Who? Who is it?"

It was then that a brilliant idea came to him. He had thought of a way to make his news even more devastating than the truth.

"I think it's that brave from the village who has been so friendly to Aaron . . . Night Walker. He has sure pulled the wool over Aaron's eyes. I . . . I hope it's not gone too far," he added with enough inflection in his voice to bring visions before Brittany's eyes. For a moment she was stunned; then suddenly she was filled with a pain she could not account for.

Had Night Walker been deceiving them all? Was he seducing her sister? Had he held Tempest as he had held her? Brittany could not find her breath, and she wanted nothing more than to run from any other words Daniel had to say.

Daniel could not have been happier. Her face had gone white and there was a stark look in her eyes, as if she had been struck.

"I don't believe it."

"It's true. She is taking her 'walks' and meeting him. They have been spending a lot of time together. You don't know what that savage could have done already."

Brittany felt as if her heart had been caught in

a vise. She didn't want to believe . . . she couldn't believe. *Night Walker!* her heart cried. Had he such contempt for what she was trying to do that he'd taken this way to bring it to an end?

He had held her, kissed her, and had taken her to a magic place where she felt sensations she had never felt before. Had it been only a game?

It was then Tempest's last words came to her . . . "Brittany, I have something to confess to you" . . . No! She could not bear it. She could not! Her sister was innocent, and Night Walker would not do such a thing. This had to be a lie! It had to!

She needed to find out for herself, and there was only one way to do that. She had to face Night Walker and see his eyes when she asked him. She had to know this was some kind of misinterpretation by someone who had thought he had seen something that was not so.

She could not go to Tempest and face her with such a lie. It would look as if she did not trust her. She knew it could not be true . . . she knew it.

"Thank you, Daniel. I shall see about this."

"I don't want to distress your sister. I wouldn't want her to think that the people here at the mission are talking behind her back. Everyone here has a special feeling for her."

"I know. I will find out for myself."

"What will you do if—"

"I shall see to it that Tempest returns home. I will not have her hurt any more than she has been. It is up to me, as it has always been, to protect her from such things."

"If I can be of any help—"

"Thank you, but I can take care of this myself
. . . I promise you."

Daniel watched her walk away. She would learn
that her sister had, indeed, been meeting someone, and she would be too enraged to listen to reason. When she found the truth, she would snatch
her sister away from here . . . and if his men completed his plan, Brittany would be with Tempest
when she left, and the threat of a teacher for the
Indians would be removed. Then Daniel could focus his efforts on eliminating Aaron and the mission altogether.

Brittany was still numb from the force of Daniel's words. She walked toward the place where
the horses were kept and saddled one for herself.
She didn't want anyone to caution her or give her
unwelcome advice. She had to see Night Walker
. . . and she had to see him now.

She found landmarks she had noticed before,
and she knew she was riding in the right direction.
Of course she didn't know how many miles stood
between her and the village, but she did not care.

She rode hard and steadily, and with no idea
that others rode behind her waiting until she was
far enough from the mission to make their move.

She was a good distance away when she realized her horse could not keep up the pace she had
set; he was breathing heavily. She dismounted
and loosened the cinch so the horse could breathe
and relax. Making sure he could not wander off,
she walked away from him and sat on a large, flat

rock. Her mind was in a turmoil, and she could not wipe Night Walker from it.

"Oh, Night Walker," she whispered, "what kind of fool am I? I cannot believe . . . I cannot." Her mind was so caught up in her own misery that she did not notice the approach of others until they were beside her. Three men, and they were smiling as they brought their horses to a halt.

Suddenly Brittany was looking up into three cold, hard faces. She bolted to her feet, fear shivering through her.

"Who are you and what do you want?" She tried to sound authoritative, but even to her, her voice sounded thin and frightened.

"Well, well," one man said with a sneer. "What do we have here? Are you lost, pretty thing?"

"No, I'm not lost, and I don't need any help, thank you."

"Real polite, ain't she?" The second man said with a coarse laugh.

"Why, boys, do you know what we got here? We got us an Injun lover. She's the gal from that mission. The one that wants to teach those redskins."

"Yeah? What's she want to teach 'em?" The three laughed at this, and to Brittany's distress they dismounted and walked toward her. She was surrounded. She felt her mouth go dry as fear coursed through her.

"You're real pretty. Maybe you'd be interested in giving us some lessons. I'd be right pleased to take a little instruction from you. I'll bet you can . . . instruct . . . real good." He reached to touch her cheek, and Brittany slapped his hand away.

"Keep your filthy hands off me."

"Now, come on. We only want a taste of what you're givin' away."

Brittany wanted to cry, but she would not give them the satisfaction. They were crowding her, reaching to touch her, and as soon as she pushed one hand away, another took its place. She could smell unwashed bodies and breath reeking of whiskey. She knew their intentions, and she knew she would have to be dead before she surrendered to them.

They were laughing, and she knew the memory of that laughter would linger in her mind for a long time. One man caught his hand in the top of her blouse, and the sound of ripping cloth brought a groan from Brittany. She struggled to gather her torn blouse together enough to cover herself, but was not successful. Her efforts brought a gleam of lust to their eyes.

As they taunted her and reached quick hands to grasp and touch, they laughed among themselves. They meant to make sure that when Brittany ran, she would run all the way back to Philadelphia. All three men wished Daniel had said they could do more than frighten her, for they were enjoying the sight of her soft, creamy flesh and were more than ready to ravage her. It was only Daniel's anger that stood in their way. That, and the cry of gold. They promised themselves that if the opportunity came, they would enjoy her at their leisure. Perhaps if Daniel had what he wanted . . .

As Brittany fought off the grasping hands, panic made her tremble, and her eyes stung with tears. She had never thought of herself as a coward, but she was so frightened that words could not come if she had wanted them to.

She was forced to the ground, and despite her struggles hands roughly caressed her, and her skirts were pushed up. This humiliation was enough to drag a reluctant cry from her, and she heard their harsh breathing and excited laughter as she continued to struggle.

Then suddenly the hands were gone, and she opened her tightly closed eyes and looked up. Her breath caught in her throat, and she could have wept in relief. All three men were looking up at the tall and very formidable warrior with the bow in his hand. It was drawn, and one arrow had already hummed past them to plant itself in the ground beside them.

All three men stood facing a man who looked fierce enough to kill . . . in fact, Night Walker was considering it. He had never been so enraged in his life as he was when he saw their treatment of a lone woman, but when he saw that woman was Brittany, he found it hard not to kill.

"Get the hell out of here, Injun, or you'll regret it," one man found the bravado to snarl. "You can't take us all."

"No." Night Walker smiled a smile that was deadly. "But I can kill two of you before you can use those guns. Now," he laughed softly, "which of you feels so brave that he will die for it?"

The three eyed him carefully, taking in the deadly bow in his hand. They looked into his eyes and saw that he was a man who would not hesitate to do what he promised.

"Come on," the man who led the group said, "let's go. Maybe he won't find so much trouble with her as she gave us. She's partial to Injuns."

When the three had mounted and ridden off and Night Walker was certain they were gone, he replaced the arrow in the quiver he wore and re-slung his bow across his body. Then he dismounted and went to Brittany's side.

The reality of what had almost happened to her was finally registering fully in her mind. Her body was shaking and there were tears in her eyes. Night Walker took hold of her shoulders and drew her slowly to her feet. He could not stand the look in her eyes, and he gently drew her into his arms and cradled her against him. He felt profoundly grateful that he had found her before . . . the thought of what had almost happened to her brought a new surge of rage.

Brittany felt the warmth of Night Walker's arms, and could not deny her need to be held within them. She rested her head against the breadth of his chest, and felt safe and secure. For a silent, warm moment they simply held each other. Night Walker found the truth of his brother's words and he knew if he were given a chance, he would choose to hold her forever like this and protect her from anything that might endanger her.

But reality was breaking through Brittany's lethargy, and she remembered her anger and why she had come to him. It was difficult to be angry with a man who had just rescued her, but she had to think of his motives and of her sister. She moved from his arms and looked up at him.

"Brittany, what were you doing out here alone?"

"I was coming to see you."

For a minute a swirl of pleasure swept over him, but then he realized that it must have been some kind of emergency to bring her into this wilderness alone.

"Why? You must know that was a dangerous thing to do."

Because the thought of his deception was painful, she fought her emotions, looking for the anger that had carried her here. His presence played havoc with her nerves. She didn't want to feel the emptiness she felt as she left the security of his arms, and yet she was grateful for it because it fueled her anger. She turned on him.

"Oh, God, how I hate you! You are a liar and a deceiving snake!"

Night Walker was stunned, and for a minute he could only stare at her in shock. He tried to think of what he might have said or done to bring about this anger, but there was nothing.

"What are you talking about?"

"I have found out my sister has been meeting someone away from the mission."

It hurt to see a guilty look cross his face. She

261

did not know that he thought she had found out about his brother and Tempest.

"I am sorry you found out like this. You should have been told long ago. But you cannot blame—"

"I blame you! My sister is young and innocent. She could not have thought to deceive me."

"Now wait. She is as much to blame as anyone, and she is not as young and foolish as you would like to make her."

"How could you do this?"

"Maybe you should look at yourself for that answer." Night Walker was getting angry now, too, partly because he felt guilty. He could have tried harder to stop what was happening, or he could have told Brittany. But he was sure she would not have understood, and her actions now were proof of that. "Maybe if you had understood her more, and not smothered her with too much love, she would not have considered doing something behind your back. She was running from you!"

Brittany gasped as if she had been struck, and her eyes welled with tears. "I was only trying to protect her."

"She has tried to tell you a million different ways that she does not want to be protected like a flower that will wilt at a single touch. She wanted to be herself, and you would never let her. You guided every step, until she could not breathe." He inhaled deeply, distressed that he was taking his anger out on her. It was not his right to hurt her like this, and he felt her hurt as if it were his own. "Now . . . she has a right to her own decisions."

"Yes, I suppose she does. And you feel you have the right to take advantage of her difficulties."

"Me? I take advantage of no woman."

"What do you call it then?" Brittany snarled. "Because I would not come to you, you took her instead."

If Night Walker had been stunned before, he was stricken almost wordless now. She actually thought it was he Tempest was meeting in the woods. He was going to fight back with denial, but then another, more pleasant, thought came to him. Which was she angrier about, the fact that her sister was meeting a man . . . or the fact that it was a man she was interested in?

"Your sister is old enough to make her own decisions," he said casually, "and you do not govern my life." Brittany lifted a hand as if to strike him, but there was more than anger in her eyes and he needed to know all her feelings. "Is it that you care so much about who your sister has been meeting . . . or that you care that it might be me?"

She looked away from him. "I hate you," she said almost to herself.

Night Walker smiled and took hold of her shoulders, forcing her to look up at him. "Do you hate me? Is that why you are so angry? When you think of me and Tempest together, do you fear for your sister's innocence, or for your own feelings? Do you lie to yourself, Brittany Nelson?" His last words were spoken too gently not to hit home.

She tried to escape his arms and those piercing dark eyes that seemed to be reading her soul. "Don't."

"Don't what? Love you? Ask me not to need my next breath. I cannot do either. I have loved you from the moment I saw you that night at Aaron's."

"You can't! You can't! Or you would not play this game of deception with Tempest."

Although she tried to resist, she was no match for his strength, and he drew her closer in his arms until she was pressed to the length of him. Helplessly she looked up at him.

"You little fool," he said tenderly. "If you do not remember, I do. The times I have held you are carved in my mind and my heart. Do you think I could have touched you and felt the need for any other? It is impossible. There is room in my heart for only one, and that is you."

"That only makes matters worse."

"How?"

"I . . . I would not hurt Tempest. If she believes she loves you . . . I know she will be devastated. I cannot break her heart."

"And for that I only love you more. But you will not break her heart, for she does not have a special love for me . . . except as a friend perhaps."

"I cannot see why she would meet you so far from the mission, and in secret, if she did not want you," Brittany said miserably. She was in the most horrible of positions. She could not deny her love for Night Walker or accept his taking Tempest's feelings so lightly.

"She would if it were someone else she was meeting and, like you, she felt she could not hurt the sister who had sacrificed so much for her."

Brittany stood paralyzed. What was he saying to her? That it was not he Tempest had been meeting? But then who . . . ? She sucked in a breath as Soaring Eagle's face came into her mind. She was swept by a sense of relief that made her legs weak, and she clung to Night Walker's strength. When she looked up into his eyes again she knew he saw the depth of her feelings. She also knew another truth. Night Walker was right: she did not want him to meet or to love anyone else, for she loved him.

"It's Soaring Eagle, isn't it?"

"Yes, they have been meeting almost from the beginning. Does this distress you, Brittany? Soaring Eagle is an honorable man. He would not hurt her. I know he loves her very much."

"But Tempest—"

"Tempest is a woman, not a child you still need to lead. Let her go. Let her find her own way and walk her own path. She is young and she is unable to hear, but she is not unable to feel what you feel or want what you want. She does not want to hurt you, and so she might give Soaring Eagle up if she thought it would hurt you. It is up to you to let her go."

All of this was almost too much for Brittany. She didn't want . . . She looked up at Night Walker and saw the hope in his eyes. She realized she had spent a lot of years trying to make Tempest helpless so she would depend on her. The truth was followed by a wave of guilt.

"Oh, Tempest, I'm so sorry," she whispered. "Night Walker . . . I'm sorry for what I was thinking."

"I am not."

"You're not sorry I misjudged you?"

"For that, yes. But I am not sorry you felt as you did, for it means you cannot deny how you feel for me any more than I can deny what I feel for you. It is good to know you were jealous." His smile was broad and teasing, and she had to smile back, for she had no intention of denying her feelings any longer. "I was on my way to the mission because I had the need to see you again, for even if you could not find it in your heart to look at me again, I could not let you go."

"Now I know why all those things were in our house. Tempest must have gotten them from Soaring Eagle."

Night Walker laughed. "He would have presented her with everything he possessed, but she would not have it. She . . . she was afraid of your reaction and she wanted to speak to you first."

"So she did go to the village."

"Yes, while you were gone. She is loved there, Morning Sun. I don't think you know how loved she is. Soaring Eagle would keep her there."

"I must go back and talk to her . . . ask her to forgive me."

"Forgive you? I do not think love needs to ask for forgiveness, and I do not think she will think so, either." His voice lowered and his arms tightened about her. "Must you go now? Can you not stay and be with me? I have missed you more than you know."

"I should . . ." The words died on her lips, for the melting heat of his eyes was holding her, and awareness leapt between them.

The breath fled her lungs as she drowned in the warmth of his gaze.

She was hotly aware of him, the strength of his arms, and the hard warmth of his sleek bronzed skin where she was pressed against him. The top of her head came to his chin and he could see the blazing emerald of her eyes darken and grow warm.

Brittany felt as if she had touched a live flame.

He reached up a hand and traced her lips with one finger. Her mouth was soft and warm and he could feel the heat of need uncoil within him.

Brittany felt a bit dazed, and a flood of sensual pleasure went through her at his touch. Her heart began to beat furiously. There was something magical happening between them. She saw it in his eyes, and felt it to the depths of her, in every bone and sinew of her body.

She could not force her eyes away from the beautiful, rough planes of his face. A flame was lit, and she did not think she would ever have the power, or the inclination, to put it out.

Night Walker did not think he had ever felt such a fierce hunger, and he molded her to him while he bent his head and gently took her soft mouth with his.

When he released her mouth, Brittany felt as if she were swimming up from the depths of a languid pool of warmth. She had felt, from the first time they had touched, that this could not be love. She had thought this sweet flame was nothing but the call of the wildness within her.

But now his arms were holding her as if she were the most precious thing in his world, and she felt all rational thought dissolving in the melting fire of desire. She wanted this man, not only for today, and not just for the passion he'd awakened in her. She wanted to laugh and to cry and to grow old with him. She wanted a man who would die for her as she would for him. And this man, so beautiful and so strong, would do that. She had seen it in his eyes when he had faced the three men, any one of whom, if he'd had the courage, could have killed him.

"How beautiful you are," Night Walker whispered against her hair. "Brittany . . . join with me."

She wondered if she was really hearing these words from him, or from the depths of her own heart.

"I . . . I must think—"

"No, think only of us and what we share. You are my woman, Brittany, and now I find it impossible to let you go."

Brittany had never in her life experienced the emotions he could stir in her. Ecstasy, excitement, contentment and, most of all, confusion.

As for Night Walker, he was bewitched. The fragrance of her, the way the sunlight sparkled in her hair, the tantalizing feel of her, created a magic that he could not question or understand, but simply felt and enjoyed.

"Night Walker, I didn't say no. I am simply asking for time to . . . to know myself. You have a way of taking every thought but you from my mind."

"That is good. I would be your husband. I love you, Morning Sun, and that is the only truth that needs to be between us. Do you share what I feel?"

She could not lie. Looking up into his questioning eyes, she knew there was only one answer. "Yes, I do."

He drew a long, ragged breath of satisfaction and crushed her to him. This time he would leave no room for the useless arguments she would present.

Hastily throwing bow and quiver aside, he drew her, unresisting, down to the soft grass and the cool shade of a tree. "We must talk—" she began. His mouth found hers, and the kiss was long, driving every other thought from her mind.

When he released her lips, he murmured, "Do you still want to talk?"

"No," she sighed softly. She could feel his strong hands seeking the softness of her breasts, and she aided him in the removing of her clothes. She wanted to cry and to laugh and to sing. She wanted to shout to the world that she loved him, and better, that he loved her.

Then his hands were stroking the ivory body bared to his gaze, and he reveled in the feel of her skin beneath his fingers. He was in a daze of contentment, his world consisting only of this slim golden body and the whirlwind of feverish desire that filled him.

She, too, wanted to hold on to this beautiful emotion. She called to him in soft sighs and sweet words.

Her body was on fire, and she ached for him to fill this heated hunger that was threatening to send her spiraling into oblivion. Then the long, smooth length of him was inside her, moving with slow deliberation in and out, stroking, sliding along the moist and welcoming passage, to touch the innermost depths of her.

She felt the fire blaze deep inside. Like an exploding volcano, it shot the molten lava of passion higher and higher. Flame red, hot gold, dazzling purples and brilliant oranges—blasts of passion soared and expanded, matching the colors of the cataclysm that was exploding in the very center of her. She moved in a world with him that no other could tread, and she heard his words of love as he carried her to the pinnacle with him and beyond.

He held her as they soared, and then the spiral of their passion gradually led them back to the moment and the realization of how perfect it had been.

She was looking up at him with an expression of wonder on her face. He took her hand in his and kissed her fingers.

"What is it?"

She reached to touch him, to lay her hand against his cheek. "Only that you are wonderful, and that I love you completely."

"I cannot believe that this is not a dream, and that I will not waken to find my arms empty and my longing for you filling me again as it has these past days."

Neither had ever known such fierce hunger or such sweet release. He kissed her gently now, her eyes, her cheeks and the sweetness of her mouth. They lay contented for a while, and he felt her relax in his arms and sleep.

But he could not sleep, for the wonder of their love held him. He would have her for his wife, and she would remain with him always. She would never return to the place from which she had come. Nothing would ever separate them as long as there was a breath in his body. That he swore with all that was in him.

His arms drew her closer, and he found himself repeating her name over and over in his mind . . . her name, and the wonder that she would be his.

Chapter Fifteen

Tempest was upset that she had not had time to finish explaining to Brittany, and more so when she found that Brittany had ridden away from the mission without telling anyone. She questioned Thomas and Skinner, but no one knew where Brittany had gone. Finally she came to Daniel, who tried to muddy her thoughts as much as he could. He pretended he could not understand her gestures until, in desperation, she reached for the pad of paper in her pocket. She had grown unaccustomed to using it.

Do you know where my sister has gone?

No, I have no idea, he wrote back.

Was she upset when she left?

She seemed a bit angry.

Tempest turned away and did not see Daniel's

look of satisfaction. Had someone told Brittany her secret before she could get a chance to?

She had worried that the news would come to her sister some other way and that Brittany would not only not understand, but would be angry. Now she felt weak, and wished she had Soaring Eagle to come and stand with her. Stand with her? As if she had done something wrong and Brittany were judge. That was unfair to both of them and she tried to force the thought aside.

She had enjoyed the days she had spent in the village, and the acceptance of Soaring Eagle's people. In fact, she had never felt so loved and so valuable.

Soaring Eagle was at her side every moment, showing her their ways, answering her questions. They had spent two joyous days together, escaping now and then to share precious moments alone. They had discussed the ways they might tell Brittany.

I will come with you and speak to her myself, Soaring Eagle signed.

No, Tempest responded, *it is my place to tell her first. Please understand. I want to talk to her and explain, not just present her with a fact as if she had been completely gone from my thoughts. It is not fair to her.*

And what of us? If she refuses to see, to understand. I cannot lose you, White Dove.

But you must see—Tempest smiled—*you cannot lose me. Nothing can come between us. But this thing I must do.*

Soaring Eagle had pleaded and pressured, but Tempest was adamant. He could do little more than agree to take her back to the mission and leave until she sent for him.

She had tried to tell Brittany, and now she did not know what to do or what might be happening. She did know she could not let Brittany go to the village angry, or to say things to Soaring Eagle without her there.

She was confused and frightened, and went in search of Aaron. He had been supervising the building of a library and was in the midst of work on the roof when Tempest came. Tempest's hands flew in sign so fast, Aaron could not follow. He reached out and grasped both her hands in his to still them, then made the sign for slow . . . slow.

Do you know where Brittany has gone?

I didn't know she had left the mission at all, Aaron signed.

She left alone.

Alone? You must be mistaken.

No, I am not. She left alone. She was angry over something.

Now Aaron stood without replying for a moment.

Aaron, please—

What did she have to be angry about?

Tempest flushed, and then lifted her chin determinedly. *She does have something to be angry and hurt about*. As quickly as she could, she told him of all her meetings with Soaring Eagle. Of how she had tried to tell Brittany, only to be interrupted. Now, before she'd had a chance to complete her confession, Brittany had gone without an explanation and was angry.

Perhaps it would be a good thing if I sent someone for Soaring Eagle. Skinner will go. The rest of us will gather a search party and follow Brittany. If she has run into any trouble, we will find her.

Aaron, I am so sorry. If anything happens to Brittany, I will never forgive myself.

Nothing is going to happen to her, child. We'll see that it doesn't. Tempest, is it true? Do you wish to wed Soaring Eagle?

With all my heart.

But you are sure Brittany opposes this?

Yes.

What will you say to her?

That I love Soaring Eagle. That I will join with him, as he puts it. And that I will be happy. I cannot say more than that.

No, I guess you can't. Aaron smiled. He turned and shouted for Skinner, who came on the run.

"There something wrong, Aaron?"

"I need your help, Skinner. I want you to ride to the village as fast as you can and bring Soaring Eagle to me. Tell him that Tempest has great need of him."

"I'm supposed to bring him back with me?"

"Does that pose a problem?"

"Only if he don't want to come. I ain't one to try and tell that boy where to go or not to go."

"Don't worry, Skinner. If you tell him Tempest needs him, he'll come on the run."

275

"Whatever you say." Skinner walked away, and Aaron chuckled. Skinner was not convinced that he would have Soaring Eagle's cooperation.

Tempest saw approval in Aaron's eyes, and she made a soft sound of relief and threw her arms about his neck. He would help her, and maybe even plead her cause with Brittany.

As she moved away from him, she could see that his attention had been drawn beyond her. She turned to follow his gaze and gasped in shock when she saw Brittany and Night Walker riding toward them.

Aaron could feel Tempest's body go tense and he cast her a quick glance. She might be nervous, but she was also courageous. He returned his gaze to Brittany to see if he could read her emotions.

Brittany and Night Walker dismounted and started toward them. Aaron and Tempest could see the condition of Brittany's clothes. The torn blouse, flushed cheeks and disheveled hair were obvious evidence that something drastic had happened. Brittany hastily explained the attack that had been made on her, and Aaron relayed the explanation to Tempest, who was badly shaken.

Brittany smiled and reached to touch her sister, assuring her she was all right. But Tempest could see deeper questions in her eyes. Aaron and Tempest exchanged surprised looks. Tempest looked at her sister and she could feel her heart pounding. Surely Brittany would understand . . . she must understand.

Night Walker had no problem reading the look

in Tempest's eyes. He turned to Brittany.

"Your sister is frightened of your disapproval. Look at her, and know the truth about what she feels for my brother."

Brittany silently embraced Tempest, and Tempest returned the embrace fiercely. Only then did Brittany turn to Aaron.

"Aaron, has Tempest told you why she went to the village while we were gone?" Aaron looked from sister to sister, and then to Night Walker. "There is no use pretending on my account. I know now what has been going on," Brittany added.

"I'm afraid I didn't know what was 'going on,' as you put it, until Tempest came to me just now and told me all about it. Brittany, she is frightened of your disapproval. She's guilty of nothing but loving. Can you find it in your heart to condemn her for that?"

"I don't condemn her, Aaron. I guess . . . I don't know. I was . . . afraid for her. Can you understand?"

"Of course. I know you have always had her welfare in mind, but we can get caught up in our protectiveness and sometimes do as much harm as we intend good."

"Aaron," Night Walker said. "Let me try to explain to Tempest."

"I'm afraid my sign is not as good as I would like it to be. I don't use it often enough," Aaron said.

"It's important that Tempest understand," Night Walker said.

"Yes, once she does, all of this misunderstanding will be washed away.

"Night Walker, I have sent Skinner for Soaring Eagle. It will make things easier if he is here to see for himself that he is not hated by Brittany," Aaron added.

"That is good. For now, I will see that Tempest understands she has Brittany's approval."

Night Walker turned to Tempest and smiled. His hands moved quickly while Tempest watched with fascination. Then she, too, began to smile.

Welcome among us, sister. I would tell you how happy you will make my brother and my whole family, when you join us. I would be brother to you.

Tempest made a soft sound of pleasure, and her hands flew in response.

I welcome you as a brother. I only worry about what Brittany will do when I say I want to wed Soaring Eagle.

She and Aaron would have me make it clear to you. They welcome the prospect as well. Soon Soaring Eagle will come, for Aaron has sent for him.

Tempest's eyes filled with tears.

Brittany does understand?

Yes. She has told me herself, even before we returned here, that she now knows her protection of you was making your life hard. She would have you know she has much trust in what you want, and will not stand against you.

"Night Walker," Aaron spoke now. "I would like

to marry them according to our custom first. I know Soaring Eagle will understand that Tempest will not feel truly married if she does not have the blessings of her faith as well as Soaring Eagle's."

"I know I can speak for my brother when I say he will have no argument with that. He is too worried that you and Tempest's sister will not allow her to marry at all. Once they have married here, we will have a celebration in our village."

Tempest laughed, and Brittany, though she didn't know what had transpired, could feel her sister's presence.

"Night Walker," Brittany said, "I need much more help with signing. I would like to be able to talk to Tempest and to Soaring Eagle. After all, he is to be my brother."

"I will be pleased to teach you more," Night Walker said. He still could not read Brittany's thoughts. They had shared something so wonderful that he knew he could never forget her. But would she come to him, join him if he asked her again? She had not answered him before, and the nagging thought filled his mind that she did not mean to answer. "Why do you not come to our village for a while? It would be easier to teach you day by day than to see you only once in a while."

"Well, we must see about the situation between your brother and Tempest before we can make any other plans. Come, let's go to our house and discuss how this situation will be handled."

The four of them walked to the small house the sisters shared. But Night Walker was well aware that Brittany had not agreed to anything. He began to worry that she did not intend to join with him.

Skinner arrived in the village on a lathered horse, and all knew his haste meant that something of importance had transpired. Skinner said that his message was for Soaring Eagle, and it was from both Aaron and Tempest. Soaring Eagle was sent for at once.

When the message was brought to him, he raced to Skinner.

"You have a message for me from the mission?"

"Soaring Eagle, Aaron says you are to come as fast as you can. Tempest needs you."

"She is well?"

"I guess so. She was crying, and Aaron said to come quick."

That was all Soaring Eagle needed to hear. Grimly he went to his horse. "Come, Skinner, we must ride quickly."

"My horse is tuckered out. He won't make the trip to the mission that fast."

"I will provide another," Soaring Eagle said impatiently. He brought another from the small herd he had, and soon they were on their way.

Skinner was not the horseman Soaring Eagle was and he was hard put to keep up with the warrior. When the mission came into view, Skinner was more than grateful. Still, he did not like the look on Soaring Eagle's face. His dark eyes were cold, and there was a look of fiercely contained anger there.

Like the wind they flew, and Skinner could do little more than follow. They came to a halt beside the house Tempest and Brittany shared, and Soaring Eagle was off his horse and at the door before Skinner could dismount.

At any other time Soaring Eagle would not have considered bursting into the house, but now there was no time for such considerations. He cared about nothing except finding out if Tempest was all right.

If necessary, he would do battle with her sister or anyone else who stood in their way. He had seen Night Walker's horse and was prepared, if the need arose, even to do battle with him. Tempest was the best of his life and he could not lose her.

He practically flung the door open. His burning gaze found Tempest at once. She was sitting on a stool near the fireplace.

Soaring Eagle saw only the traces of tears on her face, and his face froze in a mask of fury. Night Walker read his brother's thoughts and reached out a hand to stop him. But Soaring Eagle brushed it aside. Night Walker might be willing to give up the woman he wanted because of the white man's prejudice, but he would not.

He went to Tempest and knelt beside her. Gently he took her hand in his, and then he drew her up to stand beside him. He held her close and turned defiantly toward the others in the room.

"I have come to take her from here. She will remain with me and find understanding and happiness at my side. I will not let you stop us. We wish to join and it will be so, whether you will it or not. I will not let you hurt her again."

Both Night Walker and Aaron started to speak, but Brittany turned to them. "Wait, let me speak to him first." Both men remained silent and Brittany turned back to Soaring Eagle. "Soaring Eagle, I can see by the anger in you that you care a great deal for my sister."

Soaring Eagle looked from her to his brother in puzzlement. But Brittany continued talking and he returned his attention to her.

"My sister has told us about how you have been meeting, and I am sorry that I was the one who forced you to meet in secret." She came to his side and laid a hand on his arm. "I am happy that my sister has found someone so kind and understanding. She has said how happy you have made her, and for that I am grateful. Aaron and I have only one request to make of you."

Soaring Eagle was so surprised that for a minute he could not speak. When he did, his voice was filled with caution. "What do you wish? That I give up White Dove for her own good?"

"No, for I do not think she would give you up for any reason. I don't intend to ask her to. I only want the two of you to be married here first, by Aaron."

Now he was stunned to silence, and Night Walker laughed softly. "You were always in a rush, brother. What has slowed your wits now?"

"I find this hard to believe. When Skinner came, he said Tempest was crying and that she needed me. I could only think something had gone wrong."

"That was before we explained everything," Brittany said.

Soaring Eagle looked down into Tempest's eyes, and her gentle smile warmed him. It was the first time he really understood that they were no longer going to be forced to meet secretly, and that they could be together forever.

He looked back at Brittany. "I will do anything that will make her happy, even this strange . . . marrying."

"It is a simple affair. I'm sure you will find it painless," Brittany laughed.

"I think we should go and leave them alone for a while, at least until Soaring Eagle gets over the shock," Aaron said.

Night Walker was agreeable to this because he wanted to talk to Brittany alone. He needed an answer. Brittany and Aaron turned to leave, and Night Walker paused by his brother.

"You were the wise one in this matter, brother. I hope the gods give you much happiness, for the courage the two of you have shown is great." He smiled at Tempest and reached to touch her cheek. Then he signed, *I wish you many years of joy, and children to carry on your courage and your strong love.*

Thank you . . . brother, Tempest signed. She and

Soaring Eagle watched the three leave, and then they turned to each other.

There were no words or sign that Soaring Eagle could find that would speak his happiness. He simply took her in his arms and held her. Tempest closed her eyes and savored his embrace. It was coming home . . . to a safe harbor . . . to peace.

Outside Aaron and Brittany stood with Night Walker. The three were silent for a minute, each contemplating his own thoughts. Then Brittany turned to Aaron.

"Aaron, where has Daniel gone?"

"I don't know. Most likely home. Why?"

"I want to talk to him. I think I need the answers to some questions."

"If you like, I will check around and see exactly where he is."

"Yes, thank you."

When Aaron was gone, it was Night Walker who spoke next. "Why do you seek the white trader?" He was worried that there might be something between her and this handsome white man.

"I think there are some questions he should answer."

"Questions such as what?"

"Well"—she turned to face him—"for one thing, it was he who told me Tempest was meeting a brave from your village."

"His loose tongue did no harm."

"You might think otherwise when I tell you that it was *you* he told me Tempest was meeting."

"So he is the one who made you so angry with me. He is a troublemaker. To speak the truth, I do not like or trust him."

"But, Night Walker . . . why? Why did he want to turn us against each other?"

Night Walker stood thoughtfully, his brow furrowed. "I can only believe that he has come here for a deeper purpose than he has said. I have felt he also knows of the men who watch, and that his purpose is theirs."

"Again I ask, why?"

"Perhaps," Night Walker said slowly, as if he were straining for a logical answer, "it is not only you, but the entire mission that stands in the way of his achieving his purpose here."

"I don't see how it could. Even if he does have to make reports to the government, what harm can we do him?"

"I have no answers; I must give this more thought. There is a reason, but it is hidden in the shadows and I cannot see. There is something we do not know about. I wonder if it has anything to do with the men who were watching the mission. Maybe they watch for him."

"I hate to keep repeating myself, but why?"

"I do not know . . . I just do not know."

"I'll find him and ask him."

"No, it would be best if you wait for a while."

"Why?"

"If you approach him now, he will be warned that you suspect him. Let me see if there is a way for me to get some answers first. The more answers we have, the less he can defend himself. Maybe we can drive him from our land."

"What do you intend to do?"

"I will search until I find the men who watch. One of them may be willing to tell me what the white trader wants here."

"I cannot see what he has to gain. The land cannot be his unless the government pushes you from it."

"They have done that before. I think this time we will not move. Whatever this white man is after, he will find nothing but defeat here."

"Night Walker, I must tell you something. I'm ashamed that I believed Daniel's word about you and Tempest, that I thought you guilty before I gave you a chance to answer."

"It pleases me very much that you thought that way."

"It does?"

"You were angry, not because of Soaring Eagle and your sister, but because you were jealous. That knowledge was as welcome as the realization that you did not hate Soaring Eagle . . . and that you finally understood your sister's need. We have all gained much from this."

"Yes, I guess we have."

"Brittany . . . you have not answered my question."

"Question?" she said hesitantly. She looked up at him, and knew without doubt he would not let her back away from a decision . . . and she didn't know what she would decide. She realized she was not showing as much courage as the sister she had thought so helpless.

"There is much we have to say to each other."

"I know, but, Night Walker, give me time to think."

"I do not understand what you must think about. If you will say what was between us was not a strong and perfect thing, you are lying to yourself because you are afraid—"

"I am not afraid."

"Yes, you are. You had all that you thought you wanted set in your mind. What is between us was a surprise, and it did not fit into the plans you have made for your life. I will not ask you to do or give what does not come from your heart. I would only tell you that no woman has held my heart, and I have desired no woman to share the rest of my life with until you. I cannot and will not forget you, Morning Sun . . . and I cannot and will not come to you again. You must decide what you want, and both of us must live for the rest of our lives with that decision." He reached to touch her cheek with gentle fingers, then he turned and walked away.

Brittany wanted to call after him, to run to him and feel his arms close about her. She wanted to tell him that she chose to stay safe in his arms forever. But she had an obligation to Aaron . . . not only to Aaron, but to the school and the children and the promise of their future.

She knew that Aaron's plans were larger and more complicated than she had at first believed. But she had agreed, she had come this far, and she could not let her personal desires interfere with the dream Aaron had had for so long. She didn't look too closely into her heart, for she was afraid she might find fear there, and she could not bear the thought that she was much less courageous than her sister.

She returned to the house, where she found Soaring Eagle and Tempest waiting for her.

"I do not understand this way of yours to marry, but I would have it done to please White Dove. You must tell me what must be done so that I do not shame her before her people," Soaring Eagle said.

"I do not think there is anything you could do to shame her, Soaring Eagle. My sister seems to love you very much."

"If it is as deeply as I love her, it is truly much. What do I do to make this ceremony right?"

Brittany started to explain the ceremony, and the answers to the words Aaron would ask.

"That is all?"

"Yes," Brittany laughed, "that's all."

"Then we must do this now, for I would take her back with me." He had an arm about Tempest and smiled down into her eyes with such an intense look of love that Brittany felt a surge of jealousy. She need only go to Night Walker. She need only . . . She refused to let her thoughts go any further.

"I will go and speak to Aaron now, and we will see how quickly he can perform the ceremony."

She left the two together and went in search of Aaron.

* * *

Night Walker had gone to Aaron almost at once, only pausing for a few minutes to control his wayward emotions. He wanted Brittany with every beat of his heart, and he was enraged at the things that kept them apart.

But he would not try to force her to acknowledge that they belonged together. She knew it as well as he did, and he would have to wait until she had the courage to face the truth.

Aaron read Night Walker's face as he approached.

"Something troubles you deeply, my friend," Aaron said.

"Yes. I am troubled by the words of the white trader."

"Daniel?"

"Yes. It was he who sent Brittany out alone to find me. It was he who told her that Tempest was meeting me in the forest. I believe he stirs up trouble to distract us from his own plans."

"What plans? And why would Daniel say such a thing to Brittany? He didn't know who Tempest was meeting. In fact, I didn't know he was aware that she was meeting anyone."

"There is only one way he could have found this out. He is behind those men who watch the mission . . . and I wonder if they do not watch our village, as well. There is something this man wants, and it is not a trading post."

"What, then?"

"I don't know. Could it be the yellow metal you call gold?"

"But why would he make everything complicated? Why not simply stay with the men you say are watching us and remain unseen?"

"I do not know . . . but I will find out."

"Night Walker, I will be marrying Soaring Eagle and Tempest, so they can return to the village. Will you go back with them?"

"No. I will stay long enough for this marriage; then I will go and try to find the answers I need."

"Night Walker, what's wrong? I have never seen you so angry or so troubled."

"It is nothing you can do anything about, my friend."

"Is it Brittany?" Aaron asked quietly. Night Walker looked at him in surprise. "Do you think I don't have eyes? I know how you feel about her. I do not know how she has responded."

Night Walker's face closed up. "She chooses not to come to me, but to go on teaching here."

"You have asked her?"

"Yes."

"Night Walker . . . what has happened between you?"

"Aaron, you are like a father to me, but this is a problem you cannot solve. Brittany must follow the trail of her choice. It does not matter that I would choose for us to walk it together. She will have to look into her heart and make her decision."

"And if she chooses to stay here?"

"Then," Night Walker said quietly, "I will never return to this mission. It is better that way. I am not strong enough not to beg her, and that would be no good for either of us."

Chapter Sixteen

There was a sudden bustle of activity at the mission, so no one missed Daniel, who had gone to his home and then to meet his cohorts. The communal hall was decorated, and there was not a man, woman or child who did not contribute something to make the affair perfect.

But it was when Brittany and Tempest were alone that they shared a rare moment, first of laughter and then of tears. Brittany was trying to improve her sign, so she used it as much as she could.

How I wish Mama and Papa could have been here, Tempest signed.

I know they must be watching and be pleased. They know you are happy. I shall write a long letter to James and make him understand just how right this is for you.

Your signing is better than you think. Tempest smiled. *Do you think Aunt Claudia would approve of us now?*

She would be breathing flames! Brittany laughed, and blinked back tears. *Be happy, Tempest.*

Tempest hugged Brittany and began to sign something else when there was a rap on the door. Brittany opened it to find a gathering of women from the mission. They had each brought Tempest a personal gift. Tempest was touched by their generosity and kindness. Brittany thanked them, trying to push all thoughts of Night Walker from her mind.

Soaring Eagle had been mesmerized by Aaron's explanation of the wedding ceremony, and he'd tried to keep Aaron's words in his mind. The ceremony seemed so much more complicated than his people were used to.

But one custom seemed familiar, and that was the gathering of everyone at the mission. In his village, too, all would gather when he and Tempest joined. There would be a joyous celebration.

As it turned out, the wedding ceremony proved to be more of a surprise to Aaron and Brittany than they had expected. When Aaron arrived at the part of the ceremony when Soaring Eagle was to say "I do," he spoke the words clearly and firmly. But when Aaron turned to the bride, Soaring Eagle stopped him.

He faced Tempest and made a sign. Tempest smiled. Then she said softly, "I do."

Brittany gasped in shock, and Aaron looked momentarily stunned. Then both of them felt their eyes fill with tears. Both were certain they had witnessed a miracle.

Brittany ran to Tempest's side and threw her arms about her, tears now running down her cheeks. She had never felt as happy, nor had she ever appreciated Soaring Eagle as she did now, for she knew it was he and the love he had for Tempest that had created this miracle.

Night Walker felt joy, too, mostly because there was such a glow of happiness on Brittany's face.

Brittany kept her eyes averted from Night Walker, but she knew he was watching her. She remembered his words well: he would not come to her again until she had made up her mind. Had she made any decisions since the day she had met him? He had filled her thoughts and her world, and that was why she was afraid. She had come among his people for the express reason of teaching them how to get along in her world. Her own ignorance was monumental, she thought, for she did not know how to get along in his world and she was afraid to try.

The thought occurred to her that she should go home, but she knew there was no peace to be found there, not when she would consider herself a failure.

Tempest had found herself, and had found both love and peace. She would be happy. Brittany had lost herself and didn't know how to find her answers. If she were willing to give up the dream that had brought her here, she would go with Night Walker. But she had only to look at Aaron to know she could not fail him. She had more than herself and Night Walker to consider.

When the short ceremony was over, Soaring Eagle and Tempest laughed and celebrated with the entire mission.

"Aaron, will you return with us now, and remain until the celebration at my village is over?" Soaring Eagle asked.

"No, you and Tempest go along. I will follow in the morning. I want to stay for a while, and I have some things that need to be completed here first, before I am distracted."

"My family and my village will begin preparations as soon as we return. You will not be long?"

"Just a day," Aaron replied. Then he turned to Tempest and signed. *I wish you all the happiness in the world. If you should need me at any time, you need only send word.*

Thank you, Aaron. I have only one request.
What?
Try to make Brittany understand that she should seek some happiness for herself.
I thought she did understand that.
Perhaps you should look closer, Tempest signed with a smile. She kissed Aaron's cheek and turned

295

to embrace Brittany; then she went to Soaring Eagle.

He had brought both their horses, and she could see his eagerness to be off. Aaron and Brittany assured them that they would follow, and then waved good-bye as Soaring Eagle and Tempest rode away.

Brittany fought her tears and her fears, wanting Tempest to be happy but still not quite certain about all that had happened.

"I'll make preparations, and we can leave at first light if you can be ready," Aaron said to Brittany.

"I'll go right away and gather some things. I have some gifts for Never Quiet and all the other children. I don't want to forget them."

"Night Walker, will you spend the rest of the night with us?" Aaron questioned.

Night Walker knew it would be best for his peace of mind if he left now, but he also knew that after her sister's marriage in the village he might not see Brittany again. He could not cut away the feelings he had for her cleanly as he knew he should. He wanted to be with her for as long as he could; these might be the only memories he would have to carry him through the rest of his life.

"Yes, I will ride with you in the morning."

"Then let's go have supper so I can pack some things." Aaron started away, expecting them to follow. But Night Walker took Brittany's arm and restrained her gently.

"I would speak with you."

"All right."

"Walk with me?"

Brittany fell into step beside him with no argument. She felt he might be going to ask her again to consider coming with him and she didn't know what she was going to say. The temptation to agree was a force that surprised her. She wanted to go with him! She wanted to lie in his arms and forget her responsibilities and the promises she had made! She wanted to be as courageous as her sister was . . . and as obviously happy.

Still, she could not turn her back on Aaron and her promise. He had gone to a lot of trouble to come east for her, and to make her feel so needed and welcome here at his mission. It didn't seem fair to leave him stranded.

She realized Night Walker was as silent and introspective as she was. They had been walking in silence for some time.

"What's bothering you, Night Walker?"

"I need to ask you a question, and I need your promise that you will tell no one what we speak of."

"Of course I promise, but what is so mysterious?"

"I would show you something."

"What?"

"Come to the trees, where we will not be seen. This is for no other eyes than yours."

Now Brittany was intrigued. What could he show her that was such a mystery? Beneath the heavy limbs of the trees they stopped. Brittany turned to face him, questions in her eyes.

"I would not trust many, but I feel you may have the answers I need."

"Answers to what?"

Silently he took the small pouch and untied the leather ties. Then he spilled the small pebbles out into the palm of his hand. It took Brittany only moments to realize both what he held and the significance of it.

"Gold . . . it's gold. Where did you get this?"

"From the stream a short way from here. Is it something of value?"

"It is something that some men would go to any lengths to acquire. Men have killed for this."

"Why?"

"In my world this is the wealth that gives men power," Brittany replied.

"So," Night Walker said half to himself. He had an idea what the strangers were about, and that the mission was somehow a threat to them. It worried him, and he was glad Brittany was going to the village for a while. He would consider what could be done to ensure her safety later.

Before Brittany could voice the million questions in her mind, Aaron called to them again and they moved from the trees to join him.

"I thought you two were as hungry . . ." Aaron began but he stopped at the sound of someone calling his name from a distance. All three turned to see Cole and three of his men riding toward them. "It's Cole," Aaron said in surprise. "I wonder what brings him out here now."

Night Walker cursed softly to himself. If Aaron did not know what drew the tall soldier, he did. Brittany. Cole was a handsome man and one of Brittany's kind. Night Walker fought a black tide of jealousy. Although Brittany did not seem over-joyed at seeing Cole, she did smile as he dismounted and approached them.

"Cole, my friend, what are you doing out here?" Aaron asked.

"I was on a routine patrol and thought I'd stop and see how you all are faring."

"We are faring well . . . in fact, we have for generations. Why should we change just because you have come?" Night Walker's voice was calm and cool.

"Because change is coming and there's nothing either you or I can do about it. Why can't we make the best of the situation, instead of haggling over it?"

"Your people do not haggle for what they want, they simply take it. I think my people are growing tired of that."

"I cannot speak for all my people any more than you can, Night Walker. But I would like to live in peace. I do not want to fight you or your people, but I have a leader just as you have. I can't go against his orders."

Night Walker knew Aaron trusted this man completely, and it annoyed him that Cole met his eyes directly and gave every appearance that he was speaking the truth. He wanted something to battle against, and Cole wasn't giving it to him.

Night Walker did something he had thought he would never do, and he was as shocked at himself as Aaron and Brittany were when he spoke.

"You have wanted to visit our village. Aaron has told me so many times. Why do you not come for the wedding of my brother?" He wanted Cole to see his village at its best . . . and he wanted to test this man and see where his heart lay. When Cole learned that Soaring Eagle was marrying a white girl, and with Aaron's blessing, Night Walker would have the test he needed.

"That's a wonderful idea," Brittany exclaimed, her eyes glowing.

"My men, too?"

"No," Night Walker said. "Are you afraid to come alone?"

Cole grinned. "I don't see why I should be. If Aaron has spent so many years among you, I cannot see why I should be in any danger, since I come at your invitation . . . and in trust."

Cole had called his bluff, and Night Walker looked at him with the beginning of respect. "We leave at first light. Maybe you should tell your men to make camp here."

"I intended to. They will wait for my return, and maybe when I do get back, I can arrange a meeting between your chief and mine."

"I will not speak for mine until he has spoken."

"Fair enough. I'll be ready to leave when you are. I'm looking forward to it."

Brittany had been watching the two men closely, and Night Walker could feel her eyes on him. He didn't want her anger, but he didn't fully trust the soldier either.

"We were about to eat," Aaron said. "Would you and your men care to join us?"

"Yes, thank you," Cole replied. He fell into step behind Aaron, and Brittany and Night Walker walked a few steps behind them.

The meal was a strange affair, for Night Walker remained stoically silent and more watchful than ever. He seemed to be searching for something in Cole, for he considered every word he said and watched his face every time he spoke. Brittany wondered just what it was Night Walker was looking for. Then suddenly it came to her. Night Walker trusted few white men, and he knew Aaron trusted this one. He was looking for a reason to trust, himself.

The meal over, Aaron had several duties that called him. Brittany went to her house to gather the gifts she had for those in the village. Night Walker and Cole were left to consider each other and seek some common ground.

Cole was surprised, as the conversation went from hunting to arms and their uses, to find Night Walker extremely intelligent. He even felt a bit ashamed that he had considered all Indians ignorant.

He was also soon aware that Night Walker had an engaging sense of humor, and the realization came to him that under other circumstances he

301

and Night Walker could have been friends.

Night Walker was caught in the same dilemma. He liked this tall man in the blue coat. He found him interesting to talk to and hard to hate. He heard thoughtfulness in the questions he asked about the village and the way of life there.

"I should like to learn as much of your language as I can while I am here."

"Aaron has been good for those in my village. He has taught many of us your language, as well. Before Aaron came, I could not have spoken to you at all."

"I know that it is a difficult thing to exchange ideas when you cannot speak the language of those you are dealing with."

"The hunters and trappers that have come among us have taught us, as well, for some of our younger ones speak their language, too. French, so Aaron says. They did not find our language hard to learn. Many of them have shared their knowledge with us and we with them. It was good for both, I think."

"Then why do you fight our presence so hard?"

"Because you do not want to come to learn, or to share knowledge. You come to take."

"Not all of us, not Aaron . . . not Brittany, and I think there are many of us that would come to share rather than to take."

Night Walker thought of the golden nuggets he carried and the men who watched the mission. There were also many who would come for the yellow metal and destroy whatever stood in their path. Should he trust this bluecoat with the secret? No, not yet, he thought. There were too many answers yet to find. And a woman with sun hair and emerald green eyes to protect. No, he would find out much, much more about this bluecoat before he trusted him.

They spent a few more minutes in conversation; then Cole said he had duties that called and he had to see to his men. Night Walker had chosen not to sleep in one of the houses at the mission. He much preferred to sleep some distance away, where he would be alone with his thoughts . . . and not so close to Brittany that he might lose control and go to her on his knees.

Daniel was furious when he learned that Soaring Eagle and Tempest had married. He cursed everyone from Aaron to Brittany to Night Walker and his own stepmother for trying to thwart his plans. Completely out of control, he demolished piece after piece of furniture in his house before he could stop himself.

In his mind he could hear his father call him a failure, and worse, hear Josephine's derisive laughter and taunting voice telling him he had let one deaf girl destroy what he wanted.

Slowly he pulled himself together. No, he would not let that happen. He would have the gold. He would have it if he had to destroy everyone in the mission! His plans would still work. He would just have to modify them slightly.

The next morning Night Walker wakened before dawn as he usually did, and swam in the nearby river before he went back to the mission. He found that everyone was still asleep, and he drifted to the house where he knew Brittany was. He stood a short distance away from it, and thought of how easy it would be to enter and to find her warm and still dewy-eyed from sleep. To take her in his arms and make love to her until he changed her mind.

He even found himself taking a step closer and caught himself. It would not do. He could not, for if he crossed the threshold of her house and took her in his arms, he would indeed beg her to come with him.

Suddenly the door opened, and Brittany came out. It happened so fast, he had little time to react. She paused, then crossed the distance between them and spoke softly.

"You are up early."

"And you are as well."

"I usually am. I like mornings. Besides, Aaron said he wanted us to leave early. I wouldn't be surprised if he was getting ready now. Night Walker?"

"What?"

"The gold you found, do you intend to tell Aaron about it?"

"Yes, soon. But there is nothing to do yet; there are many things to consider first."

"Like the men watching the mission? If it is gold they are after, why do they watch us? We have no interest in gold, and have certainly shown no signs of looking for any."

"Maybe that is why they watch. Maybe they think you might find what they have already found. I think the presence of this yellow metal means danger for you as well as for my people."

"What kind of danger?"

"They might think you stand in the way of their getting what they want. You are the ones who might recognize what they are looking for and know its value."

"Night Walker, we must talk with Aaron."

Before Night Walker could answer her, they heard the sound of an approaching horse and turned to look in that direction. Soon Daniel rode out from a stand of trees.

"It's Daniel," Brittany said.

"Why does he come here so early?"

"I don't know. To see Aaron, perhaps."

"Or to see you." Night Walker could not control the swift surge of jealousy that prompted his words.

"No, Night Walker," Brittany said positively. "I have never encouraged him to visit me."

"I do not think he is one to need encouragement," Night Walker said. Daniel grew too close for Brittany to answer. He stopped a short distance from them and dismounted. His look at Night Walker was quick and dismissive. His smile was for Brittany.

"Good morning."

"Good morning, Daniel. What brings you here so early?" Brittany asked.

"I have to talk to Aaron. I might ask what you are doing up so early."

"Aaron and I are going to the village today. Night Walker has invited Cole to my sister's wedding. I'm sorry you missed the ceremony Aaron performed."

"So am I," Daniel said with a forced grin. "Is Aaron up yet?"

"I suspect he is by now."

"I would like to talk to him. I'd best hurry." Daniel rode away, and Brittany glanced at Night Walker, who was following Daniel with a closed and very cold look.

Daniel found Aaron was indeed up and making preparations for travel. Using his best methods, he coaxed his way into being invited to go along. Aaron was put in a strange position. Daniel knew Cole was invited, and Cole had less to do with the village than Daniel did. If Cole was invited to come, then Aaron was forced to extend the invitation to Daniel, as well. Daniel accepted with such alacrity that Aaron felt he had been used.

If Aaron was not pleased at Daniel's presence, it was nothing compared to the way Night Walker felt. Still, he told himself, he would rather have an enemy before him than behind him, and he thought of Daniel Nixon as an enemy . . . one that must be watched closely, very closely.

A rather large group left for the village. Cole, Aaron and Daniel rode together, with Night Walker and Brittany a short distance behind. Behind them were Skinner, Thomas and three of the other men with their wives. All were talking happily. It was only Night Walker who listened while he continued to study Daniel.

Travel was slow, but easy. Brittany rode as well as anyone present with the exception of Night Walker. The conversations were light, and mostly between Cole and Night Walker, or Aaron and Cole.

Brittany could feel Daniel's eyes on her and they made her uncomfortable, but not as uncomfortable as Night Walker's closed look. Something was brewing in his thoughts, and Brittany would have given a great deal to know what it was.

When they arrived, the village was caught up in the excitement of the wedding that would be held the next day. There was unrestrained laughter, and it seemed to Cole they were offered food every time they stood still for a minute.

Cole was astonished at the number of tepees in the village. But if that surprised him, the reception they received was even more unexpected. There were none in the village who did not want to display their unity and strength to the whites who rode with Aaron.

Daniel smiled and put forth every effort to be friendly. This group of people was important to him, for when he rid himself of Aaron and his mission, he would deal with the Sioux directly.

Daniel was enraged at the idea of a marriage between Indian and white, although there were a number of pretty girls present he wouldn't have minded spending a few nights with. Still, with all the control he had, he congratulated Tempest and Soaring Eagle, and wished them well.

The celebration was wild and filled with joy. Daniel might have enjoyed himself if he had not been aware of how well Cole and the chief were getting along, not to mention Cole and Laughing Thunder. Guns and assorted weapons interested them both, and when Cole gave Laughing Thunder a rifle, the young man was nearly beside himself with pleasure.

Cole was enjoying himself more then he had thought he would . . . and certainly more than Daniel wanted him to. This did not fit into his plans at all. The last thing he needed was for the village and the military to become friendly.

By the end of the day, Daniel had decided that it was time to make a move to carry out some of his plans. He had no intention of Cole Young bringing the military and the Indians together. Something had to be done, and he had decided what that something was.

Evening came and fires were lit. Soaring Eagle was quick to draw Tempest away where they could be alone. Aaron and Cole were involved in a lengthy conversation, and Night Walker had persuaded Brittany to walk with him.

Night Walker and Brittany walked for a while in silence, and then he spoke. "I have told Aaron of the yellow metal," Night Walker said.

"I know you can trust him to tell you what is

best to do. If it were me, I should like to see the gold buried and forgotten, but I know that can never be. If it has been discovered, then it means trouble."

"These men must be stopped from telling others, or I am afraid there will be a flood of whites here, and then we must fight whether we wish to or not."

"Night Walker, I'm sorry."

"Sorry? Why should you be sorry?"

"I am sorry that my people have misjudged you so much, and that they . . . some of them wish you harm."

Night Walker smiled. "It is the same among us. It is not only your people who bring trouble, it is some of ours, too."

"There were natives among those you saw watching the village?"

"I think some have joined them, but not of our village."

"You have told Flying Horse?"

"No, I will seek out these men myself and watch some more. When I find out all I need to know, then it will be time to tell him."

"I wish they had never found such a thing. I wish—"

"What?" Night Walker spoke softly, seeking to keep the longing out of his voice. He wanted to beg her not to return to the mission. He thought she might be in danger there.

Brittany looked up at him and felt his unspoken longing. It was bitter, for she knew she would have to be the one to reach out to him . . . and she knew she wanted to with all her heart. But she could not live with him in the village and continue to teach at the mission. It was impossible. It was impossible to betray Aaron's trust that way. She owed him more than that, for it was Aaron who had led her sister to Soaring Eagle and happiness.

Night Walker gazed down into her eyes and a smothering pain filled him. How could he let her go? Why did he not just gather her up and flee, and not return until he had convinced her that she belonged to him?

But he knew his answer as soon as the thought formed. He wanted her to want him with the same intensity and the same depth of love that he wanted her. He needed her to freely choose to be with him. It could never be right any other way.

What made it worse was that he understood her sense of responsibility to Aaron, and her need to impart her love of learning to his people. She was a woman with a heart filled with love, and he wanted to share that love with her more than he wanted his next breath.

"I wish I could make things different . . . or make myself different."

"No, Brittany, I would not want you different. But I wish, also."

"And what do you wish?"

Despite all his desire for self-control, despite all his determination that he would not open his heart to another disappointment, the words came.

"That whatever gods command your life and

mine would find a way to join them, so that we need never be separated again. That they would be able to grant your wish and mine as well."

"You don't ask for much," Brittany laughed softly. But the laughter had a touch of tears in it, for their wishes were not so very far apart.

"I ask for the world," he said softly. "I ask for you. If all this yellow metal that lies so close to us was mine to do as I pleased with, I would dig it up with my bare hands and give it to these whites just to send them away. And I would give it freely. I wish you could see into my heart and know what I feel, but you cannot."

"You are right about those particular whites. They want all you have. But you are wrong about one thing."

"What am I wrong about?"

"That I do not know how you feel," she replied softly. "I do. If it were not for the mission and the debt I owe Aaron, I would go among your people and teach in the village."

He looked down into her green eyes. "Aaron and I have been friends for a long time, and this is the first time I have wished the mission gone." He looked away from her and drew in a deep breath. "I think you had best rejoin Aaron and his friends, before I shame myself and you by falling on my knees and pleading for something I already know you cannot give."

"Night Walker—"

"Just go, Brittany." His voice struggled for the coldness he was using as a shield.

Brittany knew it was useless to say any more. Besides, she knew she could find no other words to ease the chasm that had opened between them. She turned away and walked back to join Aaron.

The wedding ceremony was as mysterious to Tempest as hers had been for Soaring Eagle. The women had dressed Tempest carefully in soft white leather, trimmed with colorful beads and feathers. What delighted her was how perfect and handsome Soaring Eagle looked.

She had known he was happy, for he had told her often. But now his dark eyes glowed and his hands, which held her delicate, trembling ones, were warm and firm.

Shadow Heart, the holy man, spoke clearly in the soft, flowing language of his people, and though Tempest could not hear his words, she knew every one, for his woman stood beside him and moved her hands in sign.

When it was over, there was laughter and teasing that eventually led to the celebration, which lasted long after Tempest and Soaring Eagle had stolen away.

It was in the small hours of the morning that the festivities died down and the revelers went, drunk or sober, to their beds. In the shadows of darkness Daniel slipped from his tepee, found his horse quietly and rode away from the village.

He did not have to find his men. Since he had someone watching the village, they found him. He followed them back to the camp, where Jethro was stirred awake to hear his orders.

"We have the beginnings of a problem, and it's time for us to do something about it."

"What is it . . . and what do you want us to do?"

"That old fool at the mission has gotten the military interested in the village. One of them is there right now and they are getting along too well to suit me. Listen . . . this is what I want you to do." Jethro bent toward Daniel and listened to his words.

"I want the mission wiped out and I want Aaron Abbott done away with, along with that interfering teacher, Brittany Nelson."

"You want us to kill her, too?" Jethro asked.

"Yes. You know how to make it look as if they were attacked by Indians."

"All right, if that's what you want, that's what you'll get."

"Good. See to it as soon as Brittany and Aaron get back."

The men agreed, and stood silently until Daniel rode away. Only then did Charlie and Jethro exchange looks.

"Jethro, you gonna kill that girl?"

"I don't think so. I think she'll be good company for a while and we can get a real good price for her up north. When we finish here, I don't think I want to deal with Daniel Nixon again. You can't trust the son of a bitch. We'll take care of the mission . . . but we'll take the girl along."

"Yeah." Charlie's voice was thick with anticipation.

Brittany and Aaron lingered another day, enjoying the atmosphere of happiness in the village, but the next morning Aaron insisted he had things that had to be done, and that he must go. There was a tearful good-bye between the sisters, and a promise that Tempest would visit soon and often. Then reluctantly Brittany left with Aaron. It did not surprise her that Night Walker was nowhere to be seen. She knew the good-byes would have been too painful for both of them.

From a distance Night Walker watched them leave, and he fought the urge to ride after her and take her whether she wished it or not. Still, he knew any kind of force would only destroy what was left between them. He rode away, forcing his horse into a swift gallop as if he could outrun the feelings of frustration and misery that shattered him.

Soaring Eagle and Tempest watched Night Walker go with sadness. Both understood the thing that was tearing him apart, and both knew they were helpless before it.

Aaron and Brittany, along with Daniel, Cole, Thomas and the others rode in silence. Skinner did not choose to ride back yet, but had decided to remain with some of his old friends. Each rider was caught up in his own thoughts: Aaron and Brittany with bittersweet thoughts of Night Walker; Daniel with thoughts that were much more deadly. Aaron knew of Brittany's feelings, but he knew she was a woman who had to make decisions on her own, just as he knew it was her dedication to him and the children that held her. He could not tell her that she was no longer needed, for he knew she was invaluable and that she would recognize his lie. But he knew that if she had chosen to go, he would have given her his love and gone on the best he could.

Aaron thought of Night Walker and the years of friendship that lay between them. He knew that he would see little of the strong warrior until Night Walker had conquered his hunger for Brittany . . . and he did not think that would happen. Night Walker was not a man to give his heart easily, and not one to forget once it was given. Aaron wished he had the answers to this predicament.

Although he would have liked to remain longer, if only to be with Brittany when the formidable Night Walker was not around, Cole knew he had to return to the fort.

He was surprised when Daniel said he would ride back with him, that he had to go to Sioux Falls on business. Neither Brittany nor Aaron would say it aloud, but both were relieved to see Daniel go.

When they arrived at the mission, Brittany went at once to the small house she and Tempest had shared. She had thought to gather herself together there, but all around her were reminders that she would be separated forever from the sister she

SYLVIE SOMMERFIELD

loved so deeply. She would also be close to, yet a
million miles away from, the man she had come
to love. She felt as if her heart were breaking, and
threw herself on the bed to weep the tears she
would shed before no one else.

Brittany did not come to the communal building for the evening meal, and Aaron began to
worry. He crossed the compound and knocked on
Brittany's door. For a long moment he did not
think she was going to answer; then slowly the
door opened.

It was clear that she had been crying, even
though she smiled a tremulous smile.

"You did not come to eat and I was worried
about you. Brittany," he said gently. "I am here if
you feel you need to talk to someone."

"I . . . I'm not really hungry, Aaron."

"Then come for a walk with me. It will do you
good."

Brittany thought of the walks she had taken
with Night Walker and did not want to bring more
memories to her mind.

"I'd rather not. Let's sit here and talk. I . . . I
need your advice, Aaron. I also need you to know
and understand the decision I have made. I firmly
believe it is for the best."

Aaron wasn't so sure he would agree with her,
for he was reasonably certain of the decision she
had made, and just as certain it was going to make
her more unhappy every day. Still, he knew her to
be the kind of woman who made her decisions
and lived by them, no matter what. He wished

316

something would happen to change her mind.

Brittany closed the door after Aaron entered, and motioned him to a chair. "Please, make yourself comfortable, Aaron. Can I get you anything?"

"No, thank you . . . can I do anything for you?" The question was asked so gently that it brought tears to Brittany's eyes. She went to Aaron's side and sat on the floor at his feet. "What troubles you, Brittany? Is it Night Walker?"

"Yes."

"You love him?"

"Yes."

"Then why is it a troublesome thing?"

"Because . . . I do not have the courage of my sister, and because I cannot desert your school and the children who need me."

Aaron was about to argue when the sound of approaching horses came to them.

They looked at each other in surprise. Then the night was splintered by the sound of screams and gunfire. Brittany leapt to her feet as the door crashed open. Aaron's startled words were followed by a scream from Brittany.

Chapter Seventeen

Night Walker failed to put Brittany out of his mind. He remained alone the rest of the day, and in the early evening made himself a cold and lonely camp. He didn't want to return home until he had found a way to control his emotions.

As he sat before his low-burning fire he again tumbled the glittering pebbles from the pouch. This was gold, so Brittany said. This was a thing whites would give much for. But what was the connection between this gold, the people at the mission, those at the fort, and his village?

It was obvious those at the fort had no knowledge of the gold, for they had been close by for some time and had not come for it. So those watching the mission were the only ones who had interest in it. Why then did they not take more?

And why did they continue only to watch the mission? There was a missing piece of the puzzle, and if it meant danger to the mission, he meant to find it. If he did not and something happened there, it might take Brittany far enough away that he would never see her again. It was painful to know he could not have her, but it would be worse to know that he could never look into her beautiful green eyes or feel her presence again.

In the middle of the fire he could see Brittany's face, warmed by passion. He saw her soft mouth, whose sweet taste could drive him to distraction, and the gold of her hair falling about her like a scented mist.

He closed his eyes for a moment to drive the image away, but that only made matters worse. Then memories of sweeter moments claimed him and he could feel her, soft against him, her smooth skin warm as she curled into him. He could remember with his body and his senses what his mind fought so uselessly to forget.

For this time, this moment, he would allow it. But he knew that from this night on he must force himself to forget. He was a warrior and he was needed by his people. Whatever loneliness he had to suffer would forever remain locked in his heart.

For a long and sleepless night he tried, but had no success in freeing himself. If Brittany had been there, he would have surrendered everything to have her. But she was not there.

It was well past midnight and he lay caught in a dream when suddenly a feeling of abject terror swept over him. He sat up abruptly and could actually feel his breath shorten and his skin break out in a sweat. He was panting as he stood up, but, looking around, he saw no sign of any danger. Still, he sensed danger. For a man who had never tasted fear in his life, it was a dark and mysterious thing.

He felt a calling, as if he must run, as if he must stop a dire threat. Yet the night sounds remained the same.

Slowly he eased himself back down on his blanket and tried to slow his ragged breathing. He fought for control. There was no vision, no sign, no disturbance, yet just as suddenly he was filled with sorrow and a weary kind of pain, as if he was being torn in half.

For long moments he did battle with this strange, overpowering thing, but its power seemed to grow until he uttered a groan half of anger and half of fear. Fear of this ominous feeling, and anger that he could not seem to control it.

Then, as suddenly as it had come, it was gone, as if something had been smothered into quietness. But it left him drained and filled with another emotion he could not subdue. One of immense loss. It was as if part of him had been torn away.

He could not bear it a moment longer. He rose, swept dirt over the remains of his fire, gathered his things and rode back to the village.

* * *

Brittany gazed at the intruders with stunned disbelief. Neither she nor Aaron could fathom what was happening. Fear was soon to follow, for the shouts and cries from outside told a terrible story.

But why? Brittany's mind could not grasp any reason for this attack.

"What is this? What are you about? This is a mission and we are unarmed," Aaron said in as firm a voice as he could muster.

But the words were hardly out of his mouth before one of the men stepped forward and struck him across the face, knocking him to his knees. Brittany cried out and knelt beside him to see if he was badly hurt, but Aaron was more worried than hurt. There was no one to protect Brittany from the kind of men he knew these were.

Suddenly Brittany gasped in shock, for the next men who entered were two of those who had accosted her when she had ridden to find Night Walker.

Her face was pale as she slowly stood erect. She had never thought to taste such fear again, and she was as much afraid for Aaron as she was for herself.

"What do you want?" she demanded in a voice much less controlled than she desired it to be. Aaron rose to stand beside her, putting an arm about her waist. He could feel her trembling.

"This is unbelievable. We are an unarmed and

church-protected group. What do you want here?" Aaron said.

"For starters, old man," one man chuckled, "I'll take that pretty thing there. Come over here, girl."

"Do you realize what will happen if you touch her?" Aaron said firmly. He could feel the fear emanating from Brittany.

"Sure do. I'm gonna enjoy it." All the men laughed at that. "Now you move aside, old man, before I have to move you."

"The military will find you and hang you for this."

"I don't think so. They'll have someone else to blame." He came to Brittany and grasped her arm, pulling her close to him. She tried to struggle, but the gun he held was pointed at Aaron's head. She ceased her struggling.

"Now, that's a good girl. I have an idea you're gonna learn pretty quick, and I'm the man who's gonna help teach you." He turned to the other man. "Get the old man out of here."

"No!" Brittany cried as they dragged Aaron away. She had the terrifying thought that she would not see Aaron again. She fought the man who held her, but it was useless. His strength was much more than she could combat.

Shouts and gunfire, mingled with screams and cries of agony, beat against Brittany's consciousness. But the door was closed and she was left alone with this sadistic man, whose malicious smile matched the feral gleam in his eyes. He released her and she backed away from him.

"Come on, pretty thing. I thought you were going to learn easy. You can't get away, so it's better to cooperate."

"Cooperate!" Brittany spat. "Keep away from me! What are you doing with Aaron?"

"You just concentrate on me," he chuckled as he stalked her. She backed away from him, but there was no place to go.

Tauntingly he jumped toward her and when she jerked away he laughed. She could feel desperate tears in her eyes but she refused to weep and beg. It was what he wanted and she would be damned if she was going to submit.

Suddenly he leapt at her, grasping her dress, and she could hear his taunting laugh as the sound of rending cloth filled the room. Fight as she would, and she fought with all she had, the dress was soon in shreds and she stood in her shift, trembling but unbending.

He looked at her and was happy that the others were still busy outside. He would have her to himself for a while. Not too long, but long enough to be the first to sample the lush charms that had been revealed. This time he meant to have her.

She dodged and fought, but she was caught. She could feel his hungry mouth against her skin, and nausea swept through her.

She bit as he tried to kiss her and writhed in his arms . . . but she was forced backward until a table stopped her. Now there was no further retreat and she closed her eyes and tried to control her scream as his hands began to explore. Then the door crashed open again and her tormenter turned with a curse.

"Let her go, Charlie."

"Aww . . . Jethro, come on."

"Bring her along. We'll have time for that when we're away from here. I want this place burnt now." His attention went to Brittany and the picture she made. Her clothes barely covered her soft skin and sweet curves, and her gold hair flowed wildly about her. She was enough to awaken a dead man . . . and he was far from dead. "Come here, girl."

Brittany tried to gather her torn garment close to her, but she was not very successful. She moved slowly to Jethro's side and he took a minute to caress her shoulder, pleased with the smoothness of her skin.

"Wh . . . where is Aaron? What have you done with him?"

"Like all the others . . . he's dead."

"No," Brittany whispered. Hope drained from her and pain replaced it. "Everyone?"

"Everyone but you." Jethro's smile was as evil as that of the man who had attacked her before.

"Kill me now . . . I won't—"

"Oh yes . . . you will." He gripped her arm with a force that nearly broke her wrist. "Burn this place and come on. We have a lot of ground to cover. I don't want any of this squaw's Indian friends coming along to spoil our fun." He dragged Brittany from the house and toward his horse.

Brittany was aghast at the devastation about her. The whole mission was aflame and bodies were everywhere. Her friends! All who had welcomed and been so dear to her. All lost! She closed her eyes as she was lifted up on Jethro's horse. She couldn't bear any more . . . and she didn't want to see any more blood and death. Her thoughts now were on Night Walker . . . Night Walker and how wrong she had been not to have gone with him and shared his love. Now . . . there was no chance. Now . . . she knew the real and vital truth. She loved Night Walker completely.

Soaring Eagle wakened slowly, lying still with his eyes closed and savoring the soft warmth of Tempest nestled close to him. Her head was against the curve of his shoulder and one slim, white arm lay across his bronzed body. He didn't move, but opened his eyes to look down at her. A new surge of protective love flowed over him. She was so marvelously female, so gentle and sweet that he wanted to pull her within him and shield her so that no harm, no pain would ever come to her.

Her love for him was almost too wonderful to believe. Her strength of mind and heart were unique. She had given herself to him when both of them knew the world would frown in displeasure.

Every time he was with her was a wonder to him, but the night just past had been even more incredible. It was as if all other joinings had been

325

leading here and when she had become his wife, a vital force had been unleashed. The memory of the past night made his body respond.

He thought he heard a muffled giggle and looked down again into eyes warm with love and mischief. She had been awake and aware of his thoughts and his condition. He laughed warmly in response and gathered her close. Contentment held them so for a while, but soon Soaring Eagle sought more. They made love gently and tenderly, and so differently from the fierce passion of the night before.

A short while later Tempest drifted back into sleep, but Soaring Eagle rose slowly and quietly and left her side. He meant to give thanks, at the rising of the sun, to *Wakan Tanka* for the blessings that had been bestowed upon him.

But when he stepped outside, his gaze was drawn to a tall, familiar form that stood a good distance from him, beside a horse . . . Night Walker.

Soaring Eagle walked toward him. Although he didn't turn around, Soaring Eagle knew Night Walker sensed his approach.

"Night Walker, you are up early . . . or did you sleep at all? I saw you ride away. Where did you go?"

"I am sorry I could not celebrate with you as I wished. I needed . . ." He paused, for he could not put into words what his need was.

"I know," Soaring Eagle said cautiously. He did

not want to push Night Walker into saying more than he wanted to say. These two had shared more than most brothers and understood each other completely.

"Soaring Eagle, I must tell you of something strange that happened. Something I do not understand."

"I am here, brother," Soaring Eagle replied.

Night Walker went on to explain as best he could what had happened to him. He could see puzzlement awaken in his brother's eyes.

Neither man had heard Tempest approach, nor seen her intent look as she studied the brothers. She had learned long ago to read the emotions people displayed by posture and movement. She knew Night Walker had been abjectly miserable when Brittany left, but his expression now revealed much more. There was deep trouble here.

When she came to stand beside them, Soaring Eagle smiled down into her warm, blue eyes, and a feeling of agony tore through Night Walker.

Her swiftly moving hands questioned her new husband. *Is there something wrong?*

Night Walker is denying what he feels, but I believe he intends to go back to the mission. He is . . . uncomfortable. It is the first time he has worried about the mission's safety.

Tempest's hands moved quickly. *He should make Brittany admit the truth in her heart. I know she loves him.*

I hope you are right.

327

Perhaps . . . when Skinner goes back to the mission, Night Walker will ride with him.

Tempest then turned from him to Night Walker. There were questions in her eyes he could not answer.

Perhaps, she signed, *there is danger somewhere and somehow you are being warned . . . or called.*

Night Walker's gaze returned to her. He knew of the men who watched the mission. They meant danger in his mind. Had something happened? Were he and Brittany so attuned to each other that her cry for help could reach him in some way? He remembered well that he had gotten the vivid impression that he was being called, and he had fought the urge to run.

Had he ignored Brittany's cry for help? In his heart he knew a piece of him had gone with Brittany and would forever be in her possession. Surely there was a link between them that he would never understand. Only *Wakan Tanka* knew the truth of such things.

What is it, Night Walker? Tempest signed.

I don't know, Night Walker signed to her. *I must go.* He exchanged a look with his brother that did not pass over Tempest as he had hoped.

"I will ride to the mission, Soaring Eagle, and I will have Skinner go with me. If something is . . . wrong, I will speak with you first."

"What could be wrong?"

"I do not know . . . but—"

"But you are afraid something is?"

"What I felt last night was . . . fear. Fear, and I

do not know what else. But I must know if she is safe."

"Why do you feel she might not be?"

"I have told you of the men who watch the mission." Slowly he took the pouch and again the glitter of gold lay in his palm. "This is what they are after. I have told Brittany of this, and maybe she and the mission are more of a threat than she thought . . . or I thought. I should have been more careful. I should have remained close to her."

"You punish yourself for something you do not yet know is true."

Neither man had noticed Tempest's eyes widen at the sight of the gold. She reached out and took one of the nuggets from Night Walker's hand to examine it more closely, and both men looked at her.

This is gold, she signed.

Yes. Soaring Eagle returned her sign.

Where did you get it?

Soaring Eagle quickly signed all that Night Walker had said to him, and her eyes widened in fear.

Does my sister know of this, and does this put her in danger?

Now there was no way to conceal the harsh truth, to keep from her Night Walker's belief that Brittany had somehow reached out to him for help.

"Soaring Eagle, I hate to leave this bitter explanation to you, but I must go. It has been too long and I do not want to find"—he swallowed heavily—"I do not want to be too late."

329

"I understand. Go, I will explain all to Tempest and I will bring some of the men to follow you. If there is trouble, you will need our help."

"Tell Tempest—"

"Do not worry, brother. Go and do what must be done. Tempest will know."

Night Walker ran to find Skinner. Tempest would know, and she would have the strength of Soaring Eagle's love to lean upon. But who would fill the emptiness in him if something had happened to Brittany? With fear clinging to him, he rode toward the mission.

Tempest turned to Soaring Eagle and he knew there was no way to spare her this pain. Slowly he began to explain, and tears welled up in her eyes. All he could do to ease her hurt was to gather her into his arms and hold her close. Silently he prayed that there would be no further cause for tears. But this was not enough for Tempest. She was too afraid for Brittany.

You will follow Night Walker?

Yes, with some of the other braves.

And me.

No!

Yes. This is my sister and I could not bear it if she were to need me and I was not there. My dear husband—her eyes were pleading—*I must go . . . I must.*

Whether he liked it or not, Soaring Eagle knew this was true. He could not prevent her from going to the person she loved so much. Reluctantly he nodded.

Night Walker and Skinner rode as if all the devils of hell were on their heels. Deliberately Night Walker closed his mind to the fears that tried to strangle his thoughts. He had to find her safe! He would find her safe! He had to or he could not face another day.

To him time seemed to be stretched beyond endurance. Had it ever taken this long to reach the mission before? Finally he saw that they were drawing near. Then, with a groan of despair he jerked the halter of the horse to bring him to a dirt-scattering stop. He gazed at the sky where curls of grey smoke were spiraling upward and a group of black birds circled.

"No," he muttered under his breath. "No." But he did not deceive himself about what he was seeing. He exchanged a wordless look with Skinner, whose face had gone grey. Kicking their horses into motion, they raced over the crest of the last hill and down the rough terrain toward the disaster unfolding before them.

All Night Walker could do was silently plead: *Brittany . . . Brittany, be alive, Brittany, please be alive.*

He came to a stop and gazed at the destruction. The buildings were burned . . . all of them. Only the chimneys still stood among the smoldering ashes. The school had been destroyed, too, and his heart wrenched. All that was precious to Brittany was gone.

The worst were the bodies, some lying burned and indistinguishable among the blackened ashes. But he saw no sign of Brittany or Aaron.

They dismounted and moved slowly, Night Walker's darkened eyes missing nothing. Fear kept step with him as he examined every body, reluctantly looking for a familiar face. A slow, fierce, black rage was growing in the depths of him, controlled only by the need to find the one who was so precious to him.

But there was no sign of her. He turned finally toward the school. Had she run there to protect what was so valuable to her, and died in its ruins? His heart was pounding furiously against his ribs and he fought to control the agony of uncertainty blended with the misery of draining hope.

He did not realize that tears stained his face and that he had clenched his jaw to control the need to scream out his fury and his pain.

Why had he let her go! He punished himself over and over, blaming himself for her fate. Why had he let her go!

But the ashes of the school revealed nothing, and a flicker of hope returned, for there was no sign of Aaron either. Maybe Aaron had somehow gotten Brittany away. But the hope died when he heard the groaning, half-whispered sound of his name.

The corner of the school had somehow remained standing and the sound had come from there. Quickly he circled it and dropped on his knees beside a dirty and bloody Aaron. Skinner hurried to Aaron's other side, and surprisingly his eyes were filled with tears. He took Aaron's hand gently in his. Aaron was in such a condition that Night Walker could hardly tell if he was burned or direly wounded. There was a great deal of blood mingled with the blackness of ashes.

Tenderly he lifted Aaron's head and watched his eyes flicker open; a twisted and painful smile touched his lips.

"Night Walker . . . Skinner," Aaron gasped, "I had hoped—"

"Aaron . . . how badly are you wounded?"

"I don't know. They left me for dead. Perhaps I am close to that. But I have to believe . . . I had to get help . . ."

Now Night Walker asked what he feared to know. "Aaron . . . where is Brittany? I can't find . . . I can't find her."

For a moment Aaron's eyes closed as he tried to gather his strength. It brought a soft groan of agony from Skinner. But Aaron only struck more fear into Night Walker. He was certain now that she lay dead somewhere nearby and he had not seen her.

"Aaron . . . please . . . where is she?"

Aaron's eyes opened slowly and again he fought the black cloud of unconsciousness.

"They came—" he gasped.

"Who? Who came, Aaron, who?"

"I didn't know them. They thought to make us

believe they were Indians of your village, but they were not. They were whites. Brittany—"

Again Night Walker sucked in a deep breath while he waited for the fateful words to come.

"Brittany," he prompted. "Where is she, Aaron?"

"They . . . they took her with them. Night Walker, leave me! Go after her. They took her with them!"

Now Night Walker was torn. Aaron was badly hurt and he needed help. But Brittany had been taken, and he remembered the time he had found her being attacked. He had no doubt these men were part of the group that had taken her, just as he had no doubt about what her fate would be if he didn't find her . . . and soon.

Still, he could not let Aaron lie in the dirt and die of wounds if he could aid him.

"Skinner, we will have to see that Aaron is taken to the fort as quickly as possible."

"Sure, sure, we kin do that."

"No!" Aaron groaned. "You damned young fool. Leave me. Go after her!"

"I cannot let you die."

Despite all of Aaron's protests, Night Walker set about examining the extent of his wounds. They were worse than he had thought at first glance.

Grimly he rose to his feet. He had to get some water to clean Aaron's wounds. His body and hands were busy with the task, but his mind and heart were with Brittany. He would find her . . . he had to.

Aaron begged and pleaded for Night Walker to

leave him and go, but Night Walker silently ignored him. Then Aaron breathed a sigh of relief when he heard other riders coming and Night Walker rose.

"Soaring Eagle," he said softly, giving thanks to all the gods for his brother's speedy arrival. He was not surprised to see Laughing Thunder and several other braves with them. But he was shocked to see Tempest, and only Soaring Eagle's quick look and grim shake of the head kept him from sending her back to the village immediately. Tempest wept openly and knelt by Aaron to hold his hand. The shock of all she saw about her was evident in the greyness of her face and the trembling of her body.

Night Walker was grateful for Soaring Eagle, for now he could go on with his search for Brittany. Soaring Eagle reached his side quickly.

"Night Walker, what has happened here? Who has done this?" Soaring Eagle began. Then he saw his brother's eyes. "Where is Brittany?"

"They have taken her."

"Taken her? Who? Where have they taken her?"

"Soaring Eagle, do not ask what I cannot answer. There is much that needs to be done. Aaron needs to be taken to the fort, where they can treat his wounds. And the bluecoats must know the truth of this. And Tempest must be taken from here, too."

"I will go with you," Soaring Eagle protested.

"Yes, I will need you." He turned to his younger

brother. "Laughing Thunder, you must do this for me. You and Skinner make a travois, and take this—" He took the pouch from his belt. He explained what it held and why it was so important to the whites and what they might do to have it. "Get Aaron to the fort as quickly as you can. With Aaron's words and this to help explain, the soldier Cole Young will understand. We cannot have our village blamed for this. It will cause a war between us and the whites."

"And you?" Laughing Thunder questioned, fighting the fear that twisted in him at the prospect of going to the fort.

"Soaring Eagle and I will follow and free Brittany. I will kill as many of them as I can. Then I will come to the fort. We do not know who is behind this . . . but I have my thoughts and I will find the answer. You must do this, brother, for Aaron is in bad condition."

"He will live?"

"He must live, or the whites at the fort will never believe we are not responsible for this. You walk with great danger, Laughing Thunder. Be careful and guard yourself and Aaron well. Skinner will speak to them, too, but we cannot trust that they will believe him, either."

"I will . . . but I will follow your trail later and seek you out. You will need help."

"Once the bluecoats believe you . . . if they believe you, it would be best if Cole Young and some of his men come with you."

"I will do as you say, Night Walker. But if Aaron

should die . . . if the whites do not believe, I will still follow. It has been hard also for Soaring Eagle to face Tempest, and tell her her sister is gone. Now we must find her."

"I know. Go then. See to yourself, brother. Don't let the whites catch you unprepared. I need you."

Laughing Thunder nodded and watched his brother stride toward his horse. He had seen Night Walker angry before, but he had never seen him like this. Yet he knew and understood. If any of his family had been taken, he would feel the same. In a way he felt sorry for the whites when Night Walker found them. If Brittany were hurt or dead, he would show no pity.

Night Walker and Soaring Eagle had no difficulty picking up the trail. Night Walker hoped Laughing Thunder would get Aaron to the fort safely and that Cole Young would believe him. But all his concentration was on finding the men who had committed this horror.

He fought to keep his mind from imagining Brittany in the hands of such monsters, for it would drive him out of control and he needed all the control he had.

He had fought the visions that had nearly broken him and now he was grim and silent as he followed the tracks of a number of horses. It had not been many hours since the mission had been attacked, and he was certain the riders did not think they were being followed. But if they

SYLVIE SOMMERFIELD

stopped . . . he had to force that thought from his
mind. He couldn't stand it.

Morning Sun . . . Morning Sun, gentle, sweet
Morning Sun. No matter how he tried to push her
image to the back of his mind, she crept in. Her
gentle touch, the way her eyes crinkled at the cor-
ners when she laughed, the velvet of her voice, the
way her skin felt . . . He felt a sharp stab of pain.
Had he lost her . . . had he lost her?

He reached in desperation for rage; it was the
only thing that would help him retain his sanity.
Soaring Eagle did not speak, for he understood his
brother's emotions. Had it been Tempest they
were searching for, he would be insane with fear.

The trail was not easy; the riders were not careless. But Night Walker didn't lose it. He was a cold
and relentless force. Night Walker touched the
knife at his belt and adjusted the bow strung
across his chest. A strong bow, and a quiver of
deadly arrows.

On and on they moved, and the further they
went, the more pleased he was. The riders were
afraid to stop and when they did they would be
tired, on edge and much less attentive to what was
going on around them. They would be careless.

338

Chapter Eighteen

Jethro was considering how he could decrease the number of men who rode with him. He would pay the Indians he had recently hired, giving them the guns and whiskey they demanded; he would also dismiss the extra gunmen he had hired to complete the job they had just finished. He only wanted two of his closest companions to go north with him . . . and to share the girl.

He held her before him on his horse and had been enjoying her near-naked warmth. He meant to be first . . . and to enjoy her for a long, long time before he sold her . . . if he sold her.

"Jethro?" Charlie said in a complaining voice. He just didn't like the idea that Jethro had the girl. After all, he'd gotten hold of her first. He should be the first.

"What?" Jethro replied shortly.

"When we gonna stop? Hell, they ain't nobody on our trail. Besides, I'd kind of like to start a little party with the pretty lady."

"Before too long, Charlie." Jethro smiled. "I'm going to get rid of the others before we make a more permanent camp."

"Damn good idea."

Brittany tried to ignore the words and the way Jethro continued to touch and caress her. He'd enjoyed her fighting him, and now she refused to acknowledge that he existed.

He bent to inhale the sweet scent of her hair and brushed his hand across the fullness of her breast. Brittany quivered, but controlled the reaction. She heard him chuckle softly as he bent close to her ear.

"You pretend all you want, girl, but I'll make you moan and beg when I have the time. Soon . . . real soon, all you'll have to think about is pleasing me. Maybe like you pleased that big buck who stopped my boys from havin' some fun."

"You're an animal. A beast, and Night Walker is more man than you'll ever hope to be."

"Now you don't really know that, little lady." He laughed. "Wait until I give you a sample or two. You might like it."

"About as much as I like the scent of skunk. Rape is the best a man like you can do. No woman in her right mind would want you. Murderer, thief, coward."

340

"She sure is a spicy one, ain't she, Jethro?" Charlie said.

"That's okay, I like a lot of spice. It only makes taming 'em more fun."

Brittany remained quiet, but she struggled to put the scene they had described out of her mind. She would find a way to kill herself before she gave them any satisfaction.

The trip to the fort had been slow, silent and to all but the nearly unconscious Aaron, it had seemed to go on forever.

During the journey Laughing Thunder had considered all he must say to convince the soldiers to go to Night Walker's aid. After all, they owed Night Walker nothing. For the first time in all the years he could remember, he was afraid he might fail.

Tempest could think of nothing but Brittany, and she prayed that Night Walker and Soaring Eagle would find her safe and unharmed. She refused to consider the terrifying pictures that struggled to form in her mind. She had seen Aaron . . . she could not think of her sister hurt that way, or worse, unhurt and at the mercy of the men who could do such a thing.

When they finally approached the gates of the fort, Laughing Thunder called a halt. He didn't want to sacrifice any men, so he rode closer to the gate with Tempest and Skinner beside him.

The young sentry on guard was amazed at what he was seeing. He had been at the fort for nearly

341

a year and had never seen an Indian before. Laughing Thunder was not only the first, but he was the most impressive Indian the young man had ever seen.

So impressed was he that Laughing Thunder had come within a hundred feet of the gate before the sentry even thought to call down and challenge him.

"I am Laughing Thunder from the village of Flying Horse. Tell Cole Young that I bring a wounded white man from the mission, the gold-haired, silent one and a message from Night Walker."

"Tell him it's me, too," Skinner shouted. "Skinner Mackenzie. Tell him to hurry."

"Y'all stay put right there. I'll take your message to the colonel."

Laughing Thunder had no idea of the rank among the military so he took it for granted the sentry had gone to bring Cole. Pleased that all was going to be all right, he waited.

Colonel Brady was given the message by the excited trooper and was frankly surprised. He sent for Cole at once. Cole was there within minutes, for he had already heard of the Indian outside the gates who had asked for him. It had to be Night Walker, he thought, and was more than pleased. Aaron had told him long ago that Night Walker had always adamantly refused to come to the fort, so his arrival seemed to be a good sign. He was smiling when he went into the colonel's quarters, saluted and waited to hear what was going on.

"You know an Indian named Laughing Thunder?" Brady questioned a bit belligerently.

"Laughing Thunder?" Cole questioned, surprised.

"That's what he said his name was. What the hell is he doing outside my gate, asking for you? Skinner Mackenzie's with him and that woman, the one who can't hear. She's with him. I don't know if the Indian is using them to get inside the fort."

"One woman and one brave? I doubt it. You can trust this, he wouldn't have come here if it wasn't something very important, and Tempest wouldn't be here if there wasn't a problem."

"Go. See to it. Find out what that red devil wants."

"I beg your pardon, sir. But Laughing Thunder is not a red devil, as you put it. He's an intelligent young man who would keep his distance from us if he had a choice. When I went to the mission last, Aaron took me to the village. I met Laughing Thunder and his older brothers, Night Walker and Soaring Eagle. I think we can deal quite well with them, sir."

"Do you now? Well, go and see what he wants."

"Yes, sir." Cole saluted, spun about and was gone before Brady could add anything else.

As Cole rode out through the gate he spotted the group that waited beyond Laughing Thunder, and the travois. Someone was hurt, and the chances were that, since they had brought the injured person here, he was white.

"Laughing Thunder, Skinner, what brings you

SYLVIE SOMMERFIELD

here?" Cole asked, stopping beside them.

"Much trouble, bluecoat. My brother Night
Walker has sent me. I bring Aaron to you for care.
He has been badly wounded."

"Wounded! How?"

"He needs care at once. Bring help and I will tell
you of Night Walker's words."

Cole nodded and sent for help. "Tell me. There
must be trouble if Night Walker purposely sent
you here. He is not too enamored of our fortifi-
cations."

For a second Laughing Thunder looked at him
blankly because he couldn't understand a thing
Cole had said. The whites were a mysterious lot;
they spoke circles around a problem and never
came directly to the point.

Laughing Thunder began the explanations as
Night Walker had told him to do, and watched
shock after shock cross Cole's face. When he was
finished, Cole rode to look down on the travois.
He could see that Aaron had lost consciousness.

"Come, follow me into the fort." At Laughing
Thunder's hesitation, Cole held his gaze. "It will
be all right. You will be as safe there as I was at
your village. You have my word."

Laughing Thunder considered this and nodded
his head.

The group of Indians were silent as they rode
into the fort. Laughing Thunder was certain neither he nor the warriors with him had ever been
so wary or so nervous. He wondered if Cole had
felt like this when he had come to their village.

But soon Esther Brady was bustling toward Tempest, and she took her gently in her arms and led her away. If any of the whites were upset that she had married an Indian, they gave no sign of it; Esther was a formidable force no one wanted to tangle with.

Aaron was gently lifted and taken to the infirmary. Cole led Laughing Thunder and the rest to Colonel Brady's office.

"A massacre! A damn massacre!" Steven nearly shouted.

"Flying Horse's village was not responsible for this," Cole said calmly. He was well used to anger when Steven was frustrated or shaken.

"Who is?"

"This is." Cole threw the pouch down on the desk before the colonel. It was opened and several of the nuggets rolled out. Steven gazed at it in profound shock.

"Good God, it's gold."

"Yes. It seems the gold was on mission property and someone not only wanted it, but wanted the mission eliminated."

"What's going on here, Cole? I've a feeling we're being diddled and I don't much care for it."

"Yes, sir, we are. I think someone intended to use us to make sure the mission is not rebuilt and to see that Flying Horse's people are blamed for the attack. I don't much like it, either, because I've made some friends at the village and I'd like them to be left in peace."

"Laughing Thunder." Steven looked the calm young man over carefully. "Tell me exactly what you saw at the mission."

As best as he could, Laughing Thunder told of the destruction they had found at the mission and how Night Walker had sent him to the fort while he tracked the men who had wounded Aaron. "And the men who have taken Brittany away. He will find her, this I can promise you. I do not believe that he will bring any of them back to confess."

"That is a job for the military, and as soon as we can muster a troop we'll go after them."

Cole kept his opinion to himself. He realized that Laughing Thunder had meant he did not believe they would find anyone to deal with by the time Night Walker was done with the attackers. Before the colonel could speak again, another soldier appeared in the doorway.

"Sir, Mr. Abbott is asking for . . . this man." He gestured toward Laughing Thunder. "And Lieutenant Young. Doctor says you'd best come pretty quick. He's in a bad way."

"We'd best go," Steven said.

There was no doubt in anyone's mind that Aaron was gravely injured. They gathered close to his bed and grew quiet. Aaron's face was white and his breathing was shallow. At first, no one thought he would be able to speak. It seemed a struggle, but at last the eyes of the wounded missionary did flutter open. He saw Tempest first, who had never left his bedside. She had nursed him gently and lovingly.

When Aaron began to speak, it was in short, gasping sentences. But speak he did, making it clear to Steven and all the others that it was white men who had perpetrated the atrocious attack and not Indians.

Laughing Thunder quickly made the sign to explain all he could to Tempest. Then he returned his gaze to Aaron. Aaron's worry for Brittany was voiced, and all were surprised when it was Laughing Thunder who bent to lay his hand over Aaron's.

"Night Walker has followed their trail. You know he will find them. He will bring his woman back and he will punish the men who have done this to you and to those you love. Be at peace, Aaron. Rest and regain your health. We would not spend more time here than we must. My friends and I will follow the trail Night Walker and Soaring Eagle will leave for us. All will be well." He added the last but he wasn't too sure of the truth of it.

His woman, Cole thought as he cast a look at the colonel. Steven was watching Laughing Thunder with a look that had long since gone past surprise.

"Lieutenant Young."

"Yes, sir."

"Gather a troop." He looked at Laughing Thunder as he spoke. "You lead us to the trail your brother has left and we will follow."

347

Laughing Thunder smiled for the first time since he had come into the fort. Perhaps there were some whites who might be able to listen after all.

Laughing Thunder looked back at Aaron whose eyes had closed again. He sent his prayers to every god he knew that this good, kind man would live to see what his courage had wrought.

They rode from the fort less than an hour later. Laughing Thunder knew they had to go all the way to the mission to find the trail Night Walker had left.

They rode at a steady pace, eating up the distance between the fort and the mission. Laughing Thunder and the warriors with him were silent, but they were fascinated by the rigid military bearing and the accoutrements of the soldiers.

When they came to the mission, more than one soldier's face blanched. Grimly Cole ordered a burial detail to remain behind to bury the dead.

It took Laughing Thunder very few minutes to find where his brother had began his search. From there the going would be easier because Night Walker had carefully left a clear trail.

Laughing Thunder kept his thoughts to himself but he was worried. Tempest must be beside herself, and he hated to think how frightened Brittany must be. He already had a good idea of what his brothers were suffering. He was frightened that what he might find at the end of this journey was going to be a bigger tragedy than the one they had left behind.

Jethro was successful in ridding himself of the extra men he had gathered. With several guns and jugs of whiskey they were satisfied. The white woman didn't interest them. The group consisted now of only three men. Mingo had a feeling deep inside that Night Walker was the kind of man to follow and to kill. Jethro and Charlie were more complacent. Now they had only to wait at the meeting place for Daniel and to decide how the gold was to be shared.

"Daniel's gonna be real put out about you takin' the girl and not killin' her back at the mission like he said."

"Daniel don't need to be told. What he don't know won't hurt. We'll get rid of her before he shows up."

"Yeah . . . yeah," Charlie replied. Brittany turned to look at him and he grinned. She turned her head away, disdain flushing her cheeks. She felt a wave of nausea wash over her. Daniel . . . Daniel Nixon. He was behind this terrible tragedy. His hands were red with the blood of so many wonderful people. She only prayed she would have the chance to make the world know what he had done.

Daniel sat over a brandy in Sioux Falls and smiled to himself as he savored it slowly. Savored it and the thought of what was happening while he was here. All his plans were being carried out. He need only go back and appear as shocked as everyone else. But the mission and the interfering workers there would be out of his way.

With a massacre such as this, it would not be long before the military forced Flying Horse's people to move to a reservation. The gold would be his for the taking. He had never felt so pleased or so successful in his life. No matter how many lives it had cost, the gold was his!

The sun was lowering toward the horizon, bathing the world in a red-gold glow. Brittany had never felt so exhausted, but still she refused Jethro's help in dismounting.

Her legs felt like rubber and she was intensely hungry. But she did not wish for time to pass. After the evening meal she would face hell. She wanted to curl up in a ball and cry.

Jethro and Charlie built a fire and began to prepare the evening meal. Mingo dragged Brittany to a nearby tree and tied her hands together. Then he tied her to the tree with a length of rope that gave her some space to move.

Brittany watched them with scorn as they filled their tin plates and concentrated on eating. Of course they would eat first and not even consider her well-being. She gathered her courage together. She would think of nothing but Night Walker. If she had to go through this ordeal she would cling to him. Fiercely she struggled to clear her mind of everything but him.

It was Jethro who finally brought her a plate of food. Brittany wanted to throw it back in his face. But she knew she would be needing strength, and that eating would create a delay of several precious minutes more. She took the plate after he had untied her hands, and she began to eat.

She knew their eyes were on her, and despite her best efforts, she felt fear well up in her until she could not choke down another bite of food.

When Charlie took a bottle of whiskey from his pack, her terror only grew worse. Alone and afraid, Brittany was facing three beasts who might soon be so drunk they would not care what they did with her.

Jethro, Charlie and Mingo handed the bottle back and forth.

Despite the urgency of the situation and the stubborn desire of all the men to continue, night began to fall and the trail became impossible to follow. Finally, even Laughing Thunder, who was the last to surrender, had to give up. They stopped and made camp.

After the others had rolled up in their blankets and gone to sleep, Laughing Thunder and Cole remained awake. They were seated by the fire and had not spoken for some minutes. It was Cole who broke the silence.

"Laughing Thunder?"

"Yes."

"You said Brittany was Night Walker's woman. Is that true?"

"It is true in many ways, but not all."

"I don't understand."

As best he could, and as far as he knew, Laughing Thunder tried to explain the choices Brittany had made.

"It is different between Tempest and Soaring Eagle. Soaring Eagle is fortunate that he found her and that she smiled at him."

"So Brittany decided she would stay with Aaron."

"No," Laughing Thunder said gently. "She decided she would honor the promise she gave Aaron and the decision to teach the children. She has Night Walker's love; she also has his respect."

"I wish it could be different."

"So do I."

"Well, I'm going to get some sleep. You?"

"No, I will remain here for a while."

Left to himself, Laughing Thunder allowed his mind the freedom to think of something other than the trail he had to follow.

"Where are you, Night Walker?" he said softly to himself. "What have you found? Is death there, or have the gods smiled on you?" He thought of Tempest and Brittany and how bitter it would be to return home with any other news than that Brittany had been found and was safe in Night Walker's arms . . . where he knew she belonged.

Night Walker sensed that he was closing in on his quarry. He slowed. They had to be very careful now. When the tracks had shown that several of the party had separated from the others, he'd been forced to make a choice. But he'd hesitated only for a moment. Logic had told him Brittany would be with the three who had changed direction. He'd ignored the larger group and followed the smaller one, praying he was right.

Now Night Walker was as tense as the bow he carried. Every sense he had was alerted to the sounds and scents about him. In the darkness they could no longer follow the horses' tracks, but the forest was his domain and he could distinguish every sound and smell. The scent of wood smoke drew him now. They were nearing a camp.

Night Walker and Soaring Eagle exchanged glances. Neither had any idea of what they might find, but they knew they had only the advantage of surprise, for there had to be at least three men in the camp.

Slowly and cautiously they dismounted and tied their horses a good distance away from where the glow of the campfire could be seen. When they were close enough to distinguish figures, they were pleased to find there were only three men. Night Walker smiled to himself . . . three dead men. But before they died he meant to have the answers . . . the names of the people behind this tragedy.

Night Walker motioned to Soaring Eagle, holding up three fingers. Soaring Eagle nodded. Then Night Walker motioned for Soaring Eagle to go around so they could approach the camp from two separate directions. Confusion would give them those precious seconds it would take to reduce the numbers and protect Brittany during the attack.

SYLVIE SOMMERFIELD

It took only seconds of swift hand signals for
Night Walker to make his plan clear to Soaring
Eagle, who nodded silently, his face grim and his
eyes reflecting a murderous fury. They separated.

Brittany kept her eyes on Jethro and his companions. She had never been so afraid in her life.
She had hoped they might be tired and groggy
from drinking. Perhaps they would fall asleep.

They sat close to the fire, but Brittany was firmly
tied to a tree some distance away. In her state of
near nakedness she shivered with the cold chill of
the night air.

The ropes were scraping her arms and wrists,
but she was afraid that if she moved and called
their attention to her it would be disastrous. She
remained still and quiet. Then she leaned her head
back against the tree, closed her eyes and drew
from her memory every precious moment she had
shared with Night Walker.

Mingled with these memories were thoughts of
Aaron and his dreams. Dreams that she would
carry on for him as best she could if she lived
through this nightmare.

With her eyes closed she didn't see Jethro stand
up and start in her direction, nor did she hear him
as he walked slowly to stand over her.

Jethro looked down on Brittany and felt the
blood within him begin to heat. With her soft flesh
glowing in the light of the fire and her golden hair
tangled about her, she was a vision such as he had
never seen before.

Suddenly Brittany became aware that someone was close by. Startled, her eyes flew open. She had no trouble reading his heated gaze, and an involuntary sound was drawn from her.

Jethro released the ropes that bound her and gripped her wrist in an iron hold. Relentlessly he drew her to her feet and close to him. She saw him smile at her ineffectual resistance, and suddenly a white-hot rage filled her. She was not going to submit to this cold-blooded murderer without using every bit of strength she had.

She struggled, kicking out furiously. Jethro laughed as she fought his embrace and the two at the campfire watched the conflict with interest. They knew what the outcome would be. Jethro outweighed Brittany by ninety pounds and he was a strong man. They would have their turn when Jethro had tamed her spirit a bit.

Night Walker stood just outside the range of light from the campfire with the darkness of the forest surrounding him. Jethro might have tasted fear if he had seen Night Walker's face. His eyes blazed with vengeful fury. It was obvious that Jethro led the other men, and he had put his hands on Brittany. That was enough to seal his death. The only thing Night Walker waited for was the signal from Soaring Eagle that he was in place and ready. After a few minutes it came, the calling sound of a night bird. Night Walker stealthily took his bow from his shoulders, reached into his quiver and drew forth an arrow. Slowly he fitted the arrow to the bow, drew back with all his strength, held his breath to aim, and let go. The arrow sang, accompanied by the hum of Soaring Eagle's arrow. The two men seated at the fire dropped without a sound.

Too caught up in the pleasure of bringing Brittany under control, Jethro was unaware of what had happened until Night Walker's cold voice cut the night air.

"Take your hands from my woman, white-eyes."

Jethro spun around, but he had the presence of mind to hold Brittany close to him. Night Walker stepped from the shadows and Jethro sucked in a harsh breath. He was looking into the eyes of death.

In a quick move he drew his knife and pressed the point to Brittany's throat.

"Don't come any closer or I'll cut her throat."

"Night Walker." Brittany said his name like a prayer, and her gaze met his. "I knew you would come."

"Shut up, woman," Jethro snarled. "His coming here makes no difference. He will only have to witness your death if he takes another step."

"Aaron?" Brittany asked fearfully, ignoring the prick of the knife against her flesh.

"He is alive," Night Walker said gently. "Have courage."

"Yes," Brittany replied in a whisper.

"You damn fool. Back away and saddle my horse. Your woman and I will be riding away, and if you even try to stop me or follow, you'll have her dead body on your hands."

"She will not die here this night, but maybe you will . . . after you have told me what I want to know. Think carefully, if you choose not to die."

"You're crazy. Get to that horse." Night Walker remained immobile, his hot gaze locked on Jethro, and Jethro could feel his bravery slip away. Was this man insane? Didn't he realize Brittany could die before his eyes? "I said get to that horse and saddle it."

"Why? You will not be using it."

Jethro grasped Brittany tighter, causing her to gasp as her breath was forced from her. The knife was forced a little closer until a thin trickle of blood ran down her skin. Night Walker grimaced and his jaw grew rigid.

"Saddle that horse, or by God she will die here right in front of you. It won't be easy. I'll cut her throat slow so you can see her pain." Night Walker took a step or two toward them, and Jethro's face assumed a look of disbelief. He had no choice. Anger bubbled up in Jethro. He was not going to allow this Indian to intimidate him. He held Night Walker's gaze and smiled. He drew the knife back, raising his arm to strike the final blow.

Then suddenly a tremble of shock went through him as the arm holding the knife was gripped and held. He spun about to see Soaring Eagle behind him, giving Night Walker the opportunity he'd been waiting for. He exploded, his pent-up fury released as he had released the arrow from his bow. He slammed into Jethro with the full force of his body, and Jethro found himself on the ground with Night Walker astride him and gazing down with a look that told Jethro there would be no mercy for him tonight.

Brittany was so shocked she was not able to move, and Soaring Eagle came to her and took hold of her arm. When her stunned eyes gazed up at him, he smiled as best he could, considering the pounding rage he felt toward Jethro.

"You are well, Brittany?"

"Ye . . . yes . . . yes, I'm all right." She sucked in a breath and sought to control her trembling. "Night Walker . . ."

"Stand here, Brittany. Night Walker must repay this debt . . . and he must make this white-eyes give him the answers he needs."

"Oh, Soaring Eagle, he will kill him! The military will then punish him and your people!"

"No," Soaring Eagle chuckled mirthlessly. "But this man will wish Night Walker had killed him. There is another man . . . or men connected with this, and Night Walker must find out their names. Tempest and Laughing Thunder are with Skinner; they have gone on to the fort with Aaron. They will tell the bluecoats the truth, and for once they will have to believe."

Brittany returned her gaze to Night Walker. This was the gentle man who had made love to her so sweetly that he'd made her entire being sing. This was the man whose hands had caressed her skin with infinite tenderness. She could not quite reconcile that tender lover with the coldly furious warrior who was pinning Jethro to the ground. She clung to Soaring Eagle, who could feel her tremble.

"Soaring Eagle, I know who ordered the attack. Daniel Nixon is behind all this! Jethro and Charlie told me so."

"If this is true, Night Walker will see him dead."

"It is true, and Daniel deserves to pay for what he has done."

Soaring Eagle knew his brother better than any other. Night Walker was one to control his emotions, and not a man who would kill a helpless, unarmed prisoner.

Jethro gazed up at death, he was sure of it. With a strength Jethro could hardly believe, Night Walker had him pinned to the earth. The glitter of the silver-bladed knife in Night Walker's hand sent lightning streaks of terror through him. Still, Jethro struggled for some semblance of courage.

"I'm unarmed, you murdering savage. Let me up and let me have my knife. I'll fight you."

"Why should I, white-eyes? You would have taken my woman with no mercy at all. And what about the helpless people at the mission?"

Jethro's face had gone greyer with each snarled word. "What are you going to do?"

"I will take every bit of flesh from your body, piece by piece, and you will live and suffer a long, long time before you die screaming."

There was a calm, cold deliberation in Night Walker's words that made the last of Jethro's courage and resolve disappear. He choked back an involuntary sob and began to talk desperately.

"It wasn't my idea! For God's sake, listen to me! It wasn't my idea."

"I do not want to hear excuses. You kill without heart, white-eyes, and you deserve the same." Night Walker touched the point of his knife to Jethro's cheek with just enough force to draw blood.

"No! No! Listen to me. If you kill me, that won't put an end to this! He'll only bring more men and go on with his plans. You don't understand! He's got a lot at stake and he's got a lot of power!"

"I do not believe you. You scream for your life like a child," Night Walker said with casual disregard and pricked Jethro's face again. "Tell me, did the others at the mission beg for mercy? Did Aaron plead for his life?" Night Walker's voice became a low hiss. "And did my woman not beg for her honor and her life?"

"Listen to me! Listen to me! Killing me won't stop him. He'll be after—"

"The yellow metal," Night Walker finished calmly.

"You know?"

"Yes. I know. But he will never have it, and you will not be here to help him murder anymore."

"Please! Please!" Jethro begged as the knife grew closer again.

"I have no feeling for men such as you."

"It was Daniel Nixon," Jethro screamed. "He intends to dig for gold where the mission was. He had to get rid of the mission, and start trouble between your village and the fort."

"You would have my people blamed for this ugly thing?"

"It's not my idea, I swear. It was Daniel's orders."

"Yes," Night Walker said quietly. He rose, and Jethro looked up as Night Walker towered over him. Was he really going to let him live? As Night Walker turned toward Soaring Eagle and Brittany, Jethro breathed a sigh of relief.

"Tie him up, brother. It will be good for Cole Young and the others at the fort to know what was planned and by whom." He turned to look at Jethro. "And if you value your life, remember, Daniel Nixon and all the friends you know cannot save your life if you lie. I will find you . . . and the next time I will kill you."

Soaring Eagle went to Jethro and began to tie him with strips of leather he always carried when he hunted. Night Walker walked straight to Brittany and took her in his arms.

He crushed her to him, closing his eyes and inhaling the scent of her. The relief that flooded his being was so intense that for this moment he had no words that would describe how he felt.

Brittany could do little more than cling to him. She laid her head against his broad chest and felt the steady beating of his heart.

Night Walker held her gently away from him, then cupped her face between his hands and drank in the love that was flowing from her.

It was a deep, intensely passionate kiss and Brittany gave all her being to it. The strength of him and the promise the kiss held overpowered her senses. She pressed herself to him as if she could blend the two of them into one being, for indeed she felt as if they were.

"Morning Sun . . . Morning Sun, they did not hurt you?"

"No, they didn't. Oh, Night Walker," she breathed huskily, "I thought I would never see you again."

"You should have known I would follow you forever until I found you."

"The mission! Oh, God, is it all—"

"It is gone, there was little we could do."

"And . . . and Aaron?" Her eyes pleaded with him to deny what she felt must be true.

"Aaron is still alive, or was when we left him. Laughing Thunder and Skinner are taking him to the fort now."

"Tempest . . . she will be devastated."

"She came with Soaring Eagle, and has gone to the fort with Aaron and Laughing Thunder."

"Aaron tried so hard to stop them. I can't believe that anyone could be so cold and bloodthirsty. Those wonderful people who tried so hard to do what they thought was right." Brittany was trembling and Night Walker tightened his arms about her. "They were so loving and kind. They made both Tempest and me feel . . . needed." She looked up at him and a look of determination filled her eyes. "I will not let all their work be in vain, I won't. I love you, Night Walker. I love you with my whole heart and soul. I know the mission is gone . . . but I would marry you, live with you and teach the children of your village . . . and one day ours."

For one wild moment Night Walker felt as if his heart would burst with the joy she gave him. It left him temporarily speechless.

He grabbed her up in his arms, and she laughed breathlessly and reached to pull his head to hers. Their lips met again, and all about them was forgotten as they shared a kiss so heated that both were overpowered and lost in it.

Only Soaring Eagle's soft and very satisfied laugh drew them back to the present. He smiled at their embarrassed look and waved a graceful hand toward a well-trussed Jethro.

"He will be uncomfortable, but he will be very safe for the night. Will we camp here, or will we go back to the fort now?"

"We will spend the night here," Night Walker replied. "Get more wood for the fire and we will find the supplies these men brought and have a meal. Soaring Eagle, help me." He motioned to the two who lay so still by the fire. Soaring Eagle nodded.

"Stay right here, Brittany," Night Walker said. "We will take care of this. You must be tired and hungry." His voice grew gentle and soft. "We will spend the night together here."

She could only smile and nod her head. Still, when he left her side she felt a sense of loss. Clad only in her torn shift, she shivered, partly from the cold night air and partly from the ordeal she had gone through. But it was only minutes before Night Walker returned to her side with a blanket, which he wrapped about her. He took the occasion to kiss her again.

"Come by the fire where you can be warm," he said as he led her toward it.

Night Walker, Soaring Eagle and Brittany sat by the fire, all three aware of Jethro's hate-filled gaze upon them.

Jethro was sure Daniel Nixon would deny he even knew him. But Jethro knew where the gold could be found and Daniel didn't. If he could survive this, he would have the gold for himself and to hell with Daniel, who had let him take all the chances while he reaped the rewards.

Jethro gazed at the golden-haired girl kissed by the glow of the fire. . . . If only there were a way to get free . . . to get the gold . . . to get the girl. He would teach her never to underestimate him. As for Night Walker . . . his hatred surged again. Given any chance at all, Jethro would see him dead.

Exhaustion swept over Brittany, and with the warmth of the fire she became still and heavy-eyed. Soaring Eagle took his blanket and went to a shadowed area near Jethro. He would keep watch.

Night Walker spread his blanket, and without words Brittany rose and went to him. They lay together in the blackness of the night. Holding her was enough for Night Walker. To know she was safe and that he had the promise of the years that lay ahead filled him with contentment.

Brittany felt the strength of his arms about her and drifted into relaxed sleep.

Brittany woke at dawn to the sound of Jethro's plaintive voice.

"Dammit, you red devil. These ropes are killing me. They're cutting off my blood. I can't even feel my hands."

"Consider that you are lucky, white-eyes," Soaring Eagle said with little pity. "Those at the mission will never feel anything again. If you wish to end your pain, I could send your spirit to join them."

This silenced Jethro for a while, and Brittany could hear Soaring Eagle and Night Walker continue their half-whispered conversation. She rose and walked to the newly built fire to join them.

"Will we be leaving soon?" she inquired of Night Walker as she sat down beside him.

"We were only waiting for you to wake up," he replied.

"You should have wakened me."

"You needed to sleep. You have been through much. Soon we will go to the fort."

"Night Walker . . . what if Jethro tells someone about the gold? It will bring a swarm of people."

"We must not let word of this get out. To prevent that, we must begin to trust each other. Those at the fort and we in our village must keep this secret between us."

"Perhaps it is a good thing, my love."

"Why?"

"Because something had to create a bridge between your people and mine. This secret, Tempest and me . . . maybe this will be what is needed."

"I hope you are right."

"I pray she is right," Soaring Eagle said. "As you have said, sister, you and my beloved wife will bring more to us than our happiness. Tempest has already shown me what it will mean for our children to learn your ways. It is for us now to see that we make use of what we can."

"My brother has grown wise in his old years." Night Walker grinned. "But you will admit, we have made the right choices in our women. If we must do this thing"—he reached to take Brittany's hand—"we have the best of teachers."

"I agree," Soaring Eagle laughed. "And I also think we must be going. Laughing Thunder must be very worried among all those bluecoats."

"And Aaron," Brittany said softly.

"He will be well . . . he must be," Night Walker said firmly.

"Yes . . . he must be," Brittany echoed the hope.

They began to make preparations to travel. Night Walker put the fire out and Soaring Eagle began to gather their equipment. But the sound of others approaching brought all three alert. Then Laughing Thunder, Cole, the braves who had accompanied Laughing Thunder, and several of Cole's men rode into the camp.

"Cole!" Brittany rushed to his side. "My sister . . . Aaron?"

"Tempest is fine. But you, Brittany, how are you?"

Brittany's smile faded and her eyes searched Cole's. "I'm all right. Night Walker and Soaring Eagle found me in time. Cole . . . please, how is Aaron?"

"Truthfully, I don't know. When I left the fort he was in a pretty bad way. Now that we've found you safe, I think it best we get back as fast as we can."

"Oh, Aaron," Brittany said softly. Hot tears stung her eyes.

Night Walker came to her side and put an arm about her. He looked at Cole. "Aaron is dead?"

"No."

Brittany moved away but Night Walker continued to look at Cole. "He's not dead, Night Walker, but I'm not sure he's going to be alive by the time we get back."

"Then we must hurry. It will tear her heart to be too late." Night Walker drew Cole aside. "There is more I would tell you. My brother has spoken of the need for us to learn to trust each other. You know of the gold?"

"Yes."

"This man"—he pointed at Jethro—"and Daniel Nixon hold the secret. We must not let word of this spread."

367

"Colonel Brady feels the same. We must find a way to keep Daniel Nixon and this man quiet."

"Don't worry," Night Walker said, in a voice so cold and grim that Cole was shaken. "We will see to their silence one way or the other."

Chapter Nineteen

"What is going to be done about Daniel?" Brittany asked as they prepared for the trip back to the fort.

"He doesn't know what has happened," Cole replied.

"No?" Night Walker said. "He is pretending he knows nothing and has no part in anything. It is better we let him go on pretending . . . until we can end his treachery."

"Night Walker's right," Cole said. "We have to keep our prisoner a secret until we see what Colonel Brady can manage. But to tell the truth, I don't think Brady can stop this . . . or arrest Daniel unless we can prove he is connected."

"We will prove it. That one"—Night Walker gestured toward Jethro—"is going to tell those at the white fort everything he knows. He knows all the plans Daniel Nixon made. I think it best we convince him to give us the answers that will stop those plans."

Although he displayed no sign that he had heard what was being said, Jethro did not miss a word of the conversation. Yes, he would implicate Daniel Nixon, but only if he gained his own freedom. He would claim he did not know where the gold was to be found. He would swear that only Daniel knew that. He missed the grim smile on Night Walker's face.

The ride back to the fort was silent. Night Walker watched Brittany closely and knew her heart was breaking with the fear that they might not find Aaron alive. Yet he could not make the long miles any shorter. When they paused to rest for the night, Brittany was tense and nervous, and Night Walker had to speak gently and soothe her fears as best he could. He tasted her fear and knew it matched his own. For Aaron was as much a father to him as Sleeping Wolf was.

The soldiers that Cole had brought with him were hard put to keep their eyes from straying toward Brittany. But the dark scowl on Night Walker's face was enough to warn them. Cole laughed to himself. Night Walker was no enemy to make, but Cole hoped he would prove to be a good friend.

Later the next day when the fort came in sight, Brittany clutched the reins of her horse in a white-knuckled hand. Her eyes were frozen on the fort and her heart was torn by fear. Night Walker reached out and laid his large hand over hers.

"It will be well, Brittany."

"I've prayed all the way back, Night Walker. But I cannot wipe the screams and the flames from my mind."

"If it is so, and we must face the truth . . . then we must remember why Aaron was here. We must do what is necessary to let his spirit walk in peace. If Aaron is gone from us, then we must learn to depend on each other."

Brittany smiled up at him. "Aaron was the best teacher, after all. His ideas were like seeds on fertile ground. We will do it, won't we, Night Walker?"

"Yes. We will."

The group rode down to the fort. As they rode through the gate, more than one pair of shocked or awed eyes followed their progress.

Night Walker lifted Brittany gently down from her horse, and Cole had to turn his head to keep from laughing. The dark-eyed warrior's stern presence was more than enough to divert the admiring gazes of the men.

Suddenly Brittany's attention was caught by the sound of her name. She turned to see Tempest rushing toward her. With a glad cry, Brittany ran to meet her and the sisters embraced. Their tears were hot and filled with the fear that still remained for Aaron.

Laughing Thunder stood a short distance behind them with a look of intense relief on his face. Now that everything was settled, he looked around the bluecoats' fort . . . and thought of going home. He didn't like confinement.

Soaring Eagle came to Tempest's side and quickly signed to her. *It is a terrible thing to lose so many friends. The whole village will grieve for you. Tempest, one thing is good, and that is your sister has not been harmed. Soon we will be able to return home.*

"Soaring Eagle, what of Aaron?" Brittany asked.

"I have asked Tempest and she says he has been very bad, but part of it is worry about you, and the worst is the memories of all his friends who sacrificed so much. Maybe when he sees your face he will be able to rest better."

"But he will live?"

"Yes, I believe he will live. But the white doctor is very strange. He wants to open Aaron's arm and take some of his strength."

"Bleed him? It's a common custom."

"It is foolish. Everyone knows strength lies in keeping the life flow from leaving the body. The whites are strange."

"Come." Brittany laced one arm through Tempest's and the other through Soaring Eagle's. "Let's go and see Aaron."

Tempest held back and Brittany stopped to look at her in surprise. Tempest smiled and looked at Soaring Eagle.

I believe my sister needs to find a new dress before we see the colonel or Aaron. Aaron will not believe she has not been hurt if he sees her this way.

Soaring Eagle smiled and relayed the words to

Brittany, who suddenly became aware of the stares of the men about her . . . and Night Walker's cold-eyed look.

"I'd best, or Night Walker will be causing more harm here than good." She nodded to Tempest. Then her sister's hands flew so fast she was helpless even to try to follow. Soaring Eagle chuckled and a devilish look appeared in his eyes.

"This I will not tell you. I will only say it has made me more anxious to get home."

Brittany looked across the compound and spoke softly, almost to herself. "Yes, I am anxious to get home, too."

"The village is home, Brittany?"

"Yes, Soaring Eagle . . . it is home."

"I am glad, my sister."

Brittany followed Tempest to the quarters she had been given and quickly found another dress. Brushing her hair hastily, she nodded to Tempest. The sisters embraced again and left to rejoin the men. Outside their door they met Esther, who was about to knock. She smiled at Brittany.

"Child, it's good to see you safe and sound. We were all so worried about you. When Aaron was brought to us the way he was, I had a great fear of how it might be for you."

"It was frightening for a while, but Night Walker came for me."

"Please know that we all mourn the loss of the mission. Some of the people at the mission were friends of mine, as well."

Esther did not need to be told how Brittany felt

about Night Walker. It was clear, both in her eyes and in her voice.

"So that is your young man. Is he as fierce as he looks?"

"No," Brittany laughed. "He is a very kind and gentle man."

"I don't know. If one more soldier looks in your direction, I believe a war will start right here."

It was the truth. Outnumbered as he and his two brothers were, Night Walker was too tense and much too annoyed not to have made his feelings known. It was Brittany's smile as she walked toward him that brought soothing calm.

"I think we should see Aaron," Brittany suggested. "I would go home with you as soon as I know Aaron is safe and well. He must come to us soon, Night Walker, so that we can help him survive his grief and begin his life again."

His smile was answer enough. Then Esther nudged Brittany slightly.

"Night Walker, this is my dear friend, Esther Brady. Esther, this is Night Walker."

"Night Walker. It's a real pleasure to meet you at last. I have heard a great deal of you. I just wanted to make sure these two little lambs were in good hands."

Night Walker looked totally blank for a minute. Then he realized this woman was proclaiming herself as close to a mother to Tempest and Brittany as she could be.

"I am sorry that I did not bring bride gifts," Night Walker said, feeling somewhat shamed, and the look on Soaring Eagle's face said that he, too, was embarrassed at the omission. "We will bring gifts before the winter comes."

Now it was Esther's turn to be puzzled. Brittany's laughter soon brought an end to the situation. Tempest touched Soaring Eagle's arm, and he tried to explain to her how stupid he and Night Walker had been. Tempest looked at Brittany and both women laughed.

"I will explain bride gifts to you later, Esther," Brittany said. "Night Walker, there is no need for bride gifts here. We do not have such a custom."

Night Walker didn't know whether to be relieved or to be suspicious that Brittany was simply smoothing things over for him. He exchanged a look with Soaring Eagle and Laughing Thunder, knowing they agreed. They would bring the bride gifts anyway.

Esther led them to the infirmary, where they met the doctor who had cared for Aaron for the past days.

"Doctor?" Brittany asked hopefully.

"He will live, my dear. But it will be a long time before he can function. It will be even longer before he can do any kind of mission work."

"May I see him?"

"I would appreciate it if only two of you at a time went in. I almost lost him. I don't want him under any strain now."

"I think what I have to say to him will erase all the strain. Let Night Walker and me go in."

The doctor eyed this tall, formidable man and

wondered if he wouldn't shatter Aaron's peace.
But then, he thought, who was going to argue with
a man who looked as if he could break a fellow in
two like a dry twig?

"Go in. But please, try to keep him quiet."

"We will." Taking Night Walker's hand, Brittany
opened the door and the two went inside.

The man who lay on the bed was so reduced
from the Aaron Brittany knew that she gave a
muffled cry of shock and ran to kneel by his bed.
Gently she took his hand in hers.

"Aaron . . . oh, Aaron."

Only then did Aaron's eyes flutter open, and for
a minute neither Night Walker nor Brittany
thought he recognized them. Then he smiled at
the tall man who hovered over him.

"Night Walker."

"It is good to look upon you again," Night Walker replied, "and know you will live many more
years."

"And Brittany, my dear sweet girl. They found
you in time. No one hurt you?"

"No, Aaron. I am well. I do not want to tire you."

"You cannot tire me, you can only make me heal
faster. I heard you scream and I was afraid—"

"I was afraid for you. When they said you were
dead . . ." Her eyes filled with tears.

"No, no. It's no time to cry now."

"You are right," Night Walker said. "Can you
talk more or do you wish us to return later?"

"No. I would talk now. What has happened?"

In as few words as he could manage, Night Walker told Aaron of the situation.

"So Daniel Nixon is the cause of all this," Aaron said angrily. "Daniel Nixon and gold."

"Yes. We have one of his men, but we have ended the life of two of the others. We all fear it will be impossible to keep this yellow metal a secret. I would ask you and our elders for advice. If it were left to me, I would end the lives of these two men before they can cause more harm."

"Night Walker—" Brittany wanted to doubt his words, but she read the truth in his eyes.

"I am not as forgiving as you. This Daniel Nixon left you to their mercy, and those others did not understand the word. He did not care how you suffered, and I cannot find pity in my heart for such men."

"I'm afraid," Aaron said quietly, "that Night Walker is right in many ways."

"I cannot believe you would condone murder, Aaron," Brittany said.

"No, but I foresee the ravages a flood of gold seekers will bring upon this place, if news of it leaves this area."

"There must be something that can be done," Brittany argued.

"There is." Cole's voice came from the doorway. "I've sent a troop of men to Daniel's home to arrest him. The colonel has been told the whole story and has decided to play him and Jethro against each other. He's sure Jethro will confess that Daniel ordered the attack on the mission. With your and Aaron's testimony, the trial can only go one way. They are guilty of mass murder and destruction. They will be tried by military law . . . and hanged."

"Then it will end here," Brittany said.

"Thank God," Aaron replied.

"I would see this white man's justice," Night Walker said a bit doubtfully. "It is a rare thing."

"Not so rare." Cole smiled. "Perhaps we will surprise you. We have two unimpeachable witnesses and, contrary to what you believe, all white men do not lie. Aaron should be an example."

"Then word of this yellow metal will go no further than this," Night Walker replied.

"There's no way we can be sure of that. There's no telling who was in on this with Daniel and how much they know. We can only do as much as we can, and hope nobody else back East knows enough to be sure where to find the gold."

"I do not think Daniel is the kind of man who trusts many."

"I have one question," Aaron said gently. "How are we going to keep the word *gold* from entering into the trial?"

They all knew the hunger for gold was as rife among the military and the settlers as it was among those back East. There seemed to be no way out of the dilemma.

"For now, Aaron," Cole said, "you need to rest. We can still consider answers for a time. Maybe we'll come up with something."

"I want to speak with Aaron for a while in private, Cole," Brittany said. "Night Walker . . . if you don't mind? I won't be long."

"I will wait outside," Night Walker replied. He and Cole left and Brittany turned to look at Aaron to find his gaze regarding her.

"Something bothers you, Brittany?"

"Yes. It's the mission."

"The mission?"

"Actually the loss of the mission."

"I'm afraid it will be a long time before I can rise from this bed and be well enough to rebuild the mission and start my work again."

"That's what I want to discuss with you."

"I'm sorry, my dear, I'm afraid I am too befuddled to understand what you're talking about."

"Aaron . . . I am going to marry Night Walker. And I am going to the village to live with him there. I will teach the children there."

"If that is the wish of your heart, you would be betraying yourself to do any less. Night Walker is like a son to me, and Flying Horse's people will consider themselves fortunate to have you and Tempest living with them. I'm sure this has made Night Walker more than happy."

"He has told me so."

"Go, Brittany. Teach the children. Perhaps all this is God's way to provide them with what I have been trying to provide them all along. You will become one of them and they will trust you. One day, you will see that some of their children go on to even better education. You have my blessings."

"Then hurry and get well, Aaron, for I cannot

marry without you there to conduct the service."

"I shall try. I don't want an impatient Night Walker causing more of a scandal than the gossips are trying to stir up now."

"Oh, Aaron," Brittany laughed, "when I saw the reaction of some of the ladies, I got the distinct feeling it was less gossip and scandal than downright envy."

"I wouldn't doubt it a bit."

"I shall go along now. You need your rest." She bent to kiss him, and then left the room. Aaron drifted into sleep with a smile on his face.

A few hours later, Night Walker, Soaring Eagle and Laughing Thunder stood together looking around them. None of the three liked the high walls that contained them.

"Why do they hide behind walls like these?" Laughing Thunder asked his older brothers.

"Perhaps they are afraid and think to keep enemies out," Soaring Eagle said.

Night Walker chuckled and both Soaring Eagle and Laughing Thunder grinned. "If I chose to come in here," Night Walker said, "I do not think it would be so hard to do. Maybe they are afraid to go out."

The three brothers laughed at the white man's fear of the wide world they roamed at will, yet all three were nervous in the confines of the fort and wished to be gone as soon as possible.

Tempest had gone with Esther to make room for Brittany in her small quarters, and Laughing

Thunder and Night Walker were standing on the porch before Cole's quarters.

"Have you noticed how many clothes their women wear?" Laughing Thunder asked.

"Does it make you curious, little brother?" Night Walker grinned.

"No," he laughed, "I do not doubt they are all made the same beneath them. With the exception of my two new sisters, I do not think the white women so interesting. All those skirts would give a man too much of a battle."

The three went on teasing each other until the fort doors opened and a troop of soldiers rode in.

Night Walker had been trying to convince Brittany to leave for the village at once. Now he was stirred by the strange and uncomfortable feeling that he wished they had.

The lieutenant who had led the group rode up to the front of Colonel Brady's quarters, dismounted and strode up the steps, across the porch and inside.

"There is trouble," Night Walker said quietly. "See to our horses."

Soaring Eagle and Laughing Thunder moved quickly and silently. When they arrived at the stable, Soaring Eagle helped to prepare the horses, and then he told Laughing Thunder to stay with them. He went at once to find Tempest.

Night Walker moved with purposeful intent. He sensed that something was wrong. He wanted the answers to two things: What had gone wrong, and was Brittany still with Aaron?

He did not knock on the colonel's door, but went to open it without asking permission of the two corporals stationed there. They jumped up to prevent him from entering Colonel Brady's office. There would have been a fierce confrontation if Cole had not opened the door and come out at that moment.

"Night Walker, I was just coming to find you."

"What has gone wrong, Cole? Is this more of the white man's justice?"

"Daniel Nixon's place was empty. He's gone and no one has any idea how he knew we were coming after him."

"Then there is no doubt the gold is no longer a secret?"

"I'm afraid it won't be for long. But we will do all we can to keep the gold seekers away from your village."

"You give us some hope. I will take Brittany and we will return to our village. We will defend ourselves against these gold seekers."

"I'm afraid Brittany can't leave the fort just like that. Colonel Brady has ordered that she remain here. I wish I could do something about it, but I can't. There are times he can't be reasoned with. He says if there's going to be trouble, she must remain here."

"Has she no choice in this matter?"

"The colonel says no and that she's his responsibility."

"Where is she?"

"Night Walker . . ."

"Where is she?"

"She went back to Aaron."

"I will speak with her."

"You can't take her from here. Night Walker . . . I will be under orders to stop you," Cole said help-lessly.

Night Walker held his gaze for a moment. "You may be forced to try, but it will bring more blood-shed than your flimsy fort can withstand."

Night Walker left Cole standing there and went at once to Aaron's room, where he found Brittany in conversation with him.

Brittany could see that something was drasti-cally wrong. She rose to her feet.

"Night Walker, what is it?"

"We must leave here . . . and I do not believe the soldiers at this fort intend for you to go with me."

"Good heavens," Aaron said. Painfully he raised his head. "What has happened?"

Night Walker tried to explain as quickly as he could, but his rage kept getting in the way. "My brothers and I will not be kept prisoner here . . . and we will not leave Tempest and Brittany be-hind."

"I see," Aaron said thoughtfully.

Brittany went to Night Walker and put her arms about him. "I would not have you killed for me."

"My life would mean little without you, and what of Tempest? She is Soaring Eagle's wife. Do you think he would go and leave her here?"

"But she need not remain. They cannot deny that her place is beside her husband."

"Brittany," Aaron said. Both Brittany and Night Walker looked at him quickly, for he was smiling. "Hand me my Bible."

Brittany couldn't see what his Bible had to do with the ugly situation they were caught up in. She handed Aaron the Bible and turned back to Night Walker.

"Oh, Night Walker, what have I done? I know your pride. You will die here foolishly over me! I'm not worth it!"

Night Walker caught her to him and held her for a moment, then he caught her face between his hands and held her gaze relentlessly with his.

"Brittany . . . understand me well. You are a part of me I cannot live without. You are the morning sun and the softness of moonlight. You are my breath and the beat of my heart. I cannot . . . and I will not go from here without you."

"And I don't think you'll have to."

Both of them turned to Aaron as if they had almost forgotten he was there.

"I do not understand," Night Walker said.

"Do you two trust me?"

"With our lives," Brittany replied. Night Walker nodded agreement.

"Then, Brittany, call in that harridan of a nurse who takes care of me and that young private out there. We need witnesses."

They did as he said, but the veil of mystery remained.

384

"Now, face me and, Night Walker . . . take her left hand in yours."

Night Walker still looked dumbfounded, but Brittany was suddenly radiant. Obviously she understood what this was all about.

Brittany was more than delighted to do what Aaron said. When the four were gathered facing Aaron, he began.

"We are gathered here together . . ."

Cole was explaining as best he could, and finished with ". . . and I told him your orders were that Brittany could not leave the fort if there was going to be trouble in the near future. But . . . he wasn't exactly receptive. Colonel Brady, sir . . . I'd suggest you let them all leave peacefully."

"Where is her sister?"

"With your wife, but . . . Aaron has married her and Soaring Eagle. We have no right to keep her here. Colonel, it is my . . . recommendation that we get these people out of here before the whole thing gets out of hand. This can only cause more problems and more bloodshed."

Steven paused and then smiled grimly. "Come along, Lieutenant. We will see these young men on their way, with the assurance that we will handle any gold seekers who show up to the best of our ability, but that woman will not leave here."

"I'm afraid, sir, that Night Walker already knows that, and has little regard for 'our way.' You're not going to stop him from taking Brittany back to that village, especially since she desires to go."

"I have no intention of letting her step beyond the gates of this fort."

Cole felt stymied. There was little he could do about Tempest's leaving, but he knew the colonel wasn't going to let Brittany walk into more danger if he could do anything about it.

Laughing Thunder could see the two officers cross the compound, and from their attitude he sensed that Night Walker was right about more trouble brewing. He tied the horses and followed.

Tempest and Soaring Eagle were surprised, and Esther was shocked, when Cole and Steven came so abruptly into the room.

"Steven, for heaven's sake. What has got you all tied in a knot?"

"I'm afraid we have a little problem, Esther," he said. "Soaring Eagle, it seems your brother has taken it upon himself to leave, and that's all right. He has the freedom to go with you and your wife and Laughing Thunder. But you must help me convince him that I cannot allow him to take Brittany along."

"You think my brother would leave her here?" Soaring Eagle smiled. "You do not know him well."

"I will have to stop him if he tries to take her."

At that moment Laughing Thunder appeared in the doorway. His questioning gaze found Soaring Eagle, whose hands moved swiftly. In seconds Laughing Thunder was gone.

But Tempest had seen clearly what had passed between the two, and knew Night Walker and Brittany were in danger. She gripped Soaring Eagle's arm. Then it was Tempest whose hands flew in question after question. He did his best to both comfort her and to assure her he was not going to let anything serious happen.

What of Brittany? she signed.

Night Walker will see to her safety. Tempest, all of us are going home. We can't let them stop us. Night Walker . . . me . . . Laughing Thunder, we would be nothing in this fort.

I know. I'm ready to leave with you.

Are you sure? These are your people.

No, my husband, you are my world now. I will go with you.

Soaring Eagle smiled. Then he turned to Cole and the others. "I will go speak to my brother."

"Good," Colonel Brady said, "I thought you'd see reason."

Soaring Eagle did not reply, and Cole had an idea it was not going to be easy. When they walked into Aaron's room, Cole was sure of it.

"Gentlemen," Aaron said. He lay back against his pillow and seemed to be exhausted. He held his Bible against his chest as if he were sure he were leaving the world.

"I'm sorry, Aaron." Steven spoke softly as if Aaron were already passing. "But I have to settle a little problem that's come up."

"You mean you've caught Daniel Nixon?"

"No." He flushed. "Right now we only have

Jethro to try for the attack on the mission. But I'm sure he'll turn over some of the others to us."

"What's got you so tangled up then?"

Steven looked at Night Walker and suddenly felt as if he were standing on shaky ground. "Aaron, since you brought Brittany here to teach at your mission . . . and there is no longer any mission . . . you'll have to admit her place is now here at the fort with her own kind."

"You're right, Steven, I brought Brittany here to teach. But my real hope was that she would teach some of the Indian children, the ones I found so bright and promising. It is true that God works in mysterious ways. For Brittany *will* go there and teach . . . and when I am well, I will join her there."

"No, Aaron. As much as I admire and respect what you are doing, there is no way I will let that girl leave this fort."

"But you will let Tempest go?"

"Because, you damn . . . you fool. You went and married them. I can't do much about that. All I need is this girl or her family to go complaining to the big brass in Washington that I interfered between her and her husband. But Brittany is a different story."

"I'm afraid not, my friend. You see, I have just married Night Walker and Brittany."

Cole closed his eyes and tried not to smile. Steven looked at Aaron in shock. Esther smiled, Soaring Eagle signed to Tempest what had occurred and even Laughing Thunder breathed a sigh of relief.

Brittany went to Aaron's side and bent down to kiss him. "Get well, Aaron, we need you. I cannot fill all the need. Hurry and come help me."

"Perhaps I will be well in time to baptize a babe or two."

"Perhaps." She smiled.

"Take very good care of her, Night Walker. You will account to me if you don't."

"Have no worry," Night Walker replied. "I would be a fool to do otherwise. We have captured these two beautiful doves as a treasure for our village. We will guard them with our lives. Come to us soon."

"I'll do that. Go now, before my military friend here decides to come up with another idea."

"Go on, get out of here," Steven said, while Esther hugged his arm.

They rode from the fort an hour later—Night Walker and Brittany, Soaring Eagle and Tempest, and Laughing Thunder along with the other braves. All knew there were trials yet to be faced, but all knew they would gather strength from each other to face whatever the future had to offer.

Epilogue

Three Years Later

Brittany stood near the edge of the meadow where the tall grass waved in the afternoon breeze like an undulating ocean. She stood and watched Night Walker riding toward her.

She watched the sun glint in his long, silky, ebony hair, and as he grew closer she could see the whiteness of his smile. Even before he dismounted and took her in his arms, she sensed the familiar strength of him. Her love for him had grown over the few short years they had shared together. She had not thought it possible to love him more every day, but every day she found a new facet of him that drew her.

"It is time?"

"Yes," he said. "You know she would not leave without your good wishes."

"She is frightened?" Brittany asked.

"Yes. As you must have been when you came here. But she is excited, too. I think she is more afraid that she will disappoint you."

"She could never disappoint me. I think what she has accomplished so far is nothing short of a miracle. She needn't be afraid. James and his wife will see to her care."

"It would not make much difference if we did not arrive in the village for just a while longer," Night Walker said, his voice warm and coaxing as he gently tugged at the ties that laced up the front of her shirt.

"I don't think we'll be missed for a little longer," she whispered as his mouth claimed hers and they slowly drifted down to the soft grass.

They knew each other's secrets now and sought to taste the depth of that knowledge. He made love to her, realizing as he always did that each time was unique and yet as beautiful as the first time he had ever held her.

Afterward they lay together for a while, reluctant to leave their sanctuary.

"Our son will be searching for you," Night Walker said comfortably. But he did not move.

"Tempest has become his second mother. If Never Quiet wasn't leaving, I could lie here in the sun with you all afternoon."

"There is no way for my parents to show you how grateful they are for what you are doing.

391

Never Quiet will be the first. Maybe others will follow."

"And we will bring them home every summer so they will never forget where they have come from and where their hearts should be."

"I would like to meet your brother one day."

"In his last letter he warned me that Daniel Nixon has made himself quite a reputation. Night Walker, he hates you. One day—"

"Shhh, we have promised not to worry about what the coming days hold. For now I have you, our little one, and the promise that Never Quiet can have a new world to discover. You are happy?"

"I have never been happier in my life."

"Then, for now, that is enough. Now we must go back or Aaron will be sending someone for us."

Brittany sighed, but she rose with him and they dressed. Soon they arrived at the village, where pandemonium reigned. Aaron would be leaving soon to take Never Quite to James, who would see to her care while she went on with the education Brittany had begun.

All knew that change was coming, but they had prepared for it. They would face the future together, with love to bind them one to the other.

MADELINE BAKER

Author of Over 10 Million Books in Print!

Shattered by grief at her fiancé's death, lovely Katy Marie Alvarez decides to enter a convent. But fate has other plans. En route to her destination, the coach in which Katy is traveling is attacked by Indians and Katy, the lone survivor, is taken captive. Thus she becomes the slave of the handsome, arrogant Cheyenne warrior known as Iron Wing. A desperate desire transforms hate into love, until they are both ablaze with an erotic flame which neither time nor treachery can quench.

__4227-4 $5.99 US/$6.99 CAN

ELAINE BARBIERI

DELANEY'S CROSSING

JEAN BARRETT

Virile, womanizing Cooper J. Delaney is Agatha Pennington's only hope to help lead a group of destitute women to Oregon, where the promise of a new life awaits them. He is a man as harsh and hostile as the vast wilderness—but Agatha senses a gentleness behind his hard-muscled exterior, a tenderness lurking beneath his gruff facade. Though the group battles rainstorms, renegade Indians, and raging rivers, the tall beauty's tenacity never wavers. And with each passing mile, Cooper realizes he is struggling against a maddening attraction for her and that he would journey to the ends of the earth if only to claim her untouched heart.

_4200-2 $5.50 US/$6.50 CAN

Dorchester Publishing Co., Inc.
P.O. Box 6640
Wayne, PA 19087-8640

Bestselling Author of *Frost Flower*

From the moment silky Shanahan spots the buck-naked
stranger in old man Johnson's pond, she is smitten. Yet
despite her yearning, the fiery rebel suspects the handsome
devil is a Yankee who needs capturing. Since every able-
bodied man in the Smoky Mountains is off fighting the
glorious War for Southern Independence, the buckskin-clad
beauty will have to take the good-looking rascal prisoner
herself, and she'll be a ring-tailed polecat if she'll let him
escape. But even with her trusty rifle aimed at the enemy
soldier, Silky fears she is in danger of betraying her
country—and losing her heart to the one man she should
never love.

_4081-6 $5.50 US/$6.50 CAN

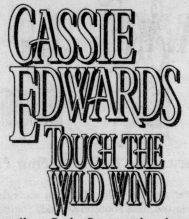

CASSIE EDWARDS
TOUCH THE WILD WIND

Alone and penniless, Sasha Seymour has thrown in her lot with a rough bunch, and she is bound for an even rougher destination—the Australian Outback, where she and her jackaroos hope to carve a sheep station from the vast, untamed wilderness. All that stands between her and the primitive forces of man and nature is the raw strength and courage of her partner—Ashton York. In his tawny arms she finds a haven from the raging storm, and in the tender fury of his kisses, a paradise of love.

____52211-X $5.50 US/$6.50 CAN

SAVAGE LONGINGS

CASSIE EDWARDS

"Cassie Edwards is a shining talent!"
—Romantic Times

Having been kidnapped by vicious trappers, Snow Deer despairs of ever seeing her people again. Then, from out of the Kansas wilderness comes Charles Cline to rescue the Indian maiden. Strong yet gentle, brave yet tenderhearted, the virile blacksmith is everything Snow Deer desires in a man. And beneath the fierce sun, she burns to succumb to the sweet temptation of his kiss. But the strong-willed Cheyenne princess is torn between the duty that demands she stay with her tribesmen and the passion that promises her unending happiness among white settlers. Only the love in her heart and the courage in her soul can convince Snow Deer that her destiny lies with Charles—and the blissful fulfillment of their savage longings.

_4176-6 $5.99 US/$6.99 CAN

ForeverGold

CATHERINE HART

**"Catherine Hart writes thrilling adventure...
beautiful and memorable romance!"**
—Romantic Times

From the moment Blake Montgomery holds up the westward-bound stagecoach carrying lovely Megan Coulston to her adoring fiance, she hates everything about the virile outlaw. How dare he drag her off to an isolated mountain cabin and hold her ransom? How dare he steal her innocence with his practiced caresses? How dare he kidnap her heart when all he can offer is forbidden moments of burning, trembling esctasy?

__3895-1 $5.99 US/$7.99 CAN

Dorchester Publishing Co., Inc.
P.O. Box 6640
Wayne, PA 19087-8640

Please add $1.75 for shipping and handling for the first book and $.50 for each book thereafter. NY, NYC, and PA residents, please add appropriate sales tax. No cash, stamps, or C.O.D.s. All orders shipped within 6 weeks via postal service book rate. Canadian orders require $2.00 extra postage and must be paid in U.S. dollars through a U.S. banking facility.

Name_____
Address_____
City_____ State_____ Zip_____
I have enclosed $_____ in payment for the checked book(s).
Payment <u>must</u> accompany all orders. ❑ Please send a free catalog.

LOVE FOREVERMORE

MADELINE BAKER

The West—it has been Loralee's dream for as long as she could remember, and Indians are the most fascinating part of the wildly beautiful frontier she imagines. But when Loralee arrives at Fort Apache as the new schoolmarm, she has some hard realities to learn...and a harsh taskmaster to teach her. Shad Zuniga is fiercely proud, aloof, a renegade Apache who wants no part of the white man's world, not even its women. Yet Loralee is driven to seek him out, compelled to join him in a forbidden union, forced to become an outcast for one slim chance at love forevermore.

___4267-3 $5.99 US/$6.99 CAN